Grumpy Old Wizards

by

John O'Riley

This is a work of fiction. Names, characters, places, and incidents either are the product of the author's imagination or are used fictitiously, and any resemblance to actual persons, living or dead, businesses, companies, events or locales is entirely coincidental.

Grumpy Old Wizards

Chapter 1

Josephine hid the rush of anticipation with a practiced air of stoicism as she clutched her half finished mug of coffee and watched her friend relinquish an ace of spades. Helen and Alice had already accumulated a higher score than her at this particular hand of rummy but she intended on somehow acquiring all four aces. She currently held two and one was now waiting for her in the discard pile. She wondered if either Helen or Alice were hogging the last ace but didn't want to let them know she possessed two of her own. She took a sip of her coffee then carefully set it down on the dining room table. For now, she chose to ignore the ace even though it drew her attention like a blazing beacon when she took her turn. The three elderly women spent every morning playing rummy or Parcheesi. Their condominiums were on the same floor and they usually woke up at an ungodly hour like most wizards and humans their age.

"This is the worst hand I've ever had in my life," Josephine said.

Unlike her two peers, Josephine had smooth, youthful skin and long black hair. Even though she was 84, she could easily pass for a thirty-year-old thanks to the side effect of slow aging that all category six wizards possessed. Her two friends were merely category three with average abilities so their age showed.

"I seriously doubt that," Helen said.

"I need more coffee," Alice announced.

1

"I'll have to make some more. I took the last of it when I refilled my cup," Josephine said.

She slapped down a card then walked into the kitchen to grind some more coffee beans. She quickly poured the grounds then set the maker to brew. Josephine returned to the living room where her two friends were waiting for her.

"Is it my turn?" Josephine asked.

"Yes," Alice said.

Josephine frowned at the discard pile. "Is someone hogging the aces or what?"

"Aha! You've got two of the aces!" Alice crowed. "I knew it!"

"I do not!" Josephine said indignantly.

"Then you won't mind if I take the entire pile in my next turn," Alice said smugly.

Josephine regarded her coolly then decided she'd better not press her luck. She grabbed the discards so she could play the aces.

"I rest my case," Alice said.

Josephine played the three aces and tried to decide which card she should let go. The phone rang and she briefly debated whether or not to answer it. More than likely, an obnoxious telephone solicitor was trying to reach her. She'd like to jinx every telemarketer in the world with severe flatulence or uncontrollable sneezing. The answering machine came online as Josephine continued to debate whether she should pick up the phone.

"This is Detective Riley. I need to talk to you about a new case. Call me back as soon as possible," Alex's familiar voice carried to the three elderly wizards' ears.

"Damn! I'm retired and I still have to drop everything at that stupid man's beck and call," Josephine grumbled. "I've worked hard for my entire life and I would like to at least be able to enjoy my retirement."

Unfortunately, one of the many drawbacks to being a category six wizard was the government consulting work required. Category six wizards could tune into subtle energies that other wizards couldn't which made them valuable in a wide range of investigative specialties. These wizards were so powerful that they couldn't control their magic so only very low-key spells were allowed for them. To ensure they weren't a danger to other wizards or humans, they were required to wear an aequitas enchantment. Josephine currently wore a topaz ring containing an aequitas enchantment which turned green if she was starting to work with magic that the Council deemed too potent for safety among category six wizards. The ring gave the user several seconds to decrease their flow of energy before a knock out spell would activate. It made Josephine feel like she was wearing a shock collar. She didn't think it was fair that she wasn't allowed to use her magic to its full potential but she didn't want to risk going to jail either. She had tried taking it off before but this had triggered a signal to the local enforcers who immediately paid her a visit and warned her to keep the ring on at all times.

The phone rang again and Josephine snorted with disgust. It was probably that obnoxious detective again. He called her far too often.

"I'm getting too old for this," Josephine said.

"Oh, please!" Helen said. "Look at you! You've got enough energy that you could have waited another sixty years before you retired!"

"At least you get paid for your consulting work," Alice said.

"I don't like working for the police," Josephine said. "Detective Whiney likes to call me practically every day."

Helen chose to ignore her friend's nickname for Detective Riley. "He hasn't called for five days if I remember correctly."

"It seems like he pesters me every day," Josephine said snidely.

"Maybe you should just answer the phone," Helen suggested.

Josephine frowned at the phone and the answering machine once again picked up.

"I know you're home. Pick up the phone," Riley said tersely. "You never leave your condo until after ten."

"One of these days, I'm going to kick his ass," Josephine grumbled as she crossed the room and picked up the phone. "Hello, detective. How are you?"

"I've got a serial killer on the loose. He's using magic to kill his victims and I need you to I.D. him."

Wizards who committed crimes used an ignotus enchantment to eliminate virtually all traces of psychic energy at the crime scene which made psychometry impossible unless you were a category six wizard.

"I'll be there in several hours," Josephine said.

"I need you here in thirty minutes," he said tersely.

"How about an hour and a half?"

"I need you here now."

"I haven't even taken my shower," Josephine fibbed. "I'm a retired woman who has an active social life."

"Just get over here," Alex said with annoyance. "Are you ready for the address?"

"Just a second." Josephine opened the desk drawer and pulled out a pen. There was already a notepad waiting for her on top of the desk. "Okay. I'm ready." She jotted down the address then promised to head over to the crime scene as soon as humanly possible before hanging up the phone.

"I think I have enough time to finish a hand," Josephine said.

"I'm not comfortable with this," Helen said. "You're going to provoke him."

"He thinks I'm taking a shower. He won't be mad," Josephine said. "Whose turn is it?"

"Mine," Helen said.

"Then hurry up and go before I get in trouble with the police." Josephine gestured impatiently.

Helen and Alice exchanged looks before continuing with the game. Unfortunately, Helen won this hand and had enough points accumulated to win the entire game.

"Maybe we can meet in the afternoon," Josephine suggested.

"Sure," Alice said.

Josephine's two friends left the condo and Josephine turned the coffee pot off. She turned the sink on and splashed water on her hair to make it seem like she'd been in the shower. After that, she grabbed her purse and made her way to her silver sedan. One of the things she hated about her consulting work is that she got lost easily. She hoped she could find this place. Josephine ended up making several wrong turns but arrived at the crime scene in a relatively short period of time. Luckily, it was Sarasota and she knew her way around the city fairly well. There were two police cars parked in front of the blue house. It had a small, overgrown and untended lawn and lacked a driveway. Josephine walked swiftly into the house to get out of the humid, tropical heat of the outdoors.

Forensics was already gathering evidence and Josephine's 28 year-old grandson was speaking with his colleague, Alex, at the far end of the room. Alex was a heavyset man with brown hair, a mustache, and green eyes. He had dark circles under his eyes and hadn't noticed her entrance. Josephine's grandson, Jake, was rapidly taking down notes as his colleague continued to discuss the case. Jake turned and smiled at his grandmother who waved back cheerfully.

"Hi, Grandma," he said.

"Hi, Jake. How's it going?" she said.

Alex frowned at her. "It took you almost an hour to get here."

"Don't exaggerate, detective, it took about forty-five minutes. You forget that I hadn't yet taken my shower and I get lost pretty easy," Josephine said dismissively.

The victim was lying beside a coffee table face-down on the floor. She was a young woman with long blond hair wearing a blue tee shirt and jeans. Josephine couldn't see any marks on her so she wondered how she'd died.

"Are you sure she's dead?" Josephine asked.

"She's dead all right," Alex said gravely. "A surge of power was forced through her hand chakras. It may be some sort of enchantment but we can't pick anything up with our tracers."

"So the enchantment used to kill this poor woman was obliterated along with the rest of the psychometric energy in the room," Josephine said.

"The entire house is clean of trace energies," Alex said.

"You mean nearly clean, Detective Whiney," Josephine said smugly. "All traces of energy can never be completely eliminated."

Alex frowned at her with annoyance. "We've waited an entire hour for you to get your sorry ass over here. Maybe you should do something."

"You young people need to learn some patience, Detective Whiney," Josephine said flippantly.

Alex continued frowning but refrained from responding to her taunt. She opened her senses to the energies of the room. She gasped in surprise because it was almost completely bereft of anything at all. This would be especially difficult. The wizard who'd done this had employed an excellent ignotus enchantment which meant the individual had purchased it or was a category four or five. This troubled Josephine just a bit because it was extremely rare for such powerful wizards to be serial killers. She noticed Alex shifting impatiently but he didn't interrupt her work. Josephine trailed the fragments of energy and reached out to one of them. Vague impressions wafted across the back of her mind but nothing substantial. She remained focused and after a moment, she saw the victim lying unconscious in her chair. Unfortunately, Josephine saw the vision through the mind of the killer so she didn't see any images of him or her.

Josephine continued to work with the energy traces without much success which began to frustrate her. She was currently tapped into the victim who was chopping carrots in the kitchen. The vision only lasted a second and was replaced by vague and meaningless impressions. Josephine concentrated harder and saw the silhouette of a man approaching. The image abruptly vanished but she knew she'd caught a glimpse of the killer. She had to get that vision back. Josephine's hands clenched into fists and power flowed through her. She tapped the trace and heard her grandson gasp with alarm. A gust of hot air whipped into the room.

"Grandma! Your ring!" Jake exclaimed.

She glanced down at her topaz ring and saw that it had turned green. Damn! She had to stop the flow of power she was currently channeling. Josephine relaxed and began blocking the magic that coursed through her. The hot wind abruptly died down and the ring turned blue. Alex stood stiff as a board and his green eyes widened with apprehension. The two forensics officers had also backed away from her so they now took up positions at the far side of the room. Josephine couldn't blame them for their fear but the Disaster that had killed so many had happened almost fifty years ago. There were safeguards in place from preventing anything like that from occurring again. If Josephine had lost control for another couple of seconds, the aequitas enchantment in her ring would have knocked her out.

"You can relax now, Whiney," Josephine said in a condescending tone. "You're safe."

Alex's tension eased visibly and his frown returned as his face flushed with embarrassment.

"Were you able to come up with anything useful?" he asked.

"No but I'm not done yet," she said.

"Yes, you are."

"I still need more time to tap more of the traces," Josephine said.

"Are you sure you're not going to blow anything up?" Alex fretted.

"I'll be fine," she said reassuringly.

Josephine tapped the few traces she hadn't yet reached. More impressions danced across her mind but few substantial pieces of information were discovered. She sighed with disappointment.

"The killer is a male. His mind feels very cold and calculating. He's very disciplined," Josephine said.

Alex and Jake scribbled down notes on their pads.

"What else do you've got?" Alex asked.

"Nothing. That's all I picked up," Josephine said regretfully.

"Are you sure about that? Nothing at all?" Alex asked expectantly as if she would fail to mention something.

"I'm sure. Except I did pick up a couple of other things," Josephine said.

"Yes?" Alex said impatiently.

Josephine pointed at one of the forensics officers. "Your wife is going to tell you this afternoon that the test was wrong and she's not really pregnant. She's pretty upset and doesn't know how you're going to take it." The officer blanched at this news and glanced at his colleague. She turned to pin Alex with an intense look and intentionally let the silence drag out before speaking. "I saw you accidentally dropping the sausages you made for breakfast on the kitchen floor but you were running late so you ate them anyway. I'll bet you pick food out of the trash too."

"She's lying. That never happened." Alex's face was flushed with embarrassment as he spoke to his colleague.

"I believe you," Jake said in a distracted tone as he jotted down what his grandmother had said.

"What in the hell are you writing that down for?" Alex said with exasperation.

"Just in case it proves useful in the future," Jake said flippantly.

Alex narrowed his eyes at Josephine. "Do you have any more information regarding this case I should know about?"

"Nothing at all, detective," she said innocently. "I've told you everything I've seen."

"You should walk around the room and see if you've missed any traces," Alex said.

Josephine snorted with exasperation but did as he requested. She opened her senses to the trace energies once again and slowly traversed the room. Alex eyed her intently and Jake was biting his lower lip to keep from laughing at her antics with his colleague. Josephine knew that it wasn't good that she hadn't come up with anything more useful and it was the first time this had happened to her. She abruptly stopped walking and shrugged.

"I'm not getting anything," she said.

"Are you absolutely sure?" Alex asked.

"I'm sure. I'd like to talk to my grandson for a moment."

"He's working. He doesn't have time to socialize," Alex said curtly.

"I didn't share everything I've picked up about you, Detective Whiney," she said in a suggestive, whispery voice. "There's something more I could share with the room."

"There's nothing more you can reveal about me that everyone doesn't already know," Alex said moodily.

"Are you sure of that?" she said teasingly. "Do you remember what and who you dreamed about this morning?"

Alex's face reddened. "Go ahead and talk to your grandson."

He strode across the room to speak to the forensics officers which gave Josephine some privacy with her grandson.

"What did you see about his dream?" Jake asked curiously.

"I was just yanking his chain," Josephine said.

"Oh." Jake looked disappointed. He enjoyed seeing his colleague squirm as Alex was difficult to work with.

"Is this the second or third victim of this particular serial killer?"

"The third."

"Do you have any idea what kind of enchantment is used to kill the victims?" Josephine asked.

"No, it could be anything."

"Normally there are telltale signs even if the magic has dissipated. Heart attack, stroke, blood aneurism, oxygen deprivation…"

"None of the typical spells. There's no sign of physical damage. It's as if the body just shut down for no particular reason," Jake said.

Josephine's eyes widened with surprise. "Just like how everyone died in the Disaster."

"We can't jump to conclusions," Jake said swiftly.

"You can't tell me that Alex hasn't thought of it already."

"Yes, he's considered that possibility but we don't have enough evidence to be sure of anything."

Alex stiffly walked over to them. "Josephine, I think you've done everything you can do here. Thank you for your help. We'll let you know when you can be of further assistance."

"Thank you, detective," she said.

She kissed her grandson on the cheek and left the house with a feeling of relief. It disturbed her that the killer possessed such a good ignotus enchantment that she hadn't been able to pick up any valuable clues.

Chapter 2

Josephine, Alice, and Helen were shopping at Publix together in the early afternoon. Josephine's friends no longer owned cars as they had both lost their license for different reasons. Helen had the unfortunate lack of ability to pay attention to what she was doing and had pulled out in front of a semi resulting in a totaled car. She'd been forced to retake the driver's test and had failed the written portion. Unfortunately, she'd retaken the test three times with the same pitiful results and given up. Alice was no longer able to pass the vision test even with her glasses. Because of her friends' plight, Josephine always took them out grocery shopping when needed. Helen was currently riding an electronic shopping cart since she tired easily while Alice pushed her own.

"You wouldn't believe how annoying Whiney was," Josephine complained. "He was so impatient and kept telling me to try again like I didn't know what I was doing."

"Young people are so full of themselves," Helen commiserated.

She accidentally bumped into a display of cereal as she turned the corner. The boxes jiggled precariously but none of them fell over. A man in his early twenties dodged the electric shopping cart and barely missed being rammed as Helen zipped past him.

"I can't believe there's another serial killer on the loose," Alice said.

"This is a big city so we're bound to have them," Josephine said.

"He must be a powerful wizard if he got rid of the trace evidence at the scene of the crime," Alice said. "Normally, you are able to I.D. the culprit."

"Yes, it's very disturbing," Josephine said.

She stopped her cart a short distance from two elderly women who were blocking the half and half. They were slowly looking through the various items as if they didn't know what they were searching for. Josephine held her hand out and two cartons of half and half slowly drifted out and dropped into her cart. The two women glanced at the cartons in mild surprise but didn't give it much attention since almost three-quarters of the population were wizards and this sort of thing happened all the time.

"And Whiney was going to refuse to let me talk to my grandson," Josephine said in an outraged tone. "I had to practically twist his arm to get some time with Jake."

"What a stupid man!" Helen exclaimed with commiseration. "Here he is having you help him out and he won't even let you talk to your grandson?"

"That's right!" Josephine said. "I'd like to kick his skanky ass."

"Me, too," Alice said indignantly.

"Did he finally let you talk to Jake?" Helen asked.

"Yes." Josephine shoved her cart forward and they turned into the canned foods aisle. "Did you need any soup or anything?"

"Yes, I need more chili," Alice said.

She stopped in front of the chili but it was placed too high for her to reach from her cart.

"I'll get that for you. How many would you like?" Josephine asked.

"Three of the roadhouse blend," Alice said.

"Okay." Josephine concentrated and three of the cans slowly rose from the shelf and drifted into Alice's cart.

"It must be nice being a category six wizard," Alice said enviously.

"Yeah, it's real nice never being able to retire no matter how old you get," Josephine said bitterly as she swept a long strand of her silky, black hair from her face. "Never being able to enjoy a nice day off without wondering if you'll be interrupted by a police call."

"Yeah, that really sucks," Alice said.

Josephine spotted a cute guy in his early thirties wearing a tropical, camp shirt and shorts. He was pulling a can of olives from the shelf. Josephine quickly used her telekinesis to make the box of cereal on his shopping cart leap onto the floor while his back was turned. He saw it as he placed the olives in the cart and bent over to pick it up. Josephine enjoyed the view as he scooped up the box.

"Nice," she said.

"What's nice?" Alice asked.

"That we're still friends after all these years," Josephine said cheerfully as she continued to admire the guy's figure. She dragged her attention back to her friends and smiled at them.

"You're so sweet," Helen said.

Alice turned her attention to the canned soup and picked out a couple of chicken noodle which was her favorite.

"I think that's everything, isn't it?" Helen asked.

"I believe so," Josephine said slowly as she surveyed the items in her cart.

"I need some more macaroni and cheese," Alice said.

"Of course." Josephine pushed off and led them to the appropriate aisle.

Alice grabbed about a dozen boxes and dropped them into her cart. Macaroni and cheese was one of her favorite foods although Josephine couldn't stand the stuff.

"Okay, I'm ready," Alice said cheerfully.

They were heading towards the end of the aisle when Robert, Josephine's ex-husband, turned the corner. Robert was a 78 year old, category five with gray, thinning hair and a mustache. His skin was dotted with liver spots and he had piercing green eyes and flabby, sagging skin on his formerly muscular forearms. He had divorced Josephine about twenty years ago and had claimed that he'd been afraid she would dump him for a younger man since she looked so young. She had been furious when she'd discovered he'd been cheating on her and given him the unflattering nickname of Spot because of his liver spots and his doglike behavior. Robert Miller stopped dead in his tracks when he realized he'd happened upon his ex-wife. He wore a green tee shirt and jeans which he'd hitched up to his stomach.

"Hello, Spot," Josephine said coolly. "What brings you here?"

Robert turned his cart around and started to walk away. Josephine flicked her wrist and his pants dropped to his ankles. She sensed a rush of power as he brought his shield up. He quickly buttoned his pants and secured the belt buckle. Josephine laughed coolly at his retreating back.

"Are you afraid of me, Spot?" she said.

Robert halted and slowly turned to face her. Helen backed her electric shopping cart so she was a short distance behind Josephine.

Alice was off to the side but positioned in between the two ex's. She eyed them both warily.

"I'm not afraid of you. You're pathetic," he said disdainfully.

"Go suck a lemon," Josephine said.

"Go to hell."

Robert turned and pushed his shopping cart away.

"That's right. Get lost, Spot!" Josephine called out sharply.

He turned the corner and was gone. Josephine narrowed her eyes with displeasure.

"He always seems to get the last word. I'd like to kick his ass," Josephine said moodily.

"Maybe we should teepee his house tonight," Helen suggested.

"No, I don't think so. When you get to be my age, you just learn to play by the rules sometimes," Josephine said with resignation.

Helen and Alice nodded silently in agreement.

"I'd like to get some rolls without the raisons," Alice said.

"You mean cinnamon rolls," Josephine said.

"Yes! But I don't want the kind shipped to the store."

"Okay. It looks like we're going to the bakery again," Josephine said with resignation.

They had already gone to the bakery for bread but apparently Alice was in the mood for some cinnamon rolls. They made their way across the store and Alice began fingering the different dessert packages. She picked up a dozen chocolate chip cookies and carefully scrutinized them.

"We came here for rolls," Josephine reminded her.

"These cookies look good." Alice eyed them for a moment then set them back on the display. She picked up a package of carrot muffins and gave them a close look. Josephine tapped her right foot impatiently while her friend made up her mind. Robert pushed his cart into the area but halted and turned when he saw them.

"That's right. Get the hell out of here, Spot," Josephine said loudly.

"Kiss my ass," Robert said just as he turned the corner.

"He really ticks me off," Josephine grumbled.

"I've noticed," Helen said wryly.

Alice didn't seem to have realized anything out of the ordinary had occurred. She was still considering the same package of carrot muffins. Josephine snatched them out of her hand and put them in her cart.

"I don't want those!" Alice exclaimed indignantly.

"Sorry." Josephine's face flushed with embarrassment.

Alice grabbed the package and put them back onto the display. She shot her friend a disgruntled look then wandered farther away. Josephine sighed with resignation and followed Alice. Finally, they reached the cinnamon rolls. Alice picked up a two-pack but it didn't seem to impress her because she put it back. She chose another one and looked it over. Josephine sighed loudly and wondered how long this was going to take. Alice was particularly choosey about her dessert and also random items.

"These look good," Alice said.

She placed a package of six into her cart and they took off.

"I guess we're done," Josephine said cheerfully.

"No, I'd like some tuna," Alice said. "I haven't had a tuna fish sandwich in quite awhile."

"Okay."

They strolled down to the aisle and Alice promptly chose four cans.

"Anything else?" Josephine asked.

"I'm good," Helen said.

"I almost forgot my grandson, Jeff, is coming with his kids to Sarasota. I should bake a cake," Alice said. "I'm afraid I don't have the patience to make it from scratch. It'll have to be one of those box cakes."

"They're just as good as the ones from scratch," Josephine said.

"Whatever you say," Alice said breezily.

The three of them made their way over to the aisle. Alice frowned thoughtfully at the choices.

"I can't decide whether I should make a lemon cake or brownies," she said.

"Lemon cake. It seems more sophisticated," Josephine said.

"Okay."

They returned to their homes and Josephine unpacked her groceries. Her mind wandered as she thought about Jake and the case she had worked on this morning. She hadn't spent much time with him lately. Josephine decided she'd do something nice for him. She baked a death by chocolate cake which she brought over to his house. She had a key to his small, white house which he'd given to her after she kept letting herself in through the living room window by peeling back the screen and using telekinesis to unlock it from the outside. The other locks were more difficult to disengage magically as they were protected by security enchantments. Jake had said that his home was more secure if she just let herself in with a key rather than possibly show a would-be criminal exactly how to break in. Of course,

18

Josephine had agreed that this was a perfectly reasonable argument and had accepted his key.

Jake loved palm trees so his front lawn had four of them. He had a lawn service come twice a week so his yard was always well-manicured. Josephine stepped inside his house and set the cake down in the kitchen. After that, she brewed some coffee and waited for him to arrive. Sometimes, he ran a bit late but never by too much. She appreciatively inhaled the aroma of freshly brewed coffee as she turned on the television. She tuned into the news then looked at his slovenly-kept living room. Several empty beer cans littered the floor along with dirty clothes strewn randomly. A pair of jeans was hanging off one of the couches and a sock was draped across the armrest of another. She gathered his clothes and brought them to the laundry room. She immediately started a load in the washing machine then returned to watch some television. Josephine heard the key in the lock of the front door and stood up to greet her grandson. Jake blinked at her in surprise before stepping inside the house.

"So how's my handsome young man doing?" Josephine said cheerfully.

"Fine. How are you?" Jake asked.

"Great! I baked some death by chocolate for you."

"Sounds good."

"You really should pick up after yourself better," Josephine lectured him. "Women don't like slovenly men. Of course, I'm not saying you're slovenly. You're a very considerate and handsome young man. I think you're a wonderful grandson. You shouldn't change for anyone."

"You sure ticked off Alex," Jake said.

"I know. I can't help myself. He's such a pain that I find myself saying things I otherwise wouldn't," Josephine said regretfully. Her thoughts went back to her shopping expedition and her expression soured. "I ran into Spot today at Publix. I hate it when that happens."

"Did you do anything to him?" Jake asked with a mischievous gleam to his brown eyes.

"I made his pants fall down," Josephine crowed. "He brought a shield up so I couldn't do anything else without making a scene."

"He usually protects himself immediately when he sees you."

"His reflexes are slow. He doesn't know how to stay sharp like me."

"It smells like fresh coffee," Jake said.

"Yes, I thought you'd want some after a hard day of work."

"Sounds good."

Jake went to the kitchen and Josephine followed him. They both poured themselves mugs of coffee. Josephine added half and half and sugar to hers while her grandson drank his black. They sat down in the living room and Jake turned off the television with a bit of telekinesis so they could talk.

"How was work today?" Josephine asked before taking a sip of her coffee.

"Fine. Alex was in a bad mood for most of the morning but it was worth it," Jake said.

"I sure got him good, didn't I?" Josephine asked.

"Yep."

"I need to make sure I remember to workout today. I skipped because of that call from Detective Whiney."

"You didn't have to spend much time. You had the entire day to go to the gym."

"You don't understand. I'm a creature of habit now that I'm retired. If I get called in to work, it throws my entire day off. I've done good work for my entire life and I think I deserve to enjoy my retirement." Josephine crossed her shapely legs and leaned back in the armchair as she took another sip of her coffee. She was wearing green cargo shorts and a tropical shirt which showed off her smooth, youthful skin and fine figure.

"You didn't have to retire when you turned 84 you know," Jake said.

"I don't know what you expected me to do! That's pretty old, you know!" Josephine sputtered in outrage. She choked on her coffee and began coughing uncontrollably.

"You know what I mean. Look at you! You look my age," Jake said. "I'm sure you have just as much energy, too."

Josephine was still coughing and she uncrossed her legs so she could lean forward a bit. Finally, she caught her breath and glared at him.

"I'm retired. End of story."

"That's fine!" Jake held his hands up in a placating gesture. "I was just letting you know that you look great."

"Thank you. You're such a flatterer." Josephine smiled cheerfully at him. "You're my favorite grandson, you know. Don't tell Bob I told you that though."

Bob was his older brother who lived in Oregon. They hardly ever saw him because he only visited once every year on either Thanksgiving or Christmas.

"You seem like you're bored sometimes. I'm not sure if you enjoy not working anymore," Jake said.

"Of course I don't enjoy retirement. Because I'm still on call at the police department. It's not fair that just because I'm a category six wizard that I have to work for the rest of my life."

"At least you have a few perks though."

"Whatever." Josephine took a larger gulp of her coffee. "I need some cheering up. Let's have some of that cake I made."

After having some chocolate cake and playing darts, Josephine returned to her condo to find a note taped to her door. Irritation made her frown and her body tighten reflexively because only one person did this to her – Dale Wallace. Dale was a seventy-nine year old who lived one floor above Josephine and strongly felt that she shouldn't be allowed to live in the retirement condominium. Of course, this outraged Josephine because she was five years older than that wind bag. As her fingers closed over the paper, anger rushed through her body. The note read: "Go back where you belong, slut."

Of course, Dale knew exactly how to push her buttons. Josephine crushed the paper in her fist and a torrent of cold air gushed through the hallway. She turned around to see if Dale was watching because sometimes he waited for her to come home and gloat over her response. She thought she saw movement from the corner of one of the hallways and suspected it was him.

"Dale! I'm going to kick your ass!" Josephine said.

He suddenly stepped out from exactly where she'd suspected he was hiding with a smug grin on his face. He had a shield up which she could take down pretty fast.

"You're going to beat up a helpless old man?" he said.

"You're five years younger than me." Josephine lashed out with a surge of power but it was out of control and branched off into three separate spells.

The cold wind continued to gush through the hallway as power continued to funnel through her uncontrollably. Dale's shield briefly became visible as a golden sphere of light surrounding his body as one of her spells knocked into it. The other two streams of power pounded against the walls making it sound like someone was knocking on them like a crazed lunatic. Dale didn't look alarmed at all as he sent off a jinx at her. She tracked it with her second sight and easily blocked it. She wasn't sure what it was. Josephine brought his shield down with her next attack but darkness was creeping along the edge of her vision. She shivered as the cold air continued to whip over her. She abruptly realized she was using far too much magic and glanced at her topaz ring which had turned green in warning. She launched another jinx at him which knocked him over onto his back. She didn't have the control to block the power flowing through her body at this point so the only hope she had was to get inside her apartment before she was knocked out.

Josephine grabbed her key and shoved it into her lock. Her hands were clumsy as the knockout spell from the aequitas enchantment in her ring took effect. Josephine passed out before she could manage to turn the key. She woke up a short while later with Alice and Helen stooped over her.

"We heard the commotion in the hall and came out to find you unconscious. You'll want to clean up," Helen said.

"I will?" Josephine asked.

They helped her stand up and her legs wobbled shakily. She slowly made her way to the bathroom and saw that Dale had written "freak" on her forehead with lipstick. She glared at her reflection and grabbed a paper towel to wipe off the annoying message.

"I'm going to kick his ass."

"You can't! Your ring will knock you out again!" Helen said warningly.

"I'll do it without magic this time!" Josephine said indignantly. "I'm not letting him get away with hounding me."

"Just leave him alone," Helen said.

"Leave him alone? I never did anything to him!"

"What about the time you made fake blood come out of his shower head?"

Josephine chortled with mirth. "That was hilarious! I wish I could have seen the look on his face."

"I think it's time for some payback," Alice cut in. "We could break into his apartment and give him some jinxes that he'll never forget."

"Let's just leave him alone!" Helen said.

"No, we're going to get even," Josephine said.

"I've got a perfect one!" Alice said with excitement. "It's a manifestation of cock roaches. They're really big and we can put it inside his cereal box. He always has cheerios for breakfast."

"Good one!" Josephine grinned with approval. "I think we should jinx his shampoo with an illusion to make it look like he's lost all his hair."

"Sounds good to me," Alice said.

"We'll have to be careful because he's probably put extra traps on his locks," Josephine said.

"We can get through them," Alice said confidently.

"Are you sure he didn't booby trap your condo?" Helen asked fretfully. "He had enough time to write on your forehead. Maybe he put a couple of jinxes in here?"

"There's only one way to find out." Josephine slowly stepped into the living room and opened her awareness to the subtle energies flowing around her.

She honed in on something underneath the couch. She began to reach out with her mind but this seemed to trigger action. A dozen huge, black spiders the size of dinner plates stormed out from their hiding space under the couch. Helen and Alice squealed with alarm. Josephine was too distracted to continue focusing on her second sight. One of the spiders tried to crawl up on right leg but she kicked it off and smashed it. Luckily, the three of them still wore their shoes. It appeared that Dale had left some manifestations behind.

"I hate spiders!" Helen climbed up on one of the other couches.

Alice and Josephine took shelter on the couch with her friends and the spiders swarmed around them in a circle.

"They're so ugly," Alice said with displeasure.

"Do you think they're poisonous?" Helen asked.

"I don't think he'd manifest venom. He isn't stupid enough to go that far," Josephine said. "Why don't you two dispel these things?"

"Okay. Let me concentrate," Helen said shakily.

She eyed the spiders and seemed to become hypnotized so Josephine tapped her shoulder. Helen flinched and squealed in alarm.

"Come on! Concentrate!" Josephine said. "I don't want to have to stand up here all night!"

"Just give me a second," Helen said.

She took a deep breath and held out her hands. Josephine sensed her friend gathering energy. Without warning, two of the spiders spit a viscous black liquid at them. The vile substance splattered against Helen's stomach and hands. She screamed and almost lost her balance. She flailed with her arms and grabbed Josephine. More of the spiders spat out the mysterious black substance which hit all three of them. Josephine cringed at the disgusting goo dripping down her blouse and legs.

"Get rid of the damn things! Please!" Josephine exclaimed.

She couldn't focus her energy enough to perform dispelling or she would have done it herself. This was one instance where she had to rely on her friends. Helen's arms shook as she held out her hands once again and concentrated. More black goo splattered on her and she flinched but continued to gather energy. When she released the spell, a small spark of white light flashed out and caused two of the spiders to vanish but the goo and the other ten spiders remained. Josephine gagged when a whiff of the odor from the black spider spit reached her nostrils. It reminded her of a backed up sewer.

"Oh God! Alice! You have to do something about this!" Josephine said desperately.

"I know," Alice said.

She held out her hands and earned herself several splatters of spider spit. A flash of white light exploded from her hands and eliminated six of the spiders and most of the goo that had latched onto the three women. Josephine was relieved that the noxious odor had suddenly dissipated due to Alice's spell.

"Good work!" Josephine patted her friend on the back.

Helen reached her hands out and furrowed her brows in concentration. She flinched when two of the spiders spit more of the black viscous liquid on her. Unfortunately, she lost her balance and fell off the couch. The spiders immediately crawled over her and spat more of the liquid on her. She brushed a couple of them off but they kept crawling on her. Josephine crushed one of the spiders with her foot then quickly raised her leg back onto the couch.

"Get them off!" Helen cried out.

Alice reached her hands out and dispelled more of the spiders so that only one remained. Josephine crushed the last one with her foot. Helen slowly sat up and wiped some of the black goo which was dripping from her face.

"We need to give Dale a taste of his own medicine," Helen said.

"I couldn't agree more," Josephine said.

Chapter 3

When Josephine entered the gym with Helen and Alice, she was the first to notice Robert. Josephine was wearing her usual workout attire consisting of pink shorts, a pink tee shirt, and a pink frilly bow in her long black hair. Helen had on black shorts and a gray tee shirt while Alice wore a white tee shirt and yellow shorts.

"Don't look now but Spot's here," Josephine said with displeasure.

"Where?" Alice looked around and saw him over on one of the exercise bikes.

Robert was wearing a white tank top and shorts. His skin was flushed and perspiration beaded along his flabby arms, neck, and legs. He looked to be holding onto the bike for dear life.

"He's so pathetic," Josephine said.

"Yeah," Alice said.

"I wish we didn't go to the same gym. It makes my stomach queasy just watching him exercise," Josephine said.

"He's pretty disgusting," Helen said.

"I don't know why I married him," Josephine said disdainfully.

They walked over to three of the machines. They liked to workout side-by-side. Helen always started on the leg extension while Alice started on her obliques, and Josephine went to the hammer which was a good abdominal. Helen carefully set her weight on the lowest setting possible. She was by far in the worst shape compared to the three of them. Josephine and Alice encouraged her to put a bit of effort into her workout but to no avail. Josephine narrowed her eyes at her ex before she began exercising. When her abs were burning and she could barely pull the weight anymore, she stopped to rest. The bottle of water she'd brought with her floated from the floor and into her outstretched hand. She took a long drink then set the bottle back down. She didn't notice that Robert had finished exercising until he approached them. Josephine stiffened and narrowed her eyes at him.

"Trying to get in shape, Barbie?" Robert taunted.

"I'm already in shape, Spot," Josephine said coolly.

"Maybe you should give your friend some pointers so she doesn't have to ride around in a shopping cart," he said as he walked by.

"Maybe you should learn to keep your pants on, maggot breath," she said to his retreating back.

"Maybe you should leave other people's clothes alone," he shot back as he continued walking away.

Josephine glared at him but he had already traversed too far away to continue their dialogue. "I'd really like to kick his skanky ass."

"Me, too," Alice said. "I think we should tee pee his house or something."

"That's so juvenile," Josephine said. "I think what I'd like to do is set a few manifestation traps loose in his house."

"We were going to get Dale back for setting that spider manifestation trap in your condo," Alice reminded her.

"That's right," Josephine said thoughtfully. "I just hate how Robert always gets the last word. It really chaps my hide."

"Who's it going to be?" Helen fretted. "Dale or Robert?"

"We'll focus our efforts on Dale, I guess," Josephine said. "Have you worked on your skunk manifestation trap yet?"

"No, I haven't had the time."

"What? You had all day yesterday to work on it!" Josephine exclaimed in surprise.

"I know but they were having an all day marathon of New Earth on the Sci Fi channel," Helen said.

"Oh, I didn't realize." Josephine shrugged and turned to Alice. "What about you? Got that vomiting toilet jinx ready?"

"No, I'm afraid not. I started on it but my dentist called and told me I hadn't paid my bill from last time. I clearly remembered paying him but it took me awhile to search the records and stuff. I couldn't let it hang over my head so when I found the paid check, I took the bus to his office and showed it to him."

"I would have given you a ride," Josephine said.

"I didn't want to put you out."

"That's okay. I don't mind. Well, I'm happy to report that I did work on the gas manifestation jinx. I'm going to make it the worst smell you could imagine. I think I'll set the trap in his kitchen cupboard but maybe the microwave would be a good choice," Josephine said. "I'd like to see him dispel a bunch of gas."

"You're right. That's pretty much impossible," Alice said.

They continued their workout then finished up and returned to their condos. Josephine had a message on her answering machine from Detective Riley which stated tersely: "Call me."

"I have better things to do," Josephine said irritably. She picked up the phone and dialed Helen's number.

"Hello?" Helen said.

"It's me," Josephine said. "Whiney called while we were out. I don't feel like working though."

"Do you think there's been another murder?" Helen asked. "Maybe you should call him back."

"I doubt there's been another murder this soon," Josephine said. "Sarasota isn't that big a city."

"You never know," Helen fretted. "I'd hate to let a killer run loose."

"I'm sure he just wants me to try to use psychometry on some items from the crime scene of the previous victims," Josephine said. "That's the standard procedure when someone can't find any trace energy at a crime scene if there have been previous crimes."

"You know a lot about this stuff," Helen said in admiration.

"That's because I have to spend my retirement working!" Josephine said in a whiny tone. "Here I am at 84 and I'm on call like a damned doctor!"

"He'll probably try calling you again."

"Let him call. I won't answer my phone," Josephine said smugly.

"That's a good idea," Helen said.

"I guess I'll talk to you later."

"Bye."

Josephine hung up with a satisfied smile on her face. She wasn't going to let Alex get his way. She'd help him when she was damned good and ready. Josephine flinched when the phone rang. She eyed it with apprehension and wondered if it was Alex. She watched the phone with anticipation as she waited for the machine to pick up.

"This is Detective Riley. I need to you to come into the station and use your psychometry on some of the items we have on previous crime scenes. We don't want this serial killer running loose."

"It's not my problem. I probably wouldn't be able to pick up anything anyway. His ignotus enchantment is too good," Josephine said. "Besides, I need some time to myself."

She turned on the television and tuned into a talk show. She found them to be informative. The phone rang a short while later and Alex left another terse message letting her know that he suspected she was at home. Josephine had a feeling he would stop by her condo so she took off. She decided to watch a movie at the theatre. Josephine grabbed her purse and sailed out the door in case Alex made another call or decided to pay her a visit. She was tempted to take the stairs but decided to ride the elevator. When the doors opened, Dale was revealed. He blinked at her in surprise and shifted uncomfortably. Josephine reluctantly stepped inside and pushed the first floor button.

"I heard your apartment had an odor problem," Dale said after a lengthy pause.

"You don't want to mess with me, maggot breath," Josephine said coolly with her back turned to him so that she was facing the elevator doors.

"You don't belong here."

"I most certainly do. I'm eighty-four and retired. Unfortunately, I can't enjoy my retirement with pond-scum like you hanging around."

"I have plenty more jinxes and I'm prepared to use them. If you think those spiders were a nuisance, you should see what else I've got," he sneered.

The elevator doors opened and Josephine turned to confront him.

"Just remember that I'm a category six so magical locks won't do much to keep me out. I can make worse jinxes than you could ever imagine," Josephine said smugly.

A cold gust of wind whipped through the elevator but she quickly cut off the flow of power that she'd unconsciously summoned. Dale blinked at her with surprise and wariness. Josephine spun on her heel and stalked away. She was pleased that he didn't throw back any sharp retorts. She loved getting the last word. Josephine hopped in her car and sped away from the retirement complex. Soon, sirens blared behind her and she realized she'd been driving much too quickly. Josephine sighed with resignation and pulled over. When the officer stepped out of his car, she recognized Howie from some of the crime scenes she'd worked at. She rolled down her window and smiled playfully at him. He grinned back at her but his eyes had a slight guardedness because he took his job seriously.

"Hey, Howie. It's so good to see you," Josephine said. "You wouldn't dream of giving a helpless old lady a speeding ticket would you?"

He laughed nervously. "You were going pretty fast."

"Did you like the brownies I made for you and Cindy last month?" Josephine said. "I know how much your wife loves chocolate."

"Yes, she loves your brownies," Howie said.

"Yesterday, there was a scene in that soap opera Evergreen Manor that really got to her. If you brought her a dozen yellow roses, she would be absolutely shocked and tickled pink," Josephine said.

Her psychometric gift was extremely useful on occasions like this one.

"I'm not much into soap operas," he said.

"You know how Cindy loves her shows. She'd really be pleased if you would surprise her."

"Thanks for the tip," Howie said.

His posture relaxed and his smile was no longer guarded.

"I'm getting a baking bug again so I'll probably be stopping by pretty soon to give you and Cindy another batch of brownies."

"That's very generous," Howie said cheerfully. "So what are you up to this evening?"

"I'm going to the movies," Josephine said.

"Which one?"

"The Hollywood 20. I just love those big screens."

"Yeah. They're nice." Howie smiled cheerfully at her. "Well, I guess I'll talk to you later. Be careful not to drive too fast."

"I'll definitely be more careful."

Howie went back to his vehicle and Josephine slowly drove away. She arrived at the theatre but didn't see any good movies so she went shopping at the mall until it closed. When she returned to her condo, there were two more messages on her machine. She sighed with resignation as she pressed the play button.

"It's Detective Riley. I need you to call me as soon as possible," he said tersely. "This is a criminal investigation and I really need your help."

The machine beeped and played back the next message which was Alex Riley again.

"You need to call me now or I'm going to come down there and drag you to the station," he said tersely.

Josephine picked up the phone and dialed Helen's number.

"Hello?" Helen said.

"It's me," Josephine said in a quivery voice. "Detective Riley is hounding me like I'm a criminal or something! It's terrible!"

"Oh, dear! I'm so sorry to hear that!" Helen exclaimed.

"Could I spend the night at your place? I don't think he'll look for me there," Josephine said. "He threatened to drag me to the station and lock me up!"

"We can't have that! Just come on over and you can use the guest room. Are you sure he won't come looking for you here?" Helen asked.

"No, I don't think so. Detective Whiney isn't too bright," Josephine said snidely.

"Okay. I'll see you soon then."

"Bye."

Josephine packed her toothbrush and a change of clothes then went over to Helen's condo which was only several rooms away. She was relieved that she would be staying with her friend because it guaranteed that Detective Riley would leave her alone for awhile.

"I've been thinking," Helen said as she and Josephine settled in the living room. "Isn't it risky to avoid your consulting work? You might end up in jail."

"No, I can just say that I didn't realize he was trying to contact me," Josephine said smugly. "Besides, I'm old and I can get away with stuff like that."

"That's true," Helen said in agreement.

"I hate to be called on a bunch of consulting work for the police. I feel like my life is being wasted away. Before I know it, my time will be up and I'll pass on," Josephine said.

"You still have many years to go before that happens," Helen said consolingly.

"I guess you're right but I feel like a freak sometimes. People act like I'm an anomaly and that I don't belong. People like Dale."

"It's okay. You're just different. There aren't very many category six wizards around and you have to remember that a category six is what caused the Disaster so even after fifty years, people will be edgy and fearful of your kind," Helen said.

"These stupid rings we have to wear keep us from doing anything worthwhile," Josephine said bitterly. "If I try to do anything cool, I get knocked out. I can't do any type of magic that's more strenuous than what a category two is capable of which isn't much."

"I know but you just have to remind yourself of the benefits," Helen said.

Josephine sighed with exasperation. She was tired of being told that she was lucky and privileged. She felt like she was constantly being punished for her genetics and she could never escape that. She heard a loud pounding out in the hall and Alex's angry voice:

"Open up! I know you're here! I saw your car in the parking garage!"

"Oh, no!" Josephine exclaimed. "What do I do?"

"He won't think to come here, will he?" Helen asked. "I don't want to go to jail as an accomplice to a crime."

"I haven't committed a crime!" Josephine said indignantly.

She flinched when Alex pounded on her door again. She couldn't risk the chance that he'd try her friend's condo. She needed to escape somehow. She gasped in alarm when someone rapped at Helen's door. She and her friend exchanged worried looks before

Josephine ran to the balcony and shut the curtains behind her so she couldn't be easily seen.

"I'm coming!" Helen called out.

Josephine wringed her hands as she stood outside and wondered if there was any way she could climb down the wall. If she used telekinesis to float down to the ground, her ring would probably knock her out before she got halfway down. She'd probably end up breaking a leg. Josephine heard Alex's voice inside the condo. He had barged past Helen and was walking through the living room.

"You have a guest here?" Alex asked.

"No, that's just in case I do have one," Helen said.

"Why do you have a suitcase here?"

"It's mine, detective."

"I don't think so. There's a change of clothes in here."

"I like to keep it for emergencies."

"Where's Josephine?"

"I have no idea," Helen said nervously.

A silence ensued and Josephine bit her lip nervously. Without warning, the curtain whipped to the side and Alex was glaring at her.

"Hello, detective! What a pleasant surprise!" Josephine said.

"You can be arrested for avoiding your consulting work," he threatened.

"I had no idea you were looking for me, Alex."

"I left two messages on your machine. You were going to spend the night here just to avoid me."

"I was just visiting her. I wasn't going to stay the night!" Josephine exclaimed. "You come up with the strangest ideas!"

"Why were you hiding out here?" Alex demanded.

"I thought Helen was having a visitor and I came outside for some fresh air," Josephine said breezily. "If you need me to work on something for you, you just have to ask."

"Let's go."

"Okay."

Josephine strode down the hall toward her condo and realized Alex was following her. She turned and shot him a questioning look.

"What are you doing?" she asked.

"I'm driving you to the station," Alex said.

"No, you're not. I'm driving myself."

Alex frowned at her warningly. "You're either coming with me willingly or I'm arresting you. Your choice."

Josephine stiffened reflexively and glared at him with open hostility.

"Okay, Detective Whiney. We'll do it your way."

The two of them headed for the elevator and he led her to his car. She'd tried to avoid him before so this wasn't the first time she'd ridden in his car. Of course, this was the first time she'd been clever enough to spend the night with a friend but unfortunately, things hadn't gone as well as she'd planned.

"I can't believe you're being so difficult," Josephine said.

Alex shot her an incredulous look of disbelief then his eyes returned to the road. His knuckles bulged as his fingers tightened on the steering wheel. He probably wanted to strangle her but she didn't care. Josephine had worked an honest, hard life and was in retirement now so if Alex found it inconvenient to hunt her down to do his work for him, that was his problem rather than hers. Josephine's chin jutted out at a stubborn angle and she maintained a chilly silence until they arrived at the station.

"Let's make this fast," she said.

Alex brought her to one of the interrogation rooms and made her wait there while he gathered the evidence from lockup. She crossed her arms over her chest and seated herself. She wished she'd had the presence of mind to bring a book because by the time he deigned to show up, she was bored silly.

"I'm really tired, Alex. I need some coffee," she said.

"We're fresh out," he said tersely.

"Make some more then," Josephine said irritably. "I'm old and tired and can't work for you without my coffee."

"You won't be able to sleep. It's getting late in the evening."

"I don't care! I want some coffee!" Josephine's chin jutted out stubbornly.

"Jesus Christ!" Alex threw his arms up in exasperation. "I'll get you your damned coffee!"

"And don't forget to add cream and sugar," Josephine called out.

She knew he'd heard her but had failed to respond. He was so childish sometimes. He was lucky she was such a professional and put up with his unruly behavior. Josephine eyed the evidence which was still in plastic baggies. They'd already been dusted for fingerprints but obviously nothing had been found. A whole bunch of everyday items lay on the table in front of her such as a broken picture, a cracked ashtray, various assortments of clothing, and other odds and ends. Alex returned with a large, gray mug of coffee.

"Thank you, sweetie," Josephine said as she accepted the cup.

She opened her awareness to the trace energies of the room to make sure he hadn't did something strange to the beverage. When she could see that it was safe, she took a sip.

"Excellent." She beamed at him with pleasure but he merely frowned back.

Josephine took another drink before she opened her second sight again. Her brows furrowed in concentration because the two closest pieces of evidence had absolutely nothing on them. She allowed her attention to wander to the other pieces. She found broken fragments on the picture frame. She zeroed in on the trace energy and received a series of broken images in her mind's eye. She hadn't attained anything useful that she could relay to Alex at this point. She focused more of her attention on the trace energy that she'd picked up on and tried to get a better reading. A pressure began to pound at her temples and a frigid wind whipped over her. Her attention was so fixed on the trace energy that she didn't notice his expression turn wary and that he'd retreated just a bit from her.

"This is so frustrating," Josephine murmured.

The wind died down when she gave up on the reading. She squeezed her eyes shut and centered herself. Maybe if she tried again, she could dredge something up. Josephine took a gulp of coffee and realized Alex was regarding her expectantly.

"I didn't see enough to give you any descriptions or any details," Josephine said.

"Tell me what you did see. Maybe it could be useful."

"You don't understand. Everything I picked up was so fractured that there's nothing to describe," Josephine said.

"That doesn't make any sense."

"You're just frustrated because this is the first time I've failed to get something for you. Well, I'm sorry but I'm doing the best I can."

"All right. That's fine," Alex said with resignation.

"Let me try a couple more times just to be sure," Josephine said. "I haven't looked at everything yet but let me try to see if I can make out anything from the trace energy in the picture frame."

Unfortunately, nothing further came to her. She was extremely disappointed by her inability to uncover any further clues. She wasn't used to such difficulties.

"I'm sorry. I'm just not getting anything," Josephine finally said.

"All right. I'll take you home as soon as I lock this stuff back up," Alex said.

Chapter 4

Josephine nodded her head in agreement as she took another drink from her mug of coffee. She, Helen, and Alice were lounging in her living room reminiscing over the past. Her thoughts turned back to Robert and she cringed. She couldn't believe she'd wasted so many years with him.

"Sometimes, I wish I could go back knowing what I know now and change things for the better," Helen said wistfully.

"If anyone could do that, they would probably discover that alternative actions would lead to consequences that are just as bad or even worse," Alice said.

"You're such a pessimist sometimes," Helen said.

"I'm a realist. There's no point in wishing you could undo the past. It just makes you frustrated."

"Maybe if I could use the full potential of my abilities, I could do go back in time," Josephine said.

"I doubt it. You don't have any control over your wicked-ass powers," Alice said.

Josephine cocked a bemused brow at her friend as she took another drink of coffee.

"Have you finished your prep work for our attack on Dale's place?" Josephine asked.

"Yes, I'm ready," Helen said.

"Me, too," Alice chimed in.

"Great! As soon as we've finished our coffee, we can get him," Josephine said.

"Assuming he's not in his condo," Alice said.

"Of course," Josephine said airily.

Alice's gray hair was held in a pony tail by a pink ribbon. She also wore a pink tee shirt and pink shorts which were reminiscent of a Barbie doll. Josephine had on a turquoise shirt with a picture of a medicine wheel and black shorts. Helen dressed in a black tee shirt and shorts but with white tennis shoes. They lapsed into silence as they finished their coffee. Josephine jumped up from the table and announced her intention of calling Dale's condo. She dialed the number and waited patiently to see if he'd pick up. If he failed to answer, she could assume he wasn't home.

"Hello?" Dale said after the fourth ring.

Josephine hadn't planned on what to say on the off-chance that he was home. She should have anticipated this type of situation but discovered she was completely unprepared.

"Hello? Is this some sort of prank?" Dale said impatiently. "I can have this call traced and press charges for harassment."

"Be my guest, maggot-breath," Josephine said.

A short silence ensued followed by an outraged response. "How dare you call me in the early morning like this and wake me up from a sound sleep."

"You weren't sleeping, you old grump. You've been up for at least an hour."

"That's not the point!"

"Then get to the point, grumpy," Josephine said coolly.

"You're a freak!"

"You're a retard," Josephine retorted.

"Slut!"

"Bitch!" Josephine shouted and slammed down the receiver before he could reply.

She turned to see both her friends regarding her with speculation.

"I think he's home," Alice said.

Josephine sighed glumly and nodded in confirmation.

"He's such an obnoxious old man! Did you ever notice how women are so well-behaved when they get to be our age but men turn out to be such a pain in the ass?" Josephine asked.

"Yes, I've noticed," Alice said in confirmation.

"I'm glad I'm not married. I'd hate to be a nurse-maid to some old geezer," Helen said disdainfully.

"Yeah. We'd probably be shacked up to some grump like Dale," Josephine said. "I wonder when he's going to leave his condo. I hope he's not really lazy and spends most of his time hanging out at home."

"We'll have to call back later," Alice said.

"I guess so."

"He probably leaves his toilet seat up all the time," Helen commented.

"Robert used to do that all the time. I wanted to slap him silly," Josephine said with disgust. "Thank God I'm not married to him anymore!"

"Have you heard from Detective Riley about the case you're working on?" Alice asked.

"No, not since the day before yesterday. I can't believe I couldn't pick up anything useful from the evidence locker. It's so strange. Whoever used the ignotus enchantment at the crime scene knew what they were doing. I couldn't pick up anything useful," Josephine said.

"It's pretty rare that anyone can destroy the trace energies at a crime scene so that a category six can't pick anything up," Helen said.

"Energy can't be destroyed; only transformed or converted from one form to another," Josephine corrected her friend automatically.

"It sounds to me like if it's changed, it might as well be destroyed," Helen argued.

"Whatever," Josephine said. "I think we should see if Dale is still home in the early afternoon."

"This is hopeless. We have no way of knowing when he leaves his condo," Helen said. "Maybe we should just give up."

"No, I don't think so." Josephine's chin jutted out stubbornly. "He's not going to get his way."

"He'll probably leave you alone now that he's done the last prank on you."

"I think he'll continue dogging me until he thinks he's got me to move away," Josephine said. "And I'm not going to let that happen. He's going to get what's coming to him."

She drank the last of the coffee and got up to refill her cup. The phone rang and she cringed. She hated to think who could be calling her. She suspected that it was Alex and she didn't want to deal with another murder. Josephine ignored the phone as she added cream and sugar to her coffee. The machine picked up and beeped.

"Hey, Grandma. It's me," Jake's voice drifted into the room. "I have something to tell you but you have to promise to keep it a secret. I'll talk to you later. Bye."

"Why didn't you pick up the phone?" Helen stepped into the kitchen with a puzzled expression on her face.

"Alex is probably tricking him into getting me to answer the phone. When I do that, he'll tell me to stop by the crime scene. There's probably been another murder that their standard psychometry skills won't work on."

"Alex only got Jake to call twice. I don't think he'll do that anymore. He's more of a direct guy," Helen said.

"I'm trying to enjoy my retirement," Josephine said in a martyred tone. "The police just won't leave me alone. It's like I'm their star detective except I'm supposed to be retired. Instead, I get harangued every day by Detective Whiny because he isn't competent enough to find his ass with both hands."

The three of them sat down and chatted for awhile longer before leaving. Josephine decided to go to the Siesta Key beach and jog. She started by walking briskly and enjoyed the warm sun caressing her skin. A power vortex was located at this particular beach and the tempting thrum of its energy sang against Josephine as if tempting her to tap into its unlimited strength. She probably shouldn't come here so often but it felt invigorating. Not very many people spent much time at the beach. Even after so much time had passed by since the Disaster, few humans or wizards felt safe in close proximity to a vortex. The United States had three of them; one in Sedona, Arizona; one in Seattle Washington, and one in Sarasota, Florida. Josephine's body thrummed with potential as she jogged along the beach. If she ever gave into temptation, the aequitas enchantment in her ring would knock her out before she could do any damage. Josephine felt certain that she could control the power if she tapped into it but there was no way of convincing the Council or the government of that fact.

Josephine continued running along the shore until her sides burned and she was forced to rest. She breathed heavily and sank into the warm, crystalline sand. Her body craved for her to take in the power that flowed so invitingly nearby. It would be so easy to tap into it. Just a thought and it would be hers. She opened her second sight and gazed at the vortex swirling a short distance ahead of her with a quarter of it laying hidden beneath the water. It was massive and beautiful as a myriad of colors swirled in its depths. Josephine closed her eyes and reveled in the feeling but also felt the temptation to connect with it increase exponentially. She would be knocked out before anything bad could possibly happen. She should try it out. But then some of the nearby wizards may sense what she'd done or see her pass out. It was expressly forbidden for a category six to tap into the energy of a vortex for any reason. She would be doing community service for a long time if she was ever caught and furthermore, she could end up in jail. Dale and Robert would probably visit her cell every day.

Josephine leapt up to her feet and walked briskly back in the direction she'd just came. She rinsed her feet off at a resting point and then hopped into her car. Even this far away, she could feel the vortex and it was still tempting. She didn't know why she tortured herself like this. A craving had awakened inside her and made her want to go back to the beach. She'd tapped into the power about half a dozen times without anyone catching her in the act but she shouldn't tempt fate. Josephine wondered if she could connect with the vortex from this far away. She reached out with her mind and power flooded through her. She reveled in the feeling and didn't notice that the topaz in her ring instantly turned green. Before she could really enjoy herself, darkness crept along the edges of her vision. She turned her gaze to the ring and focused on it, instinctively probing the enchantment for weaknesses so she could unravel it.

Josephine abruptly awakened and quickly took stock of her surroundings to make sure no one was paying attention to her. Fortunately, she had lucked out. Josephine could feel the power enticingly close-by and the craving stirred within her again. She started the engine and quickly backed up. She needed to leave this place quickly. Vortexes were like catnip to category six wizards. It was generally a good idea to stay away from temptation. Josephine could still feel the vortex until she'd driven for about a dozen blocks. She chastised herself for her foolish behavior and returned to her condo. Instead of going to her own room, she knocked on Helen's door.

"Hi," Helen said.

"Let's call Dale and see if he's home," Josephine said.

"You seem different," Helen said.

"Really? I've been to the gym," Josephine said dismissively.

"That's probably it. It's like you've really worked out hard but you aren't tired," Helen said musingly.

"I can't wait to give Dale his comeuppance," Josephine said.

Helen went to her phone in the living room and picked up the receiver. She dialed the man's number and sat there waiting. She finally hung up and smiled hesitantly at Josephine.

"He's not home," Helen said.

"Great! I'll get my manifestation that I've prepared. You call Alice and let her know."

"Okay."

Soon, the three of them stood outside Dale's locked door in the hallway. Josephine opened her senses to the subtle trace energies surrounding them and focused on the door. She could see three security enchantments protecting the locks from being picked or opened with magic. One by one, she probed each enchantment for its weakness and temporarily disabled it. This was a time-consuming process but no one ventured out into the hallway to see what they were up to. Josephine grinned triumphantly as she finished her work and telekinetically unlocked and opened the door.

"Good work," Alice said.

"Thanks," Josephine said.

They stepped through the doorway and into the living room. Dale stood there with two wooden wands held ready. It looked like he'd been waiting for them. Neither Josephine, Alice, nor Helen were prepared for this so they had all of their enchantments in their pockets. Before anyone could react to his presence, Dale activated an enchantment in his left wand. Instantly, a powerful telekinetic wave swept Helen and Alice off their feet and hurled them through the doorway. Another burst of magic caused the door to slam shut and lock. Helen and Alice pounded on the door but there was no way they would be able to unlock the door magically.

"It's just you and me now, freak," Dale crowed.

Josephine activated the protection enchantment in her crystal pendant that she wore around her neck and reached in her right pocket for her black obsidian stone which contained a telekinetic enchantment. Dale activated his own shield and launched another telekinetic wave at her. Gold light briefly flickered around her as her protective enchantment warded off the attack. Josephine suspected he had an arsenal of enchantments at hand. Unfortunately, she hadn't brought much with her except for the pranks. She would need to use one to escape. Since she was a category six, she didn't have to actually hold the enchantments in her hand to activate them. She sent a burst of telekinetic energy at Dale and was satisfied to see his shield weaken considerably. One more hit ought to take it down. Dale brought up another shield that he must be wearing on one of his rings. Josephine counted five rings on his hand which meant she was seriously outgunned. Her shield fizzled out against his next assault and the remaining telekinetic force made her stagger backward several steps.

Josephine immediately activated the enchantment she had in her back pocket wand. She directed the spell in between herself and Dale. Instantly, a foul black mist materialized from that spot as if pouring out from an invisible portal. The worst smell that Josephine could imagine drifted to her nose which confirmed that her manifestation was working exactly as she had hoped.

"What in the hell is that stuff?" Dale asked with revulsion.

"Your essence," Josephine said flippantly.

The black mist was now completely blocking her from view so she rushed to the door and unlocked it manually. She sensed a knockout spell explode toward her and warded it off with a casual thought. Josephine threw open the door and slammed it shut behind her.

"Are you all right?" Helen said shakily.

"We need to get out of here!" Josephine exclaimed.

"I'm going to kick your butt, you stupid freak!" Dale shouted.

Josephine reached out with her mind and temporarily jumbled the security enchantments on the locked door. The enchantments would revert back to normal after about ten seconds but that was enough time to make their escape. Helen, Alice, and Josephine dashed to the elevator and pushed the call button.

"Maybe we should take the stairs," Helen fretted.

"It's only four stories in this building. The elevator can't be far," Alice said.

They heard Dale swear savagely and pound on the door.

"How long will it take for him to get out here?" Helen eyed the door across the hallway fearfully.

"Not long," Josephine said. "Maybe we shouldn't wait."

Alice walked briskly partway to Dale's door and held out both hands. A puddle of black fluid bubbled up from the carpet directly outside his door. Alice rushed back to the elevator. Dale's door suddenly swung open and he burst through the doorway. His bare feet flew out from under him as they slipped over the black, putrid substance. Black smoke poured from the open door of his condo which partially obstructed him from view.

"You slut!" Dale shouted.

The elevator doors parted so Josephine, Alice, and Helen rushed inside and quickly pushed the button for the third floor. Josephine giggled as Dale picked himself up off the floor and started toward them.

"See you later, bitch," Josephine said as the elevator doors slid shut.

"I'm going to take you down!" Dale shouted.

Josephine laughed and exchanged high fives with Alice. Helen reluctantly raised her hand when Josephine eyed her expectantly.

"Wasn't that great?" Josephine asked as the doors slid open again.

"That was something," Alice said.

They gathered in Josephine's apartment. Josephine made sure to engage her own security enchantment on the locks which she normally remembered anyway. It wouldn't do to forget when Dale was so pissed at her. He was liable to come up here and try to break in. She wasn't surprised when Dale failed to make an appearance though.

"Well, that didn't go quite as expected but it was still fun," Josephine said.

"I don't think we should keep playing pranks on him," Helen said.

"Nonsense! We were just paying him back. As long as he goes after me, he can expect the same in return," Josephine said haughtily.

"What do you think he's going to do next?" Helen asked.

"I don't really care. I'm ready for him."

"This makes me kind of nervous. I wish we'd just leave well enough alone."

"We will as long as he doesn't do anything else to us," Josephine said. "What you need is a nice relaxing cup of chamomile tea. I'll have coffee instead though because chamomile makes me sleepy."

"That sounds good," Helen said.

"Okay. Why don't you both sit down and I'll get things rolling," Josephine said.

She prepared a mug of tea for Helen in the microwave and made a pot of coffee for herself and Alice. They played some rummy as they settled with their drinks at the dining room table.

"Are you going to call your grandson back?" Helen asked.

"I will eventually," Josephine said.

"If I were you, I'd talk to him so you keep in communication," Helen advised. "It's easy to drift apart. You hardly ever talk to your daughter and she lives in Bradenton."

"I keep in touch with Jake pretty well," Josephine said defensively. "I do favors for him all the time. I think he can live for a day or two without me calling him back. It's not like I'm loaded with lots of spare time."

"You could call him back now."

"We're in the middle of playing cards. I don't want to be rude to my guests."

"I don't mind," Helen said.

"You don't speak for everyone. Alice might not like it if I stopped in the middle of a hand of cards to talk to my grandson."

"That's okay. I can wait," Alice said.

"You should go and call him," Helen pressed.

Josephine sighed loudly. "It would be rude. I know you both say you don't mind but it's the principle of the thing that counts. It's not good etiquette."

Helen played four kings and then discarded. Josephine rolled her eyes with annoyance.

"You probably have three aces in your hand, too," Josephine said accusingly.

"I know what that means," Alice said knowingly.

"No, I don't have any aces I'm holding onto," Josephine said.

"Sure you don't."

They finished their hand with Alice in the lead. Josephine was a close second and Helen was trailing quite a ways behind.

"Now is the perfect time to call Jake," Helen said.

"I'll call him later," Josephine said. "It's your deal."

"All right."

When they finished playing, Helen and Alice left. Josephine decided to make a couple batches of brownies so she could give away some treats to Howie and several other officers at the station. She was in the process of preparing them when the phone rang. She ignored it and the machine picked up.

"Hey, Grandma, it's me," Jake's voice drifted into the room. "You'll really want to talk to me about this. Call me soon."

Josephine snorted in derision.

"If Alex thinks I can be fooled that easily, he can think again. I don't know why he just doesn't call himself and tell me to get down to the station," Josephine said.

Alex probably wanted her to look at the same pieces of evidence as before. Well, she could safely say that if she couldn't pick up anything useful one time, she wouldn't miraculously tune into something if she tried a second time. It just didn't work that way. Alex was a human so he didn't really understand how these things worked. She would stop by the station tomorrow with brownies and Alex couldn't accuse her of avoiding him this time because he hadn't deigned to call.

Chapter 5

Josephine had six large plastic containers filled with brownies that she'd baked yesterday. She was wearing a tropical, blue blouse with white shorts and sandals. It was still pretty early in the morning. She decided to take a jog at the beach. Her recent visit there had served as a reminder of just how much she missed it. Josephine put the brownies in the trunk of her car and drove down to Siesta Key beach. She went jogging and only a smattering of people were there. Most of them were exercising like her. Josephine laughed out loud when she remembered the black, odorous cloud she'd manifested in Dale's living room. He'd probably spent quite awhile trying to get rid of it and finally had to just let it die out on its own. It had probably stank up his condo for a good two hours.

Josephine's body tingled as the power from the vortex thrummed temptingly against her. She didn't jog too far before returning back to her car. She didn't want the brownies to melt. The Florida heat was already reaching its peak. She drove about six blocks then pulled over and turned off the engine. She was parked in front of a bank and no one would notice if she passed out. Josephine reached out with her mind and could sense the vortex. She'd never tried to access it so far away before. She wondered if it was within her reach. She shivered with delight when she finally connected with the vortex. Power coursed through her body and her topaz turned green in warning. She flowed power into a shield to see if she could isolate the ring from her body. The knockout spell activated and she grinned when she realized that her spontaneous plan had worked. The knockout spell couldn't get past the energy barricade she'd placed.

Josephine felt her mind expanding and she became aware of all the trace energies flowing around her. Her awareness continued to expand and she made sure to focus on placing more energy into the barricade around her topaz ring. The knockout spell was continuing to emanate against the protection she'd summoned. Josephine was annoyed by the constant attention required to keep herself conscious. It was detracting from her enjoyment of being linked with the vortex. Her awareness continued to expand farther out and she could sense the life around her. Her concentration wavered and the knockout spell seeped past the cracks in the barricade surrounding the topaz ring. Her body went limp and darkness quickly gathered along the edges of her vision. Before she could reestablish the barricade, she had passed out.

Josephine awakened a short while later feeling refreshed. She looked down at her topaz ring and frowned at it. She would have to try this again some time. She looked around her to make sure no one was paying any attention. Josephine smiled with satisfaction as she pulled out of the parking lot and headed for the police station. She parked her car and pulled out the containers of brownies.

Josephine stepped into the lobby and warmly greeted Anita, the receptionist. Anita was a short, woman with dark brown hair, warm brown eyes, a generous smile, and a myriad of freckles on her face.

"Hey, you!" Anita said as she rose from her chair.

She ran out from behind her desk and gave Josephine a warm hug.

"I've brought some brownies for you." Josephine handed her a container.

Anita squealed with delight. "You're wonderful! Thanks!"

"You're welcome. How are things going?"

"Pretty good. It's been very quiet lately," Anita said. "How've you been?"

"I've been kind of troubled, actually. I've consulted for a case where I couldn't pick up any useful information from my psychometry," Josephine said.

"Really? That's never happened to you before," Anita said with a puzzled frown.

"No, it hasn't. That's why it bothers me so much."

"Don't worry about. I'm sure the case will be solved with you working on it," Anita said.

"Thanks. Can I go back and see the others?" Josephine asked.

"Sure. Go right ahead." Anita pulled out her remote and unlocked the door.

Josephine went back to the small office area where five desks were scattered in different locations of the room. Only one was currently occupied and it was Howie's.

"Josephine! It's good to see you!" he said.

"Hi, Howie. Like I said, I felt like baking."

She handed him a container of brownies and passed the rest around to each desk.

"Thanks for the tip on the yellow roses. Cindy was absolutely thrilled!" Howie said.

"I'm glad I could help." Josephine sat down on the chair in front of his desk. "How are things going? Anything new happening?"

"Cindy and I found a new house we want. It's larger with a nice yard," Howie said.

"That's really good. I'm happy for you." Josephine was about to continue when she sensed something strange behind her and lost her train of thought.

She turned to see Detective Riley enter the room with a teenager who looked to be maybe eighteen. He was lanky with black hair and brown eyes brimming with anxiety. Josephine opened her second sight and immediately saw a strange magical shield around him. It wasn't the typical protection and it was practically skin-tight. She sensed a barely contained potential of energy within the kid which could mean only one thing – he was a category six wizard. His head turned and his gaze locked with hers. He halted and stared at her with a dazed expression for several seconds. Detective Riley spotted her and frowned with displeasure.

"What are you doing here?" he demanded.

"I visit the station from time to time," Josephine said defensively. "Do you have a problem with that?"

"Yes, I do. You shouldn't be visiting unless you have a job to do," Alex said.

"You didn't tell me there was another category six in the county," Josephine said accusingly.

"I don't have to tell you anything."

Josephine turned to face the kid. "I'm Josephine, by the way. It's nice to meet you."

"I'm Gary," the teenager said reluctantly.

Of course, since he was a category six then he was probably much older than his teens. He could be anywhere from 18 to 40.

"We should go out for lunch sometime," Josephine said.

"I don't think so. I'm pretty busy," Gary said nervously. "I'll talk to you later, Detective Riley."

"Thanks for your help today," Alex said.

Gary swiftly left the room and Josephine cocked a brow at Alex.

"You never thank me for my work," Josephine said.

"That's because you're a pain. Besides, you're wrong. I do thank you sometimes."

Alex went over to his desk and started typing on his computer.

"What are you doing?" Josephine started to walk over behind his desk to peer over his shoulder.

Alex turned the screen off and regarded her pointedly.

"Fine!" Josephine held up her hands in a placating gesture and sat down at his chair on the other side of the desk.

Alex still didn't start working. He frowned at her impatiently.

"Did you want something?" he asked.

Josephine slowly rose to her feet and manifested a cool breeze that gently brushed over him. He stiffened and his expression turned anxious which was just the reaction she was looking for.

"I just wanted to let you know those brownies are from me," Josephine said. "Good day, detective."

She waved cheerfully at Howie as she left the room. She drove back to the condo while thinking about Gary and wondered why Alex had kept him a secret from her. Jake must have known about him too and he hadn't said a word either. Josephine couldn't believe her own grandson had kept a secret like that from her! She headed over to Jake's house but he wasn't home. Of course, she'd known he was working. He was rarely at his office unlike his partner, Alex. Josephine made a pot of coffee and watched television until Jake finally came home.

"Hello, young man," Josephine said with a touch of ire. "I met Gary today."

"Really? Alex wanted to keep him a secret from you."

"And you helped him to cover him up! I can't believe you would do this to me!" Josephine said indignantly.

"I found out about Gary yesterday. He just moved to Sarasota several days ago. That's why I called you. I couldn't risk leaving a message like that over the phone," Jake said.

Josephine's face reddened with embarrassment. "Well, that's okay. I knew you weren't trying to keep any secrets from me."

"He certainly is skittish. Alex didn't want you to know about him because he thought it would give you an excuse to procrastinate when he called you in to take a look at a crime scene or to the police station to look at evidence."

"It certainly is annoying to be kept out of the loop," Josephine said haughtily. Her eyes widened with realization as she thought back to Gary's strange shield and suddenly figured out what the purpose was. "Gary's one of those types whose second sight is always on! He needs a shield to keep from constantly being bombarded by psychic energy from everyone around him!"

"Yes, that's true," Jake confirmed.

"The poor man. How old is he?"

"He's thirty-four."

"Interesting." Josephine slowly paced the room. "I assume that Alex showed him the evidence from the previous crime scenes on the case I couldn't solve. I'll bet he didn't pick up any clues from the evidence."

"Nope, he didn't."

"Alex just doesn't understand how good I am," Josephine said.

"He thought it was worth a shot," Jake said.

"But he was wrong as usual."

Jake shrugged and helped himself to some coffee.

"Well, I guess I'd better be going. I'll talk to you later," Josephine said.

"Okay. Bye."

Josephine returned to her condo and called Helen to tell her about Gary. Helen was suitably impressed and Josephine ended the conversation feeling upbeat and excited. She still felt the buzz from her connection with the vortex earlier. She wished she could go more often but knew she was tempting fate by visiting the beach too frequently. After Josephine hung up, she spent a couple of hours working on a knockout enchantment contained in a wand. Even though she couldn't flow much power at one time, she spend a much greater time working with it than most wizards. Josephine wasn't even exhausted by the time she'd finished with the wand. Most wizards would need to recuperate for awhile after using magic for fifteen minutes straight. It was one of the benefits of being a category six. The aequitas enchantment in her topaz ring kept her from working with stronger magic and that really irked her. She locked up the wand in the desk of her guest bedroom where she kept about half of her tools.

The phone rang and Josephine reluctantly answered it. No one spoke on the other line and after several seconds the dial tone sounded in her ear. Josephine frowned with annoyance then pushed *33 to determine who'd just called her. The number was Dale's. It looked like he planned on breaking into her condo while she was away and jinxing it. Josephine wouldn't let him get away with that. She'd be ready for him and when he came, she'd let him have it. Josephine dialed Helen's number.

"It's me," Josephine said. "Can you believe Dale just called to see if I was home? You realize what that means, don't you?"

"Yes, he wants to play a prank on you," Helen said. "Maybe we should just apologize to him. Maybe he'd stop bugging you."

"Oh, no! That won't help! I'm not going to give him the satisfaction," Josephine said. "Besides, he'd turn right around and prank me anyway. Well, I've got news for him. I'm not going to let him get away with it."

"What are you going to do?"

"I'm going to get him good," Josephine said.

"How?" Helen asked.

"I'll figure out some plan," Josephine said breezily. "But if he comes here to get me, I'm going to pay him back big time."

"This seems to be getting out of hand," Helen said with concern.

"Why do you say that? We're just playing harmless jokes on each other," Josephine said. "You're such a wet blanket."

"What does Alice think of all this?" Helen asked.

"I haven't told her yet. I called you first."

"Oh. Well, why don't you talk to her now?"

"Okay. I'll talk to you later."

"Bye."

Josephine quickly dialed Alice's number.

"Hello?" Alice said.

"It's me. Dale just tried calling me to see if I was home," Josephine said without preamble.

"That bastard! I think we need to teach him a lesson!" Alice said.

"My thoughts exactly!" Josephine said enthusiastically.

"I'm going to prepare a nice jinx so we can get him back if he's dumb enough to try anything," Alice said. "In fact, why don't you call me over if he calls you again? This time, don't pick up the phone and he'll think you're away. We can ambush him."

"Great idea." Josephine grinned wickedly at this plan. "I'll talk to you later."

"Okay. Bye."

Josephine waited with keen anticipation for the entire day but the phone never rang. She tried distracting herself with the television but that didn't work. Late in the evening, she was extremely disappointed. This had been a real letdown. She woke up early the next morning, showered, and fixed a pot of coffee. When Helen and Alice came over, she didn't have any news to report.

"Don't worry. He'll probably call sometime today," Alice said.

"We usually go to the gym today," Josephine pointed out.

"Yes we do," Alice said thoughtfully. "I'd hate for him to break into your place while we're exercising."

"Do you really think Dale will be able to get rid of the security enchantments on your door?" Helen asked. "It's really difficult and he's only a category three."

"He probably won't be able to. He may have created an unraveling enchantment to help him out but it will still be very difficult," Josephine said.

"Unraveling enchantments are pretty hard to make. If he has one, he probably bought it. Those things are expensive," Helen said.

"Yes, they are. I suppose my condo should be safe while we go exercising," Josephine said.

"Maybe he'll wait for tomorrow to try anything. He'll probably want plenty of time to pass by so you won't be expecting him," Alice said.

"You're probably right. Besides, I'm not going to skip a trip to the gym because of him. It's important for people my age to exercise regularly," Josephine said.

Alice and Helen nodded in approval and took a drink from their mugs. They lapsed into a companionable silence, finished their coffee, and went to the gym. When they returned to their condos, Josephine was glad to find that the security enchantments were still in place. She opened her second sight just to be on the safe side. There were no signs of tampering so she unlocked the door and stepped inside. She checked for any signs of jinxes or for uninvited guests but there was nothing. Maybe Dale would play it cool for a few days. Josephine felt like going to Siesta Key but didn't want to get in the habit of daily trips to the beach. On the other hand, she didn't think there was much chance of her getting caught. Josephine drove down to the bank on Siesta Key and parked her car.

She tapped into the vortex easier this time and her ring instantly turned green. She immediately formed an energy barricade around the ring and concentrated on keeping it isolated. Josephine enjoyed the buzz she was receiving from the connection to the vortex but also felt dizzy and knew the knockout spell was seeping past the energy barricade somehow. She focused more of her attention and the dizziness dissipated. She felt like laughing with delight as power rushed through her. Her awareness expanded like before and she became aware of the thoughts of those around her. No one was paying any attention to her. No one had an inkling of what she was doing. Josephine's attention slipped and the knockout spell took affect. She awoke a short while later feeling wonderful. Tapping into the vortex really did wonders for her wellbeing.

Josephine pulled her car out and headed back to her condo. She found a message on the machine from Detective Riley. She wondered if the serial killer had struck again. She dialed Riley's cell phone number and waited for him to pick him.

"Detective Riley," he said.

"It's Josephine. I'm returning your call."

"There's been a murder. I need you to take a look at the crime scene."

"Is it the serial killer?"

"No. This is different."

"Are you sure?" Josephine asked.

"Yes, I'm positive."

"Maybe this murder is related to the others. You won't know until I read the trace energies," Josephine said.

"Trust me. This is different."

"I'm going to keep an open mind," Josephine said.

"Will you please just get over here," Alex said wearily. He told her the address.

"Wait a second. I don't have a pen ready." Josephine picked up the pen and poised it over the pad of paper on the desk. "What's the address again?"

Alex repeated the information. Josephine thanked him and hung up the phone. She felt certain that this murder was committed by the serial killer. She was tempted to call Alice and tell her the latest news but decided she'd better head over to the crime scene. It was easier to read trace energies before too much time passed. On the other hand, what would a few minutes matter? Josephine dialed Alice's number.

"It's me," Josephine said. "I've got some interesting news. Apparently, the serial killer has struck again. Alex doesn't think it's the same one but I'm sure it has to be."

"That detective is so clueless I don't know how he functions," Alice said. "I'll bet you could do his job for him. Maybe you should think about being a detective yourself."

"I wouldn't like that," Josephine said dismissively. "Besides, I'm retired."

"That's true but you'd make a good detective."

"Thanks. Hopefully, I'll pick up some clues this time and solve the case."

"Good luck!"

"Thanks! Bye!"

When Josephine ventured out to the parking garage, she could see the heavy rain. It would be difficult to drive in. She hopped into her car and slowly pulled out into the street. After several moments, the rain intensified and she could barely see ten feet ahead of the vehicle. A truck was following so closely behind her that she suspected he wanted to kiss her bumper. Josephine's fingers tightened reflexively over the steering wheel as she struggled to see ahead of her. Sheets of rain plummeted to the ground and pounded against her car. She wanted to pull over but there wasn't room at the moment. She slowed down even more and the truck blinked his lights at her.

"This guy is unbelievable!" Josephine said.

She slowed to an almost standstill so he would pass her and he eventually did. She finally pulled into a shopping center parking lot and waited for the rain to stop. Josephine listened to the rain pounding against the car and gazed outside. She wondered how long she'd have to wait. She supposed that Alex would probably be trying to call her in order to demand that she get her butt over there immediately. Well, she had news for him; her safety was more important than someone who happened to already be dead! Josephine's chin jutted out at a stubborn angle as she continued to watch the rain. She finally turned off the engine since she figured it would be a long wait. Josephine supposed she should get a cell phone again so that when she was caught in predicaments like this she could at least call Alex to let him know. Maybe he would cut her some slack.

She chewed nervously on her lower lip as time dragged on. It was a good twenty minutes before the rain thinned out a bit. Josephine decided she could probably navigate in this weather now. She had a terrible time reading the street signs and the address was in an unfamiliar part of the city. By the time she found the villa where the murder had occurred, she was extremely late. Anxiety stirred in her stomach as she parked her car across the street. She wondered if Alex would reprimand her or even give her a ticket for failing to cooperate. He'd done that to her several times. Maybe she shouldn't have avoided him so blatantly from the last case. Josephine decided to go with a plan she'd tried before. She sagged her shoulders in case the officer was watching and bent forward so her face was down and couldn't be seen from the outside.

She flowed energy and created a cold, biting wind that blew steadily into her face and eyes. She stared unblinkingly into it until tears were streaming down her cheeks. Josephine immediately ended the spell and got out of her car. She made a show of trudging across the street and saw Howie standing in front of the door. He had a worried and sympathetic expression on his face. Josephine sniffed loudly as she approached him.

"I don't know what's going to happen to me," Josephine said in a quivering voice. "The rain was so scary to drive in. Somebody almost hit me from behind. He was going way to fast. It was so hard to see I got lost!"

Howie patted her awkwardly on the shoulder.

"It'll be okay," he said reassuringly.

"Alex is going to throw me in jail!" Josephine wailed.

She covered her face with both hands so he couldn't see her grinning. He was falling for it just like he usually did. She made sure not to blink her eyes as her shoulders shook and she pretended to sob loudly.

"Don't worry about anything! I'm sure Alex will understand!" Howie gave her a quick hug and a pat on the back. He pulled away from her and she dropped her hands so that he could see the tears were still streaming.

"Alex hates me! He's determined to punish me for something I had no control over," Josephine said in a quivering voice. "I don't know what's going to happen to me."

"Let's go inside and talk to him."

Howie opened the door for her and she stepped inside. Alex spun and glared at her.

"It's about time you showed up," he said moodily.

He blinked with surprise when he saw her tear-filled, reddened eyes watching him.

"I'm sorry, detective! I couldn't see with all the rain and some guy almost hit me with his truck," Josephine said in a quivering voice.

Jake was standing a short distance from Alex and immediately threw his partner a disgusted look before crossing the room to his grandmother and giving her a quick hug.

"It'll be okay," Jake said.

Josephine hugged him back and forced a broken sob from her quivering lips since she knew Alex was still watching.

"I think you should back off, Riley," Howie said in a stern voice. "She was almost hurt and anyone would have a hard time seeing in the rain. It was coming down very hard for quite awhile."

"I wasn't going to do anything to her," Alex said.

"You said you were thinking about making her spend a few hours in a cell to 'clear her head.' Was I imagining things?" Jake asked.

"I was just exaggerating," Alex said defensively.

"Does anyone have a tissue?" Josephine asked in a shaky voice.

"Here, Ms. O'Connor." Howie pulled one out from his pants pocket.

"Thank you," Josephine said in a squeaky voice.

She blew her nose into the tissue then excused herself to find the trash which turned out to be in the kitchen. She returned to the living room which was small and cramped with a large couch taking up most of the room and several pedestals taking up positions in the corners and boasting large angel figurines. One of the figurines was lying on the floor beside the deceased woman. She was average height and build and wearing a blue blouse and jeans. Her long black hair was had a smear of blood near the nape of the neck where Josephine could see a wound. The angel figurine positioned beside the woman had blood splattered on it.

"It's obvious how she died," Josephine said quietly.

A cold, uncomfortable sensation settled in the pit of her stomach. She hated to see murders and wished she didn't have the gift of psychometry. The detectives had obviously already tried using their own limited abilities on the crime scene but had failed; otherwise, Alex would never have called her. Josephine opened her mind to the trace energies in the room and could see numerous strands floating around them. Josephine began to hear the voices of the deceased and her friends and family in the back of her mind. Anger and fear commingled with flashes of images and bits of random knowledge. Josephine distanced herself from the psychic input so it wouldn't overwhelm her. She needed to remain objective so she could more easily sift through everything. Josephine lost awareness of her surroundings as she analyzed the bits and pieces of clues that flashed in her mind's eye.

Josephine flinched when Alex cleared his throat but she was deeply entrenched in the psychic stimuli. She didn't realize how tense she'd become until she closed her second sight and the trace energies were no longer visible to her. A faint pounding had started in her temple, her hands were clenched into fists, and her throat had constricted into a painful knot. She swallowed and forced herself to relax.

"The victim's name is Sandy Dupris. She's been dating Max Winthrop for quite some time now. Her last relationship was abusive and Max started losing his temper and hitting her about a month ago. She had reached the point where she was ready to confront him and end the relationship. She knew he'd probably lose his temper so she had half a dozen wands with telekinetic enchantments embedded in them hidden in one of the drawers in her kitchen. She thought she would be ready for him but he took her by surprise. He killed her with the first hit from behind. He had seemed to take it well until her back was turned," Josephine said in a hoarse voice. "Max lives on Pinecrest Circle."

"Okay. That's good enough," Alex said gently.

Josephine took an unsteady breath and slowly let it out. The negative emotions and jumble of images always took their toll. She wished she didn't have to do this or that there was some way it could be easier.

"If that's all, I think I'll be going," Josephine said quietly.

"Yes, that's all. Thank you," Alex said.

"Bye, Grandma." Jake gave her a quick hug.

"Bye, sweetie," Josephine said.

She slowly walked out of the room feeling weak and drained. Josephine climbed into her car and sat there for a moment. She took several more deep breaths, starting the engine, and slowly pulled out onto the street.

Chapter 6

Josephine drove aimlessly for awhile as the turbulent emotions she'd picked up from the murder tore through her. The rain started to pick up again and she decided to stop by the beach. It always made her feel better. She took off her shoes and stepped outside. The rain gently tapped against her skin as she walked along the shore. Performing psychometry on murders always drained her and this one was no different. She abruptly halted when she saw a man lying on his back floating a couple of feet from the ground. She cocked a bemused brow and stepped closer to him. Soon, she recognized Gary whom she'd seen at the police station. She noticed that the rain mysteriously bounced off a point about an inch away from his body which left him completely dry.

His eyes were closed and he was breathing deeply. Josephine cleared her throat but he just lay there. After a moment, he opened his eyes and slowly lifted upright and his feet gently landed onto the wet sand. The ocean waves lapped at the shore energetically and the rain continued to fall.

"How are you doing that?" Josephine asked.

"Doing what?" Gary asked calmly.

"You were floating a minute ago and you still have some sort of shield keeping the rain from hitting you," Josephine said. "That takes up a lot of power."

"I'm connected to the vortex."

"And that gives you more control of your magic? I would think it would become uncontrollable when more and more power is being channeled through your body," Josephine said.

"Actually, you temporarily gain more control the longer you hold a connection to a vortex until you reach the burnout point," Gary said.

"I can't believe you're risking this when you know how strict the laws are," Josephine sputtered with outrage.

Gary smiled and suddenly the rain was landing on him as his shield gave away.

"I'm not worried that you'll say anything. After all, you've gotten yourself in the habit of tapping into the vortex and wouldn't want me to report your illegal activities," he said.

"That's true but I wouldn't report you anyway," Josephine said. "I'm just surprised that you're willing to take such a risk."

"When I'm tapping into the vortex, it's the only time I feel completely at peace," Gary said. "As you could probably determine by the type of shield I have, my second sight is always open and I'm not able to shut it off. I'm constantly receiving disjointed images and emotions that make no sense. I'm taking medication that helps calm me and reduces the pain but that doesn't make it go away completely. I also have a shield that helps screen out trace energies; my older brother makes it for me. I don't really know how to perform magic except for the basics."

"You're a category six and you don't know how to make enchantments?" Josephine asked with astonishment.

"That's right. Just the basics." Gary shrugged. "There's no point in knowing when I'm never going to be allowed to use my abilities."

His gray shorts and yellow tee shirt were soaking now just like Josephine's clothes. She glanced down at his right hand and saw his topaz ring was blue rather than green.

"How can you tap into the vortex without your aequitas enchantment knocking you out?" she asked.

"My brother helped me to deactivate the enchantment. When an enforcer ever audits me to be sure I'm wearing the ring and that it's working, I can easily activate the enchantment again. It's just a matter of charging it up with some power."

"How did you manage to deactivate the enchantment without destroying it?" Josephine said curiously.

"I'm not sure. My brother helped. He had to make enchantments ahead of time but they basically put an energy barricade around the ring which protected me from the knockout spell. I generated a lot of power to activate the aequitas enchantment and it burned itself out after a period of time," Gary explained.

"Wow." Josephine wondered if she could keep control of her ability long enough to burn out her own aequitas enchantment.

"Normally, I don't come this close to tap into the vortex but I knew no one would be here while it was raining."

"That's a pretty good idea. You wouldn't want to get caught." Josephine smiled warmly at him. "I'm glad we're having this talk. You were so skittish at the police station that I didn't think we would ever get this chance."

"I don't like to be around people much." Gary's face tensed up a bit and his eyes became guarded. He activated the same skin-tight shield that Josephine had sensed at the police station. She now realized that it protected him from trace energy but apparently it only offered limited screening. "I need to go."

"We should talk again sometime. Let me give you my phone number," Josephine said.

"Why?" Gary asked.

"Because there aren't very many people like us and we should stick together."

"Okay." Gary gazed at her cautiously.

"We'll have to go back to my car. I have some paper and a pen in my purse," Josephine said.

"All right."

They walked back to her car and she quickly jotted down the phone number. She asked for his and he hesitated. She wondered if he would to tell her. After a long pause, he finally did.

"It was nice running into you again, Gary," she said.

"Yes, it was." He smiled nervously at her.

"Where did you park? I didn't see any cars." She took a quick look to see if she'd somehow missed a car.

"I parked across the street over there." He pointed and she saw a green Honda a short distance away. "I didn't think it would be a good idea to have my car in the beach parking spot because then people could see that someone is here."

"That's very cautious of you," Josephine said thoughtfully.

"Yes. You should be careful, too. I don't know if you'll ever figure out how to deactivate your aequitas enchantment."

"I think I might."

"Good luck. Well, I'm going to be heading off. I'll talk to you later."

"Yep. I'll see you later."

Josephine watched him walk away then slipped into her car. She still felt lousy but she'd had an interesting conversation.

Additionally, she was hopeful that she could deactivate the aequitas enchantment in her ring. All she needed to do was keep the energy barricade up when she tapped into the vortex for a long enough period of time. Josephine was certain that she could learn to do this if she exercised enough patience. She opened her awareness to the subtle energies flowing around her so she could feel the power vortex more fully. She'd come here to soak up a little comfort but the negative psychic impressions from the crime scene still clung to her. She drove to a restaurant about seven blocks from the beach and parked her car. No one would notice her here. She concentrated on the vortex and found it even easier than before to connect with it even though she was quite a distance away.

She immediately created an energy barrier around the topaz ring on her right hand as power rushed through her. Josephine didn't allow her concentration to waver as her body sang with potent magic. The topaz ring had turned green and was now emitting the knockout spell. So far, the energy barricade was protecting her from the aequitas enchantment. Josephine's mind expanded but she forced herself to concentrate on maintaining the protection that kept her conscious. The emotions and thoughts from the customers in the restaurant became a huge distraction as the myriad voices spoke loudly in her mind and the psychic impressions pulsed erratically. Josephine chewed on her lower lip and furrowed her brows in concentration. She was determined to make this work. There was no reason she should be restrained from her full potential.

Tension set into her body as this feat became more difficult. It was so hard to focus on one spell like this when her mind continued to expand and every piece of trace energy within a block was stimulating her metaconscious mind. After awhile, she relaxed a little when she realized that it was becoming easier to keep the energy barricade up. Her focus was now improving along with the flow of psychic input. After a moment, she observed that the aequitas enchantment was dormant as it had expended all of its available energy in trying to knock her out. The enchantment was still intact and could become active again if she charged it up just as Gary had described. Josephine couldn't believe she'd done it on her first try. Of course, she'd practiced creating the energy barrier several times and hadn't realized it was possible to do this until her discussion with Gary.

An intense sense of freedom made Josephine laugh with delight. She relaxed and reveled in the sensations. She was barely aware of her body now as she allowed her mind to drift in the sensations of energy around her. This experience was completely different from using her psychometry in the crime scene as the psychic impressions were a static background noise. She wondered what kind of enchantments she could perform while being tuned into the vortex. A category six had caused the Disaster using the potent power of the vortex in Seattle, Washington but Josephine wasn't planning on doing anything destructive. She was certain she could control her ability. Josephine realized her thoughts were taking a dangerous turn. There were strict laws against category six wizards tapping into the power from any vortex for an important reason. She needed to be careful. Josephine allowed herself to enjoy her current state for awhile longer than released her connection to the vortex.

She felt rejuvenated as she pulled the car out into the road and hummed quietly to herself. She couldn't believe she had actually managed to deactivate the aequitas enchantment! She was free and the negative affects from using her psychometry at the crime scene were completely gone now. She returned home and flopped down on the couch. Guilt was starting to take the place of euphoria. She should probably restore the aequitas enchantment. After all, the laws that restricted a category six wizard's power were written for a reason. They were extremely dangerous and needed to maintain control of their abilities. If they lost control, the aequitas enchantment knocked them out so that they couldn't harm anyone or themselves. On the other hand, it still didn't seem fair. Josephine had never come close to hurting anyone.

She flinched when the door knocked. She got up and went over to see who was there. Alice smiled at her from the doorway and stepped inside. Her gray hair was frizzy and poofed out like a mad scientist's. A mischievous gleam dominated her eyes. Josephine closed the door and smiled warmly at her friend as she forcibly brushed aside her doubts and worries.

"How did it go with Alex?" Alice asked. "Was it the serial killer?"

"No, it wasn't," Josephine said regretfully.

"You seem different." Alice examined her shrewdly. "I can't quite figure out how. You seem more relaxed somehow."

"I have no idea what you mean," Josephine said dismissively. "Unfortunately, Alex is still clueless about the serial killer. Too bad he has no talent."

"It's a pity," Alice said.

They sat down in the living room to chat. Alice sighed and leaned back against the couch.

"It's been a rough day," Josephine said. "I hate reading murders."

"I know. It's terrible."

"Maybe I won't be called in as often now that there's another category six in town," Josephine said.

"Yes, that should help." Alice nodded with agreement.

The phone rang and Josephine rolled her eyes with annoyance.

"That's probably Detective Whiney asking if I can come back to the crime scene. He's so obnoxious. He threatened to lock me up today," Josephine said.

"That scumbag! I'd like to kick his ass!" Alice said indignantly.

"You and me both."

The phone continued to ring until the machine picked it up. The caller never left a message so Josephine didn't know if it had been Alex or not.

"I'm so glad I was able to read the crime scene and solve the case," Josephine said fervently. "I've felt off kilter ever since I couldn't pick up anything useful from the serial killer."

There was a faint click and the front door swung open. Dale stepped inside the room and gaped at them with stunned disbelief.

"What are you doing here?" he asked.

"I live here, you skanky old coot. What's your excuse?" Josephine said haughtily.

Dale raised a shield as Josephine cast a knockout spell. She rose from the couch and released a wave of telekinetic energy which caused his protection to falter. He pulled out a long, wooden wand and a bright golden spark leapt from the end. It hissed and spat smaller sparks as it bounced on the floor then erupted briefly and transformed into a dozen large, black spiders the size of dinner plates. Alice launched a telekinetic burst at him which dropped his shield. The black spiders scuttled madly across the floor and Josephine leapt onto the couch with Alice. Dale chortled with laughter as he backed away from them. Josephine waved her hand in his direction and sent six spiders hurtling through the air at him. They bounced against his body and two of them clung to his shirt. He smashed one of them with his hand which exploded with black, viscous goo. The other spit the vile substance into his face and he tripped backward out the door.

The rest of the spiders circled around the couch which Josephine and Alice stood on. Dale had programmed the manifestations well. Josephine raised her hand out and funneled power through her body in preparation to dispel the creatures. She carefully formed the energy matrix and released the spell. A bright, white flash of light erupted over the floor and the spiders exploded. Black goo splattered the walls and Josephine brushed off a couple of spider legs that had stuck to her shirt. Alice brushed off a pile of the viscous fluid off her cheek. A repulsive odor permeated the room.

"There's no way I can dispel this mess," Alice said.

"It'll take several hours for the manifestations to disappear. Maybe we should wait this out in your place," Josephine suggested.

"Where's Dale?" Alice asked irritably.

Josephine couldn't see the obnoxious man through the doorway. She walked over to gaze down the hall but there was no sign of him.

"He's gone," she said.

"We really need to get him," Alice said.

"Yep. It's payback time," Josephine said. "I just remembered that the phone rang about five minutes or so before Dale paid me a visit. I'll bet that was him checking to see if I was home."

"You're right! The phone rang and no one left a message! I should have realized it was him!" Alice said passionately. "That skanky old toad is really going to get it! I'm taking him down!"

Josephine and Alice took a shower in her condo to remove the black spider gunk from their bodies then visited with Helen at her place. They all sat down in her barren living room which only had a television and one medium-sized, baby blue sofa. The carpet was beige and had just been put in a couple of months ago. The walls were freshly painted a soft, baby blue like her sofa. Helen frequently had the carpet changed and the walls repainted.

"We should put a stop to this madness," Helen said nervously.

"My thoughts exactly! We're going to really get Dale this time and he won't have any choice but to leave us alone," Josephine said passionately.

"That's not what I meant." Helen fidgeted in her place at the edge of the sofa. "I think we should stop pranking that man. It's not worth it!"

"I'm not going to let him get away with his shenanigans." Josephine's chin jutted out stubbornly.

"Me, neither!" Alice chimed in. Her eyes suddenly filled with mischief as she held her right hand over the carpet and concentrated. "Watch this."

"What are you doing?" Helen regarded her anxiously.

"Just watch."

Alice's brows furrowed as she aimed her palm at a portion of the floor nearby. A huge, black cockroach the size of a beach ball rippled into existence. It solidified after several seconds and hissed loudly. Helen shrieked in alarm and brought her legs up onto the sofa.

"Calm down. It's just an illusion," Alice said. "I'm going to create a jinx that will make about a dozen of these nasty critters pop out of Dale's kitchen cupboard the next time he goes for a bowl of cereal."

"Perfect!" Josephine smiled with delight.

"And it will spit out a chunky brown fluid at the old fart."

"Fantastic! Will you make it smelly too like he does with the spiders?" Josephine asked.

"I sure will," Alice said smugly.

"I have an idea on an enchantment. I'll make it snow in his condo," Josephine said.

"You can't do that," Alice said. "You're a category six. Your ring will knock you out if you generate that much power."

"You know how some enchantments can be made pieces at a time. I'll make this happen," Josephine said confidently.

"You can't make complicated spells like that without major power flow. It just can't be done."

"Sure it can. I figured out a way," Josephine said.

"Whatever."

Josephine was a bit offended that her friend sounded so dismissive about her ability but actually, she had a point. If Josephine's ring hadn't been deactivated, she never would have been able to try something like this. It will take some prep work but she no longer had a leash so she could really work with the energy now. It shouldn't take more than a couple of days to prepare a wand with that particular enchantment.

"What about you, Helen?" Alice said. "What type of jinx will you be making?"

"I'll make another telekinetic wand in case Dale should happen to catch us like before," Helen said.

"That won't happen. We'll be more careful this time," Josephine said confidently.

Helen's attention returned to the nasty, bad-ass cockroach which was still hissing at them. The creature's body rippled and it slowly faded away. She sighed with relief and relaxed.

"I wonder if Dale hates cockroaches," Josephine said.

"I think everyone hates those things," Helen said with revulsion. "Especially if they're huge like that."

Chapter 7

Josephine carefully set the wand she was about to program on top of the dining room table. Giddy anticipation coursed through her veins as she stared at the wand for a moment. This was the first time she'd ever had the opportunity to use the full extent of her abilities. Her goal was to program a snow storm enchantment inside the wand. Josephine flowed power through her body and concentrated on creating the proper energy matrix. Tendrils of white, silver, and red light slowly twisted around the wand as she shaped them into the proper alignment and frequency. More power rushed through her and the matrix began to take shape more quickly. This was going much faster than she'd anticipated. Normally, it took category five wizards a couple of days to finish this particular enchantment but it looked like she'd finish it in moments.

Hot, scorching wind swept over her as even more power flowed through her. Josephine tried to ease down on the amount she was channeling but discovered it wasn't having any effect. She ignored the wind which was now whipping her hair wildly and focused on the energy matrix she was still in the process of shaping. Unfortunately, a couple streams of magic were leaking out of her uncontrollably and one of them brushed against the wand which twisted the energy matrix out of alignment. Josephine chewed savagely on her lower lip and concentrated on realigning the enchantment. Sweat beaded along her forehead as she finished her work. Finally, she sealed up the enchantment in the wand and backed away from the table. Power was still channeling through her at an alarming rate even though she'd finished.

The hot torrid wind continued to swirl wildly through the room. Josephine focused on closing the flow of power but nothing happened. She closed her eyes and concentrated harder. Josephine was suddenly thrown backward against the wall as fire exploded in front of her in mid air. She cried out and slumped to the floor. Part of the carpet and one of her chairs had caught on fire. The scorching wind continued to whip violently through the room and threatened to spread the hungry flames. Josephine reached her hands out and directed her power into a cold stream of wind. Frosty, wet air flew from them and put out the flames. Josephine let out a sigh of relief when the magic that channeled through her body suddenly petered out.

The door pounded wildly and Josephine reluctantly walked over to answer it. She found her two friends standing outside with wild-eyed looks of panic. Obviously, they'd heard the racket and wondered what was going on.

"Are you all right?" Alice said.

"What happened in here? Did Dale attack you?" Helen asked.

Josephine was tempted to lie and say that Dale had in fact done this to her condo but decided she should stick with the truth.

"No, I was working on the snow storm enchantment and things got out of hand," Josephine said.

"But how could this happen? A massive energy release had to have occurred to create this kind of mess," Alice said.

"I was using three of my telekinetic wands to augment my power," Josephine fibbed. "I guess it wasn't a good idea."

"I would say not! What on earth possessed you to try such a crazy stunt?" Helen asked.

"I'm tired of being restricted. I've had to pass up countless opportunities to cast some really fantastic spells and I'm tired of it!" Josephine exclaimed.

"I see," Helen said thoughtfully. "I can understand that."

Josephine's thoughts went back to the successful completion of her snowstorm enchantment. She had finished it in a fraction of the time that it would take a category five wizard. She was more powerful than she had imagined. She wondered what she would be capable of if she tapped into the vortex at Siesta Key.

"You need to be more careful. Don't worry about Dale. Helen and I will help you take care of him," Alice said.

Josephine felt a stab of guilt over her recent conduct. She had illegally turned the aequitas enchantment in her ring dormant and was performing dangerous magic. She thought she could control her abilities but maybe the Council knew what they were doing when they'd banned this type of magical ability in category sixes like herself. Josephine should probably reactivate the aequitas enchantment but couldn't bring herself to do it.

"What's wrong?" Alice asked.

Josephine forced a smile on her face and brushed aside her unpleasant musings. "I'm fine. I'm just shaken up by the accident."

"That's understandable," Alice said. "Maybe we should have some chamomile tea to calm down."

"I'd rather have coffee. It's always helped to calm me when I'm stressed," Josephine said briskly.

"Coffee isn't relaxing," Helen said. "You should have some nice, relaxing tea."

"I'm having some coffee." Josephine raised her chin in the air as she crossed the room to the coffee maker.

"I'll have some coffee too," Alice said.

"Okay," Josephine said.

Her mind wandered as she measured out the grounds. Gary had obviously been without his aequitas enchantment for quite some time. She wanted to know if he'd had trouble controlling his abilities. If he could do it, so could she. Josephine would need to talk to him again. She finished with the coffee preparation and turned on the power.

"Oh my God! The enchantment is set already!" Helen exclaimed from the dining room.

Josephine whipped around to face Helen and saw her friend holding the wand she'd finished working on. Helen displayed a mixture of awe and fear as she gazed at the wand with fascination.

"This is extraordinary," Helen finally said.

"I'd better lock that up." Josephine reached over and gently removed the wand from her friend's grasp.

"How did you do that?" Helen asked.

"I told you. I used three telekinetic wands to augment the power and shape the matrix faster," Josephine said breezily.

"That's impossible," Helen said adamantly. "There's something you're hiding from me."

Josephine locked the wand in the antique desk and turned to regard her friends who both wore identical expressions of suspicion. She supposed she couldn't hide the truth from them anyway.

"I discovered a way to temporarily deactivate the aequitas enchantment in my ring," Josephine said slowly.

Helen's mouth flopped open with shock.

"That's wonderful!" Alice exclaimed joyously. "Why didn't you tell us?"

"I was afraid you wouldn't like it," Josephine said.

"I know you can control your abilities. You deserve to have your leash taken off," Alice said.

"You're wrong. You don't have control of your magic. Look at what you did in the dining room," Helen said shakily.

"It was the first time I worked magic without restraint. I can do better next time," Josephine said weakly.

"Hell, yeah! You're going to kick some butt!" Alice said enthusiastically.

Helen regarded them both with disbelief but dropped the argument. Josephine hoped her friend wouldn't nark on her. Of course, if she did then Josephine could always activate the aequitas enchantment and there would be no proof of what had happened. There was no way she could be caught.

"Do you think you could help me with my cockroach manifestations?" Alice asked.

Sometimes, Josephine helped her friends by transferring power to them via hand chakras. Josephine would serve as a type of battery which helped to boost Alice's ability temporarily.

"Sure! I'd love to."

"Great!" Alice smiled cheerfully. "Why don't I bring the wand over tomorrow morning?"

"Okay. Or better yet, we can do it now," Josephine suggested.

"Not a good idea," Alice said. "You've overexerted yourself. I can wait just a little bit."

Josephine nodded in agreement even though she felt ready for another enchantment. She prepared Helen's mug of tea and set the cup in the microwave. It wasn't until everyone was sitting down with their coffee or tea that Helen spoke up again to break the companionable silence.

"Did either one of you read the weekly paper?" she asked hesitantly.

"No, why?" Josephine shot her a questioning look.

"Because Margaret just sold her condo."

"My other next door neighbor, you mean?" Josephine said.

"Yes, that's her," Helen confirmed.

"I could care less who my neighbor is," Josephine said.

"Well, I don't think you'll like this one."

Josephine sighed loudly. "Just tell me who it is."

"Robert Miller," Helen said quietly.

"That two-timing slime ball!" Josephine exclaimed.

She accidentally unleashed a short burst of energy which made the lights flicker for several seconds.

"Why would he choose to live next door to you?" Alice said.

"He probably doesn't realize I live here," Josephine said.

"Well, he's in for a big surprise," Alice said.

"I can't believe I have to live with Spot next door. My life just keeps getting suckier and suckier," Josephine said in a whiny voice.

At least she wouldn't have to see Robert with his wife since she'd dumped him several months ago. He was probably having severe financial problems and had to sell his house which was why he was moving in the first place.

"Maybe it's not too late. If he discovers I live here, he'll probably change his mind about that condo," Josephine said.

"No, the mortgage has gone through. It wasn't in the weekly until everything was finalized," Helen said.

When Helen and Alice ended their visit, Josephine tried calling Gary but he wouldn't pick up. She left him a brief message then hung up the phone. Josephine gazed out the window and could see dark clouds gathering in the azure sky. She drove down to the Siesta Key beach hoping to run into Gary. She walked along the shore and tried to ignore the tempting power waves emanating from the vortex and brushing seductively against her. She walked briskly from one end of the beach to the other but didn't see Gary which was a big disappointment. She'd wanted to know more about her abilities and wanted to know what Gary had experienced. Josephine returned to her car and drove to a busy restaurant which was located about eight blocks from the beach. She didn't find it challenging at all to tap into the vortex. Power instantly flooded through her. Her body felt relaxed and invigorated at the same time.

She could sense the myriad trace energies milling about and random impressions danced in her mind. Josephine gasped in surprise when an image of a thin, pale, young woman rocking on the floor appeared. She wore jeans and a pink tee shirt and had a crazed look on her face. Her brown eyes brimmed with madness and spittle dripped down her chin. Josephine recognized this category six as Brenda Kirkland from the picture in the history books she'd read. Brenda was the infamous wizard who'd caused the Disaster and unwittingly ushered humankind into a new state of being. In Josephine's vision, Brenda was frantically muttering something to herself as she rocked more and more violently. Abruptly, she lost the image which was replaced by other impressions. Josephine tried to get it back but couldn't. She was surprised that a trace energy of Brenda Kirkland had existed for so long.

"Interesting," Josephine said to herself.

She was still tapped into the vortex and could feel her mind expanding further. Surface thoughts of nearby humans and wizards buzzed in the background. Josephine lost track of time and soon felt as though she was floating. She reached out for any trace energies similar to the one that had caused the vision of Brenda to appear. It was difficult to focus as her attention scattered in multiple directions the longer she stayed connected to the vortex. Another vision appeared of Brenda in a small bedroom with a minimum of furniture. She huddled in the far corner of the room wearing jeans and a white tee shirt. A wizard was approaching her with his wand pulled out and a shield in place. Brenda abruptly rose to her feet and the plastic bracelet around her wrist broke into pieces that disintegrated into a sandy substance as it fell to the floor.

The plastic bracelet had contained the aequitas enchantment and she had somehow managed to destroy it at that moment. The wizard who entered the room was short with sandy hair and green eyes. He was one of her care-takers who watched over her to make sure she didn't escape and expose the humans to magic. Wizards had still lived in secret during this time period.

"You want to kill me!" she screamed shrilly.

"Everything is okay," he said reassuringly. "I'm just here to help you."

"You're a liar! You're here to stop me from completing my Mission!" Brenda shouted furiously.

Two more wizards slowly stepped into the room with their wands pulled out and shields already in place.

"You need to calm down. Everything is fine," the man said calmly.

A determined expression dominated Brenda's pale face as she stared the three wizards down. They all fired knockout spells at just about the same time and all of them bounced harmlessly away from her. She held her arms out in front of her with palms extended toward them. The protection enchantments of all three wizards melted away.

"How'd she do that?" one of the wizards asked.

In the next instant, all three of them crumpled to the floor as she struck them all with a knockout spell. Brenda turned toward the window which was protected by steel bars to keep her from escaping. She had been preparing for this moment for months. Josephine could sense this in the vision. More wizards were racing down the hall toward the room. Brenda raised her left hand toward the door and it slammed shut. She turned her attention back to the window and the glass shattered. The steel bars screeched loudly as they slowly twisted and tore out of the frame. The vision wavered and vanished before Josephine could see more. A pervasive chill and a sense of dread washed over her. She hadn't realized she had this potential. The history books had never described exactly how Brenda had escaped from her prison in the house.

Josephine maintained her connection to the vortex but dismissed all thoughts of Brenda. She no longer wished to see anymore of this madwoman's plight. Josephine abruptly realized she was floating a couple of inches above her seat. She lowered herself back down so she wouldn't draw attention to herself. Another vision took hold and she could see Brenda walking toward a shopping mall. Before the Disaster had occurred, the mall had been entirely encompassed by the power vortex of Seattle, Washington. Brenda had a Mission to perform. She would save humanity from destruction. She walked purposefully toward the mall and was transfixed by the swirling blue, silver, and green lights that surrounded the mall. Many customers were milling about and browsing inside the many stores and others were outside either leaving or entering the large building. She reached out with her mind and tapped into the vortex.

As Brenda's consciousness expanded, she sensed the danger around her as a large group of wizards arrived in the parking lot. She created a large dampening field that would hopefully fend off any magic attacks. Brenda breathed deeply and focused on the spell which would allow humankind to ascend to a greater existence. She was doing God's work and knew that was her very purpose in life. That was why the wizards had locked her away. They were jealous of her abilities and brainwashed by the antichrist. Once she accomplished her Mission, everyone would know that she was their savior. The complicated energy matrix formed within the vortex itself and interacted with it. Potent, red tendrils of energy commingled with the blue, green, and silver swirls. The wizards launched a massive telekinetic spell at her. Brenda's attention split between her work and the incoming attack which seemed to occur in slow motion.

As the combined telekinetic waves struck her dampening field and dissipated the destructive spells, she could see that it wasn't enough. Brenda flicked away the remaining pieces of the telekinetic spells which hurtled violently in the opposite direction. The windows of several cars shattered and a wizard was thrown backwards into the air. Brenda strengthened her dampening field at the same time as she worked on finishing the energy matrix of her spell. The energy of the vortex was now dominated by angry tendrils of red which twisted violently. A smile of accomplishment spread across Brenda's face as the energy matrix of her spell snapped into place. She finished casting the powerful enchantment which caused a huge explosion of energy to rush out in a powerful wave from every vortex in the world.

No one in the mall or parking lot had time to register the fact that they were in mortal danger because they died instantly. Brenda didn't realize the folly of her ways as she, too, perished in the angry wave of red energy that swept over her. The vision abruptly ended and Josephine realized she'd cried out in horror. She severed her connection with the vortex and squeezed her eyes shut. She breathed deeply and calmed her thoughts, struggling with her guilt and self recriminations. She was putting everyone in danger by messing around with the vortex. She shouldn't be doing this. It would slowly drive her insane in the same way that Brenda's sanity crumbled away over time. Brenda had snuck to the vortex in Seattle and had tapped into the vortex many times before she'd been caught. Josephine couldn't believe she was making the same mistake.

She started the engine and carefully backed out of her parking spot. She would stop making these trips to the beach and would make damned sure she never tapped into the vortex again. It just wasn't right to continue doing this. Josephine arrived at her condo, went into a deep meditation to calm herself, and fell asleep early in the evening.

Chapter 8

Josephine, Alice, and Helen traversed the bakery section of Publix. Josephine decided she'd buy a couple of cinnamon rolls. Usually she tried to keep away from desserts because it was too tempting to overindulge. Alice had wanted to look at the cinnamon bread but had changed her mind after inspecting several loaves. She grabbed a package of carrot muffins instead.

"These look kind of good," Alice said in a noncommittal tone.

"I've had them before. They're very tasty. Of course, practically everything in a Publix bakery is delicious," Josephine said.

"I've been thinking about getting a cat," Alice said.

"Why?" Helen asked.

"I think it would be nice. I heard they're good for your health."

"That's just a myth," Helen said.

"No, I think Alice is right. I've read some articles that show cats can help calm a person with mental disorders or depression," Josephine said.

"I don't have any mental disorders," Alice said indignantly.

Several nearby customers glanced over at her speculatively. Alice frowned at them as she left the bakery.

"We should stop by the produce section. I need some salad stuff," Helen said.

"You eat like a bird," Alice said.

"I like salads. Besides, they're good for you," Helen said.

She was pushing a cart instead of riding in one of the electric ones today. This was a good idea because Josephine believed when people reached a certain age, they should be careful to remain active. That was why she insisted on going to the gym on a regular basis.

"We need to find out a good time to booby trap Dale's place," Josephine said, changing topics abruptly.

"Yes, I can't believe I was able to finish that manifestation enchantment on my wand. With your help, I can really accomplish a lot," Alice said. "I never realized how much that stupid ring was crippling you."

"Shh!" Helen hushed her warningly. "We shouldn't be talking about this in public."

"You're right. But I can't wait to give Dale his comeuppance," Josephine said.

They ambled on down the aisles until they reached the produce section and Helen began perusing the various vegetables. Josephine had no intention of buying anything from this area except for maybe some juice. She strolled away from her two friends to look at the drinks. She picked out a couple of tropical blends and placed them in her cart. Helen was still laboriously trying to decide on which zucchini to purchase. After a time, she finally set one in her cart and moved on. Josephine let out a soft sigh of impatience as Helen frowned at the display of lettuce. God, my friends can be slower than snails, she thought with annoyance.

"I'm feeling really tired and dizzy," Helen said.

"You are?" Alice gazed at her in concern.

"Yes, I think it's an ongoing problem," Helen said.

"I remember you mentioning that before," Josephine said slowly.

Unfortunately, Helen was just a bit of a hypochondriac and she seemed to think she was suffering from anemia. She still hadn't decided what kind she'd developed but she occasionally brought up the subject and stated a general intention to see the doctor about it at some point in the future.

"Maybe we should get you to the hospital," Alice said sharply.

"No, I think I can make it," Helen said bravely. "We're almost done here."

"Why don't you go to the damn doctor and get it over with?" Alice asked.

"I can't afford it. I have to be careful how to spend my money."

Alice's irritation dwindled and she nodded sympathetically even though she suspected the anemia scare was another false alarm. A couple of months ago, Helen had suspected she was developing breast cancer but a doctor's visit had showed no sign of it. Helen shoved her cart forward and they moved on toward the checkout lines at the front of the store.

"Why in the world do you think you have anemia?" Alice finally asked.

"Because I have all the symptoms. Dizziness, weakness, and fatigue," Helen said.

"You really should go to the doctor."

"I can't afford to go this month. I'll try to go next month," Helen said.

"I'll pay for the visit!" Alice said.

"No! I won't take your money!" Helen said firmly.

When they paid for their groceries and returned to their condos, Josephine quickly put away her purchases and went back to the parking garage to see if Dale's green sedan was in his spot. She grinned with triumph when she saw that it was absent which meant he wasn't home. She rushed back to Alice's place and told her. Soon, Josephine and her two friends were standing outside Dale's locked door. Josephine concentrated on deactivating the security enchantments and unlocked the door. She reached out, turned the knob, and stepped inside his condo.

"I'm not sure how long he'll be gone so we should hurry," Josephine said.

"Let's set my trap first." Alice eagerly walked to the kitchen and thrust her wand out so that it pointed at the closed cupboards above the sink. A flurry of blue shimmering sparks shot out from the tip of her wand. The trap snapped into place which meant that the next time Dale opened one of these cupboards, a bunch of huge cockroaches would come pouring out. Alice chortled with mirth as she followed her comrades into the living room.

"I'll set the snow storm to manifest when Dale walks underneath the point of origin," Josephine said.

She pointed her wand at the center of the living room and drew in a gentle flow of power. The enchantment in her wand released and a large blue spark surged from it to hit the ceiling. The temperature in the room instantly plummeted.

"It looks like you messed up on the delay setting," Helen said nervously and shivered in the sudden chill.

A mist was rapidly developing against the ceiling as the room grew colder. Josephine activated her second sight to gauge how far the spell was progressing. If it wasn't too far in the process, she could reset it and add the delay. Josephine was surprised to see that the matrix had already stretched out completely into a net of energy that was rapidly gaining strength. She doubted she could stop it at this point but believed she should try. She focused on the energy net and willed it to collapsed back into its original form. Instead of shrinking in on itself, the energy patterns shimmered wildly and drew on the power she was using to try to contain it. Josephine furrowed her brows and concentrated harder but soon had to give up.

"It was worth a try," Alice said sadly. "I guess Dale won't get to experience the snow storm."

Suddenly, the door opened and Dale stepped into the room holding a bag of groceries. He halted and stared at them in surprise. Snow began to fall gently and the door slammed shut behind him. Dale flinched in surprise and Josephine tuned her senses to the magical environment once again. She gasped in alarm when she realized the net had extended from the ceiling to curtain down on the edges of the room. It was enclosing the living room like a prison which hadn't been her intention.

"What in God's name are you doing to my condo, you stupid freak!" Dale shouted.

"I'm just paying you back for your stupid prank, you skanky troll," Josephine said in a chilling tone.

Dale activated his shield as he lowered his groceries to the floor. Snow was gently falling from the ceiling.

"I'm going to kick your sorry ass," he said heatedly.

"Let's see you try." Josephine's lips curved in a challenging smile.

Dale released a volley of telekinetic energy from a wand he whipped out from his shorts. Josephine easily deflected the attack. Alice shot a knockout spell at him which bounced off his shield. Josephine flowed in a stream of power through her chakras without trying to limit her ability. She shot out a huge blast of telekinetic energy which made short work of his shield and shoved him backward against the door. Dale remained on his feet and unleashed a stream of telekinetic energy back at her. She easily halted the attack and dissipated it. Dale's eyes widened with surprise and panic. Josephine swallowed guiltily as she realized her display of power without using any magical tools was very intimidating. Only a category five or an unrestrained category six could accomplish what she was doing.

Dale backed away from her and stood near the end of the arm chair at the far corner of the room. She suspected he was about to duck for cover. Josephine turned her attention to the door and reached out with her mind to sense the intricate patterns of energy that were blanketing the door. When she was ready, she carefully created a temporary opening and enlarged it so that the door would be released. Dale chose this moment to fire both his wands at her. Five enchantments hurtled at her and she had to pull her attention away from the door to deflect them. Unfortunately, one of the enchantments struck her in the arm. She promptly lost consciousness before she had time to register that it was a knockout spell. She awakened shivering with snow falling heavily on her. Alice and Helen stood nearby facing Dale who was crouched behind a couch.

"You're going to get it!" he said.

"Good, you're awake," Helen said.

"I can't believe this," Josephine said.

She slowly picked herself up off the floor and brushed some snow off her chest. Dale waved his wand and a black viscous fluid shot out. It splattered over Josephine, Helen, and Alice and left behind a putrid odor that nauseated them.

"You are such a disgusting troll!" Josephine shouted.

She generated a flow of power and held out her right hand toward Dale. He raised another shield but it flickered out of existence after only several seconds. He slowly lifted into the air kicking and shouting obscenities at her.

"You like disgusting smells, do you?" Josephine said softly.

"I think I can get him good if you can hold him there," Alice suggested.

"Do your worst," Josephine said.

Alice held both hands out and a black blob the size of a beach ball materialized in front of her. The blob slowly drifted toward Dale as he waved his fists in the air threateningly. Bubbles oozed to the surface of the manifestation as it drew closer to him. When it was almost within arm's reach, it suddenly picked up speed and splattered against his chest. Josephine released her hold on Dale and he dropped to the floor in front of the couch cursing savagely.

"What a filthy mouth," Josephine said.

Dale had a bunch of the vile, black substance clinging to his clothes and body. He wrinkled his nose in revulsion and abruptly stopped talking. Josephine opened her senses to the energy patterns in the room and sensed the energy net had begun to dissipate a bit. It was slowly drawing back up into the ceiling towards the spell's point of origin. The room was no longer sealed.

"We can leave now," Josephine said.

"Good," Helen said with relief.

The three of them hastily headed for the door and left the condo.

"I'm going to get you for this!" Dale shouted after them.

"Whatever," Josephine said with unconcern.

She and her friends gathered in her condo. She and Alice exchanged high fives while Helen frowned with worry.

"We shouldn't be doing these pranks. We need to start acting our age," Helen said.

"Who says there's an age limit on a good prank?" Alice asked.

"I just don't like how things are going. That snow storm seemed kind of dangerous. We need to stop egging him on," Helen said.

"I didn't start anything with that troll," Josephine said.

"We need to just let things lie," Helen said.

"I will now that I evened the score."

"You know he's going to retaliate," Helen fretted.

"So what? I can handle it," Josephine said confidently.

"That's not the point," Helen said.

"You worry too much. I think you need to sit down with a cup of tea and just forget all your problems. Learn to relax," Alice said bluntly.

"I can make some tea for you," Josephine offered.

"No, thanks. I'm going to take a nap," Helen said.

"Sweet dreams," Josephine said.

As soon as Helen had left, Alice sighed with exasperation.

"She's such a stick in the mud sometimes," Alice said.

"She means well."

Alice chuckled and shook her head. "That was a freaky snow storm enchantment you conjured up. If you would have gotten the time delay working right, it would have been fantastic!"

"I know! I wish I could see the look on his face when your cockroaches come scurrying out of his cupboard," Josephine said.

"Are you in the mood for some rummy?" Alice asked.

"Sure."

Josephine got out the deck of cards and the two of them played as they planned strategies for payback if Dale played any more pranks on them. When the doorbell rang, Josephine carefully set her cards face down and crossed the room. She opened the door but no one was there. A movement out of the corner of her eye was the only warning she received before a spell struck her in the stomach. She flinched and turned to see that Dale stood about twelve feet down the hall with his wand extended. She opened her mouth to hurl an insult at him but instead of words, a loud belch erupted from her lips. Dale burst out laughing as he backed away from her then ran down the hall and turned the corner. Josephine tried to shout again but another belch spilled from her throat instead.

She ran after him but had only managed to traverse several steps before she was knocked backward by an invisible barrier. Josephine slipped and fell onto her butt. She quickly rose to her feet and opened her second sight to identify the spell that had blocked her pursuit of the troll who had had the nerve to hit her with a belching jinx. That was such a childish ploy, he should be ashamed of himself. Alice stepped out into the hallway as Josephine quickly identified an impedimentum enchantment. Unfortunately, it took her a moment to dispel this blockade before she could continue her pursuit of Dale.

"That stupid troll! I'd like to kick his ass!" Josephine said irritably.

"Me, too," Alice said fervently.

They returned to Josephine's condo and finished their game of cards. Alice had managed to win by only ten points which irked Josephine. She wanted to play another hand but Alice had some errands to run. Josephine went to the phone and dialed Gary's number again. She wondered why he wouldn't return her call. She sighed with irritation when the answering machine picked up. Why couldn't he answer his stupid phone? It rang as she stood there frowning at it. She swiftly picked up the receiver.

"Hello?" she said.

"It's Alex. I'm at a crime scene that I need your expertise on."

"Okay. What's the address?" Josephine asked. She jotted down his reply on a notepad. "Is this the serial killer from last week?"

"It looks likes it is," he replied. "If so, he's breaking his pattern. Normally, he waits about a month in between each victim."

"This isn't good."

"No, it's not. I'll see you soon."

The dial tone sounded in her ear and Josephine hung up the phone.

"That was rude," she said.

Josephine would like to set a few jinxes on Alex but knew that wasn't a possibility. She heard some pounding and loud voices in the hallway as she headed for the front door. Josephine wondered what was the source of the commotion as she stepped out of her condo. She immediately saw three men carrying a couch toward the opened door beside her condo. Obviously, Robert Miller was moving his belongings into his new home. Josephine sighed with annoyance at the reminder of her new neighbor. The movers heaved at the couch as they tipped it at an angle to try and slip it through the door. Josephine could see that it wasn't easy.

"Okay, guys. It's time to use one of our teleportation enchantments," one of the movers said.

Teleportation enchantments required massive amounts of power to generate and were limited to small distances. The three men carefully set the couch down and one of them pulled out a wand. He pointed it at the couch and it vanished in a flash of gold light. Instantly, a gold flash emitted from inside the condo. The three men stepped into the living room and shove the couch against the far wall. Josephine continued on her way toward the elevator which had just opened to reveal her ex. He gaped at her with disbelief but recovered and stepped forward.

"Hello, Spot," Josephine said.

"What are you doing here?" he said warily.

"I live here." Josephine rushed past him so she could enter the elevator before the doors slid shut. She was amused to see the look of dismay on his face and she was further pleased that she had gotten the last word for a change. She got lost twice trying to find the house where the murder had occurred. Finally, she pulled up in front of the correct address. It was a small beat-up gray house with a small, unkempt yard. Howie stood at the front door keeping vigil. He smiled a greeting as Josephine approached him.

"How's it going?" she said.

"It's kind of freaky," Howie said.

"What do you mean?" Josephine asked.

"You'll see," Howie said.

Josephine stepped into the living room which was trashed. The television screen had shattered, the lights had blown up, and the entertainment center had two shelves which had somehow caved in. Gary sat on an armchair with his arms crossed over his stomach in a protective gesture. His face was pale and his expression haunted. He didn't seem to be aware of anyone in the room. Jake waved his grandmother over.

"What's going on?" Josephine asked.

"Gary is having an incident," Alex said.

Josephine stepped around the body which showed no signs of damage. It was a young woman with brown, short, curly hair wearing a green tee shirt and jeans. She was sprawled face down in the middle of the floor. Josephine dragged her attention back to Alex.

"What's wrong with him?" Josephine nodded at Gary.

"We were hoping you could tell us," Alex said.

Gary's eyes rose to meet Josephine's. "You're here."

"Yes, I am," she said.

"Be careful," he said.

"Excuse me?" Josephine asked.

Gary's eyes lost their focus and he no longer seemed aware of her.

"It must have been a violent attack on this woman. The psychic trauma must have put Gary in a fugue state or something," Josephine said.

"None of us could pick up on anything with our psychometry," Alex said. "And the broken lights and furniture was done by Gary when he was reading the trace energy in the room."

"So the room wasn't trashed before he started?" Josephine asked.

"No."

Josephine opened her second sight and furrowed her brows in concentration. The trace energies were faint but they seemed readable. Josephine began to read one of them and immediately heard a shrill, blood-curdling scream as agony coursed through her body. The room twisted savagely and folded in on itself. Josephine retreated from the trace energy but it was too late to protect herself. It was an excrucio lector enchantment that was causing this torment. Josephine could barely think straight as she worked at separating the energy matrix that had wrapped itself around her. She struggled to extricate the excrucio lector enchantment from her etheric body. The screaming and whirlwind of voices continued to thunder at her mind as the pain wracked her body. The room suddenly snapped into focus as she rid herself of the spell.

Josephine breathed heavily and realized she was being held upright by Howie and Jake. She drew away from them and smiled weakly in reassurance. Her legs felt weak and shaky as she stood there trying to regain her voice. Her body felt cold and fatigued. Gary was still staring off into space.

"The killer managed to set an excrucio lector enchantment on the room. There is absolutely no way I can read the trace energies without being hit again," Josephine finally said.

"Excrucio lector?" Alex asked.

"It's very difficult to cast that type of spell. It's like the ignotus enchantment except that any trace energy that remains is bound with an extremely painful psychic residue," Josephine said. "I've only experienced this one other time in my life."

"The wizard who performed this spell has to be at least a category four. He's probably a category five," Jake said.

"Yes, probably," Josephine confirmed.

"Can you help Gary?" Jake asked.

"Yes, I can remove the excrucio lector enchantment from him." Josephine centered her attention on Gary as she opened her mind to the subtle energies in the room. She made sure to keep away from the dangerous trace energies as she felt out the patterns of angry energy that had enmeshed themselves over Gary. She abruptly halted her efforts as she noticed something strange about the victim. Josephine's attention swerved to the victim and she gasped in surprise. "That woman is alive!"

"What?!" Alex exclaimed. He shook his head emphatically. "That's not possible. They checked her for a pulse. There was nothing."

"But her body was kind of warm, wasn't it?" Josephine asked.

"It was just cooling down but still kind of warm," Alex said. "She's definitely dead."

"No, she's alive. She's in a coma," Josephine said.

Alex got out his cell phone and called for an ambulance.

"How could they not know?" Alex asked when he'd hung up the phone.

"Because there is something very odd about her condition," Josephine said. "Only someone with very acute psychometry would be able to tell she was alive. She is in some sort of coma."

"Jesus!" Alex said with horror. "Is she going to make it to the hospital?"

"I don't know," Josephine said pensively.

"Can you help her?" Jake asked.

Josephine carefully scrutinized the odd energy patterns dominating the woman's body. She had never seen anything like it. She slowly shook her head when she realized she was way out of her league.

"I wouldn't know where to even begin trying to dispel it," Josephine said.

"All right," Alex said.

"Let me work on Gary."

She easily isolated the angry red energy strands weaving through his etheric body. She carefully pulled them away from him and they disintegrated into the air. Gary's eyes cleared and he looked up at her with startlement.

"Thank you," he finally said.

"Are you all right?" Alex asked.

"Yes, I'm fine now," Gary said cautiously.

His eyes took on a guarded look as he slowly rose to his feet. The ambulance siren could be heard and soon the woman in the coma was taken out of the room.

"What's her name?" Josephine asked.

"Vickie Richardson," Jake said.

"Something is very strange about that spell," Josephine said. "The poor girl. I don't know if she has any chance of living through this."

"There are plenty of qualified medical wizards at the hospital. If anyone can save her, they can," Jake said.

"Is there any way that you and Gary can dispel the excrucio lector enchantment?" Alex asked.

"No, it's not possible," Josephine said.

Alex regarded Gary expectantly and it was obvious he wanted a different answer. Gary shifted uncomfortably and avoided meeting the detective's eyes.

"It can't be done," he said quietly.

"Why?" Alex pressed.

"The energy from the excrucio lector contaminates the trace energies. There's no way to get rid of it. The evidence is completely contaminated," Josephine said. "It's rare to be able to successfully cast an excrucio lector spell and I doubt the killer will be able to do it again."

"This is unacceptable," Alex said.

"Those are the facts," Josephine said. "I can't change reality for you."

"Whatever."

"Can I go now?" Josephine said brusquely.

"Fine," he said dismissively.

Gary followed her outside and once they had crossed the street, she turned to him.

"Are you feeling okay?" she asked.

"No but I'll be better soon," he said.

"Your shield that protects you from trace energies is gone."

"Yes," Gary said.

"What are you going to do?" Josephine asked.

"I can fix it."

"How?" Josephine pressed.

"I need to go."

Gary started to walk away but she grabbed his arm. He reluctantly turned to face her.

"Where are you going?" she said.

He glanced nervously at the house and realized Howie was watching.

"I can't talk now," he said.

"Where are you going?" she said. "I'll meet you there."

Gary furtively checked to see if Howie was still watching. He let out a weary sigh and returned his gaze to Josephine.

"I'm going to the beach."

"I'll meet you there," Josephine said.

"Why? I need to be alone," Gary said.

"There will be people there."

"I don't want to talk to anyone now. Can't you leave me alone?" Gary said with frustration.

"No, I can't."

Gary stalked off and Josephine hopped in her car.

Chapter 9

Josephine followed Gary to Siesta Key but he parked a good twelve blocks from the beach. He pulled into a parking lot for a condo complex. Josephine frowned as she stepped out of her car and went over to his. He rolled down the driver's side window and regarded her warily.

"I'm going to tap into the vortex now," he said.

"You shouldn't do that. It's dangerous. I realized that when I saw a vision of the Disaster. We're doing the same thing Brenda did. We'll lose control," Josephine said.

"I saw visions of the Disaster many times. The problem with Brenda is that she was crazy," Gary said. "It wasn't tapping into the vortex that made her lose her mind."

"But it's addictive and we're liable to do something dangerous by accident," Josephine said.

"We're not trying to cast any spells. She was trying to change the world but we're not making that mistake," Gary said. "The only way for me to feel better and to put my trace energy shield back up is to tap into the vortex."

"Are you sure it's safe?" Josephine asked.

"I've been tapping into the vortex for over five years. It's perfectly safe. I'm always in control," Gary said.

Josephine took a deep breath and mulled this over. "Let me watch you."

"All right," Gary said. "The passenger door is unlocked."

112

Josephine circled the car and sat down next to him. She opened her second sight and realized he'd already connected with the vortex in the time it had taken her to get into the car. Power coursed through his body and radiated from him with breath-taking beauty. Josephine closed her eyes and reached out with her mind toward the vortex. It took her a moment to connect but it wasn't difficult like she'd anticipated. Power flooded through her and she reveled in the feeling. Her mind expanded swiftly and she could sense the minds of those nearby. She became aware of more and more of the minds that surrounded her from farther and farther away. Guilt stirred within her as she remembered the addiction category six wizards had to tapping into the vortex. Obviously, she and Gary both suffered from this affliction. Their vulnerability to this condition is why the laws existed in the first place.

"We can't keep doing this," Josephine murmured.

She felt oddly detached from her body as she floated in pleasure. She couldn't believe how wonderful it was to be connected to the power vortex.

"I don't see any reason we shouldn't," Gary said.

"It's against the laws. You have to realize we're succumbing to addiction."

"I could stop any time I want."

Josephine laughed in spite of herself. "Aren't you worried that we'll cause a Disaster?"

"It's not going to happen," Gary said. "Brenda was a psycho."

"You've been in the same classes I have. We've been warned of the addiction and how it changes you."

"It's just a scare tactic. I've been tapping into the vortex at Siesta Key for over five years on a regular basis. I'm still the same person I was. I'm not addicted. I don't have to go every day. When I lived in Saint Petersburg, I was only going once a week or so. Addictions aren't like that."

"Maybe this isn't the typical addiction. It's magic."

"It's not an addiction. What would we have to do to make you feel better about it? Stop cold turkey for a month?" Gary said sardonically.

"That would be enough proof for me," Josephine said.

Gary closed his eyes and lapsed into silence. Josephine waited for him to respond but he allowed the quiet to drag on.

"Well? Aren't you going to say something about it?" Josephine finally said.

"I'm not willing to give this up for a month."

"Why?"

"I don't believe it's an addiction. I've been able to easily handle living without a connection to a vortex for a week and sometimes longer. I don't feel I have to prove myself."

"I see," Josephine said slowly. "So you think that the classes we're required to take that warns us of the dangers of tapping into the vortex and using our magic too much is just a pack of lies?"

"Yes, exactly."

"I'm not so sure about that."

"I have over five years of experience with a power vortex that says otherwise. Last time I checked, I didn't create a Disaster like Brenda. Furthermore, I'm not crazy."

Josephine had to admit that Gary didn't seem insane although he was certainly flighty.

"I thought your brother made the trace energy protection spells for you. Why do you have to connect with the vortex to get yours up again?" Josephine asked.

"Dan is mad at me for moving here. He doesn't want to have to commute to work from Sarasota so he hasn't moved here yet. I don't know if he will. He hasn't made any more of those protection spells lately," Gary said.

Josephine mulled this over then realized her connection with the vortex was slipping. She concentrated on maintaining the link and wondered how long she could hold it. When she finally lost her connection, she couldn't believe how wonderful she felt. Her body buzzed with exhilaration and joy. She smiled at Gary and wondered if she was wrong in her assumption that they were addicted to the vortex. It seemed kind of absurd at this point.

"How is your trace energy shield doing?" she asked.

"It's great," Gary said. "I may not need my brother's spells as long as I come down to the beach often enough."

"I'll see you later," Josephine said.

"Bye."

Josephine drove to the beach parking lot, slipped off her shoes, and strolled across the white, powdery sand. She smiled pleasantly as she neared the gently lapping waves of the ocean. She stepped into the water and basked in the euphoric feeling of the aftermath of her connection with the vortex. She could sense its power gently thrumming over her body but didn't feel the pull like usual since she'd just tapped into it moments ago. She became aware of a young woman sitting cross legged on the beach nearby. She had long blond hair and wore a white and blue striped swimsuit. She was obviously connected to the vortex as Josephine could feel it power radiating from her. Glowing blue and red butterflies had materialized around the young woman and she lifted off the ground several inches.

Josephine wished she could openly tap into the vortex without fear of being caught. Her life would have been so much simpler if she'd been a category five wizard rather than a category six. She could have tapped into the vortex as much as she pleased. So many spells were out of her league because of the aequitas enchantment that she was forced to wear. Of course, now that it was neutralized she had new possibilities opening up for her. She would always have to be careful not to lose control though. The glowing butterflies fluttered their delicate wings and weaved between each other as they circled the young woman. Josephine stared at the breathtaking colors for a moment then returned her attention to the ocean. When she returned to her condo, she could hear a dog barking from the room on her left.

Josephine frowned with mild annoyance when she realized her ex had brought a dog with him to the senior complex. She picked up the phone and dialed her friend, Helen.

"Hello?" Helen said.

"Hi, it's me."

"What's wrong?" Helen said.

"Spot brought a stupid dog with him. It's barking it's head off right now," Josephine said grievously.

"Why don't you just talk to him?"

"I shouldn't have to put up with this stuff. I've worked hard my entire life. I'm old and tired now and trying to enjoy my retirement," Josephine said.

"Sometimes we have problems we have to deal with," Helen said.

"When you reach my age, you don't feel like handling life's daily problems any more." Josephine ran a hand through her silky, black hair and sighed dismally.

"The only thing you can do is talk to Robert and see if he'll take care of his dog. After that, you can send a complaint to the office."

"That's what I should do. Complain to the office," Josephine said. "I better be going. I'll talk to you later, Helen."

"Okay. Bye."

Josephine hung up the phone and called the office.

"Live Oak Meadows Community Center. This is Paula, how may I help you?" said the elderly receptionist.

"This is Josephine O'Connor and I have a complaint to lodge against my next door neighbor who has just moved in," she said grimly.

"I haven't heard from you in quite awhile," Paula said. "You're having problems with your new neighbor?"

"He has a dog that's barking its head off."

"Let me check his records," Paula said slowly.

Josephine began pacing back and forth in the living room. She stepped in front of the window and peered outside. The sun caressed the smooth, unwrinkled skin of her face as her brown eyes sparked with impatience.

"I'm too old for this kind of stress," Josephine said with exasperation. "I've lived a long, hard life and now I just want to be left alone. I want things to go easy and to be able to relax. Instead, I have a stupid neighbor with his damned dog giving me a headache. I don't know what's going to be next. Is it going to be acceptable for him to have parties late at night and to blare loud music?"

"Robert does have a dog registered," Paula said regretfully. "However, we do have noise restrictions so I'll send him a letter informing him that a complaint was made and that he needs to take care of the situation."

Josephine's jaw tightened and she jerked away from the window. She sighed loudly with exasperation because this wasn't the reaction she'd been expecting.

"You're just going to send him a letter?" Josephine said evenly.

"Yes and that usually takes care of the problem," Paula said.

"Does it really?" Josephine said quietly as anger made her fingers tighten over the receiver of her phone and her knuckles to bulge.

A scorching wind burst into the room from nowhere but Josephine was too distracted to care about controlling her abilities.

"Don't worry. He'll receive the letter tomorrow," Paula said reassuringly.

"Okay then. Have a nice evening," Josephine said evenly.

"Good bye."

"Bye."

Josephine carefully hung up the phone as the dog continued to bark repeatedly. She walked over to the wall in the dining room and pounded on it loudly to get Robert's attention.

"Make that damned dog shut up!" Josephine shouted.

The dog barked even faster if such a thing was possible. Josephine seethed with fury and walked swiftly to her door which opened of its own accord. She marched over to Robert's door and reached out with her hand. She could sense the security enchantments in place but for some reason discovered that she was able to deactivate it instantly. The door swung open violently and she stepped inside. The dog was a small white poodle which ran excitedly toward her. It snarled viciously when it came within six feet. Josephine concentrated on the obnoxious beast and it abruptly lifted into the air. It soared into the bathroom and the door slammed shut.

"Okay, Spot! I need to have a word with you!" Josephine shouted.

In the absence of the constant barking of the poodle, the condo was disturbingly silent. This only irritated her further. Robert was probably cowering in his bedroom. Josephine crossed the living room and quickly found his room which was devoid of his presence. She abruptly realized that he must not be home. In her anger and haste, she'd failed to consider this possibility. Josephine whirled around and swiftly left the condo. She locked the door and reactivated the security enchantments once she was standing in the hallway. She crossed her arms across her chest and stared at the closed door pensively. She wished there was some way she could reach Robert. As if she'd summoned him, he turned the corner of the hallway and walked towards her. He abruptly halted when he noticed her.

"Hello, Spot." Josephine smiled tightly at him. "You're stupid dog has been barking his head off all day."

"I've only been gone a couple of hours," Robert said defensively.

"Is that so? Well, it seems like an eternity."

"What did I do to deserve you for a neighbor?" Robert sneered.

"Maybe it's because you thought with the brain in your pants and slept around like a dog. Maybe it's because you left your faithful

wife for a younger woman who happened to be a slut like you!"
Josephine said.

Robert's face flushed with anger. Josephine turned on her
heel and swiftly returned to her condo. Robert wisely chose to keep his
thoughts to himself or at least voiced them very quietly so she couldn't
hear. Josephine went to the gym and rode on an exercise bike until
she'd worked out her frustration. The next day, she awoke very early
in the morning and feeling perkier than usual. She took a quick shower
and prepared the coffee maker. She was sipping her first mug of coffee
in the dining room when Alice arrived.

"This was taped to your door," Alice said as she held up a
folded piece of notebook paper.

"How strange." Josephine cocked a bemused brow as she
accepted the paper. She unfolded it and read the message aloud. "I
know you were in my home last night and you'll pay for messing with
my dog, bitch."

"Oh my God!" Alice exclaimed. "What happened?"

Josephine flicked her wrist and the door closed. The two of
them stepped into the kitchen.

"That stupid dog was barking and I sort of broke into Robert's
condo to confront him," Josephine said sheepishly.

"And?" Alice asked as though this news was perfectly normal.
"What happened?"

"It turned out that Robert wasn't home. I locked his dog in the
bathroom and searched for him but he wasn't there," Josephine said.
"He came back after I'd left and we exchanged some words."

"Tell me what he said!" Alice said.

Josephine told her and Alice regarded her with sympathy.

"That stupid man! I think he needs to be taught a lesson!"

"I was thinking that exactly! If we prank him like crazy, maybe we can drive him out of here."

"That's a good idea. I'm sure he'll want to move if you give him a lot of grief," Alice said. "I'll make as many pranks as possible."

"Good. If we work together, we can triple the amount of jinxes," Josephine said.

Alice joined them a short while later and they filled her in on the latest news.

"I think we need to be careful here. Technically, if we break into people's homes to set up manifestation traps and jinxes, we're breaking the law," Helen said. "We could even end up being kicked out of the complex."

"That will never happen," Josephine said confidently. "We'll never get caught."

"Dale has caught us pranking him. We've been lucky so far."

"That's completely different because we've caught him," Josephine argued.

"I don't like this at all," Helen said stubbornly.

Josephine took a swallow of her coffee and narrowed her eyes at her friend. Sometimes, Helen was too much of a wet blanket for her own good. However, they'd been friends for years and Josephine didn't want to jeopardize their relationship.

"Let me tell you what happened yesterday at another crime scene," Josephine said. "There was another murder – or so the police thought. Alex was completely wrong about the victim being dead!"

Josephine explained what had happened which elicited gratifying gasps of shock from both Helen and Alice.

"I can't believe it! So the killer messed up this time!" Alice said with excitement. "Maybe he left a witness! Do you think she'll be able to identify him?"

"Who knows? She's in a coma," Josephine said.

"That's a shame. She may be a vegetable," Helen said.

"I have a feeling she'll wake up eventually," Josephine said. The phone rang and she sighed grievously. "Who in the hell could be calling me so early? It's only eight in the morning."

"It's Detective Riley, I need you to meet me at the Sarasota Memorial Hospital as soon as you get this message," Alex's terse voice came over the machine.

"Why can't that man leave me alone? I worked at a crime scene yesterday! Does he want me to work every day now? I might as well not even be retired anymore," Josephine grumbled.

"Maybe there was another murder. You'd better drive down the hospital," Helen advised.

"I'll go to the hospital when I'm good and ready." Josephine's chin jutted out stubbornly and she took another sip of her coffee.

Helen's eyes reflected her concern but it wasn't her decision to make.

"I think you have enough time to finish your coffee," Alice said. "A dead body can wait another fifteen minutes or so."

"That's right," Josephine said.

Helen frowned and sipped some more of her coffee. Josephine sighed and took another gulp of her drink. Of course, she couldn't enjoy herself knowing she had a job hanging over her head.

"It feels like I'm not even retired," Josephine said.

"Maybe it would be better if you had a job," Alice said speculatively. "You wouldn't be required to leave your work if you received a call from the police unless it was an emergency. They have to follow the laws like you do."

"I'm retired! I can't go back to work! Besides, I'd end up working my butt off. I'd have to put in a full week and then do all the odd job police work, too! That would really suck!" Josephine exclaimed.

"If you weren't available on a whim, Alex may not be calling you so often. It wouldn't be convenient for him to hold a crime scene all day while you're at work."

Josephine took another drink from her mug as she mulled this over. "That's not a bad idea actually. Maybe I'll look through the want ads some time."

When she finished her coffee, she drove down to the Sarasota Memorial Hospital. The receptionist at the lobby was expecting her and told her which room to go to. Unfortunately, it was in ICU and a nurse was required to escort her. A middle-aged woman named Patricia appeared after only a couple moments. Josephine followed her down a long hallway. Finally, they arrived at the room which had two police officers posted just outside.

"What's going on?" Josephine asked.

"Alex wants you to go inside," one of them said.

Josephine stepped into the room and found the woman she saved lying on a hospital bed with an IV tube attached to her arm. Gary leaned against the wall nearby and had a weary expression on his face. Alex had his back to the door. Vickie was wearing a white hospital gown and her pallid skin made her seem close to death.

"What's going on?" Josephine asked.

Alex whirled around and frowned at her belligerently. "It took you long enough to get here."

"I got here as fast as I could." Josephine ignored the stirring of guilt that awakened at his rebuke.

"I need you to try to see if you can read the trace energies around Vickie. See if you can find out anything useful," Alex said.

Josephine was surprised by the request and realized she should have thought of this course of action on her own. Since Vickie was alive, she would be generating trace energies which may contain information about the recent attack. If she'd seen the killer's face then the case may come to a fast conclusion.

"Okay," Josephine said.

She opened her second sight and sought out the trace energies emanating from the unconscious victim. She noticed that Gary had dropped his protection in an attempt to use his psychometry but he had no way of raising the shield back up. He was vulnerable to all the trace energies in the room. Josephine tapped into something useful. She could sense that it was related to the attack. In the vision, everything was dark and she couldn't move. Josephine realized that Vickie had been attacked with a spell similar to a knockout spell but it had left her partially conscious. This had been the killer's intention. Josephine struggled to pick up more information but failed. She kept herself tuned to psychic impressions but couldn't obtain anything else. She sighed with frustration and shook her head.

"The killer used a knockout spell but kept her partially conscious," Josephine said. "Actually, it's a variant of the knockout spell. It was necessary for some reason."

"He probably enjoys knowing that they can feel him killing them," Alex said grimly.

"Maybe."

"Did you see anything else?"

"Nothing," Josephine said.

The lights flickered and a gentle but frigid breeze wafted through the room for several seconds. Alex shivered and eyed Josephine suspiciously.

"It isn't me," she said.

Alex shot Gary a questioning look.

"No, it's not me either," Gary said.

The lights flickered again and a stronger breeze shot over them. It abruptly stopped and Vickie's eyes opened. She abruptly sat up as a strangled cry escaped her lips.

"Where am I? What happened?" she asked.

"You're safe now. You were attacked," Alex said.

Vickie's gaze centered on him and the lights flickered again. Josephine opened her second sight just as another cold breeze whipped over them. She caught sight of strange energy discharges dancing along Vickie's body. This only occurred in category six wizards when they were losing control of their ability. However, Vickie wasn't wearing a topaz ring. Before Josephine could ask about it, Vickie passed out. Her body tipped over the side of the bed but Alex caught her before she could tumble onto the floor. Gary helped him to position her back onto the bed. The energy discharges no longer emanated from Vickie and she seemed to have fallen deep into the coma again.

"What just happened?" Alex asked.

"I don't know," Josephine said. "She's a category six though."

"No, she isn't. She's a category two," Alex said.

"She's definitely a six."

"You're wrong."

Josephine explained what she'd just seen. Alex stared at her with a mixture of irritation and reluctant acceptance.

"She's been changed because of the near death experience," Alex said. "It's happened before but I've never heard of someone becoming a category six."

"Maybe she'll recover from the coma and tell you what happened and identify the killer," Josephine said.

Alex snorted doubtfully. "There's no way I could be that lucky."

Chapter 10

Josephine gazed up at the dark ceiling of her bedroom as the living room phone rang once again. She groaned grievously as she shoved herself out of bed and stumbled toward the doorway. The only individual inconsiderate enough to call her this late at night was that jerk Detective Whiney. She'd helped him out at the hospital several days ago and now he was calling her yet again. Josephine made her way to the living room and picked up the phone.

"Hello?" she said in a disgruntled voice.

"Help me," Gary said fearfully.

"What's going on?" Josephine's anger immediately transformed into concern. "Where are you?"

"I'm in my apartment. Someone just attacked me. I think he's waiting outside. I'm not sure," Gary said.

"Call the police," Josephine said.

"I will but you're the only one who can help me."

"Why?" Josephine asked.

"You're a category six. Sometimes you just know things that other people would dismiss. Please, help me."

"Okay. I'll be right over."

Gary told her his address which was on Stickney Road only a mile from Siesta Key.

"I'll be there in about ten minutes," Josephine said.

She hung up and didn't bother with changing her clothes. She always slept in shorts and a tee shirt so it didn't matter anyway. She rushed out the door and to her car. Soon, she parked in front of the apartment complex where Gary lived. She knocked on his door and he opened it.

"Thank you," he said quietly.

"No one's out here," Josephine said.

"I think he left," Gary said.

Josephine gasped in horror as she stepped inside his apartment. All kinds of debris littered the floor including broken light bulbs which had shattered in the ceiling. One of the armchairs had collapsed as though a giant weight had crashed down on it. The television had fallen off the entertainment center and was lying in the middle of the floor with the rest of the debris.

"Did you call the police?" Josephine asked.

"Yes," he said. "They'll be coming soon."

"Did you get a good look at the attacker?"

"No, he did this from outside my apartment. I think he was on the other side of the door though."

"So he employed psychokinesis," Josephine said with dismay.

Psychokinetic spells could manipulate matter from a distance and didn't require a direct wave of energy unlike telekinetic spells which required a direct line of sight. Only category fives could create psychokinetic enchantments although anyone who was a category two and up could use them. Purchasing these enchantments was extremely expensive.

"I think it was the serial killer," Gary said.

"What makes you believe that?" Josephine said sharply as fear lodged into her chest.

"Why else would someone attack me?"

Josephine hated to admit that he was probably right. Howie and Jake arrived before she had a chance to respond.

"Josephine? What are you doing here?" Howie asked.

"Gary called me," she said.

"I think the serial killer attacked me," Gary said.

Howie and Jake gaped at the mess in the room.

"A psychokinetic enchantment was used," Josephine said.

"Even for a category five, it's difficult to work one of those spells," Jake said.

"I know," Josephine said.

"Have either one of you tried using your psychometry?" Jake asked.

"Not yet but we can try now," Josephine said.

"I can dust for prints outside but it's a public place and I doubt we'll get anything we can use," Jake said.

Gary's eyes filled with panic over the prospect of using his psychometry. Josephine knew he was dreading lowering his trace energy shield. She didn't blame him. Receiving all that overwhelming psychic input must be brutal. She opened her awareness to the subtle energies of the room and searched for clues. Impressions came to her as she carefully sifted through the area. A vision of part of the attack sprang into her mind. Debris had already started to litter the floor and Gary had stumbled across the living room toward the kitchen. The television flew from the entertainment center and smacked into his side. Gary yelped with pain as he was thrown off his feet. The lights shattered and he covered his head to protect himself from the raining shards. Josephine saw several more scenes of Gary being attacked but no impressions of the attacker.

"I'm sorry but I didn't get any clues from the serial killer," she said.

"We're going to post a guard with you every night," Jake said.

"I'll take the first watch," Howie said.

"I'm not staying here. I don't feel safe," Gary said shakily.

"You can stay with me," Josephine said.

Gary regarded her with a mixture of surprise and relief. "Thank you."

"No problem. Let's get you packed up so we can go."

"Grandma, can I talk to you for a minute in private?" Jake said.

"Sure, honey," Josephine said.

Gary left the room to pack and she walked over to her grandson who had taken up a position a short distance away from Howie.

"Are you sure this is a good idea?" Jake said.

"What do you mean?" Josephine asked.

"The serial killer obviously views Gary as a threat. You're probably a threat to him as well. If he follows you to your home, he'll know how to get at the both of you."

Josephine stiffened reflexively and her heart beat a little faster. She couldn't abandon Gary though. As a category six, she knew how alone and persecuted he must feel. She wouldn't make him fend for himself.

"I'm taking Gary with me."

"Howie will be following you to your condo. Keep an eye out for anyone else who might be tailing you," Jake warned.

"I will," Josephine said.

She drove Gary to her condo and noticed he was extremely nervous during the entire trip. Once they arrived at her place, he started to relax a little though.

"You have multiple security enchantments on your door," Gary said.

"Yes, I do." Josephine raised her hand toward the door and activated them.

"Most people just have one if any," Gary said.

"I like to be prepared," Josephine said. "Let me show you the guest room."

The guest room happened to be down the hall on the end directly across from her room. It was spacious and she hadn't filled it with much furniture. It had a queen sized bed, several pictures of her family hanging on the wall, a rocking chair in the corner, and a dresser which she kept empty.

"Thank you for letting me stay here," Gary said.

"Sure." Josephine smiled reassuringly at him. "Let me know if you need anything. I'm going to bed."

"I'll be fine. Thanks."

Josephine couldn't help but feel somewhat tense when she lay in bed. She stared up at the ceiling and tried to relax. Now that she'd had time to process the situation, she realized she'd put a target on her back for the serial killer. If he was going after Gary, she was conveniently putting herself with him so he could take care of them both at the same time. Of course, Gary and Josephine were two powerful wizards without the constraint of an aequitas enchantment. That offered a protection which the serial killer wouldn't know about. Josephine mentally went through the reasons why she was safe but it didn't help her anxiety. It wasn't until a long time afterward that she drifted into a troubled sleep. She woke up a bit late and had only just stepped out of the shower when the door knocked.

Josephine quickly threw on some shorts and a blouse so she was presentable and answered the door. Helen greeted her warmly and stepped inside. Luckily, Josephine had started the coffee before showering so it was already brewed at this point.

"I have something to tell you," Josephine said.

Gary stepped into the living room clad in only a tee shirt and red boxers. Helen's eyes widened with astonishment and she shot her friend an embarrassed look. Josephine's face flushed as she realized what this looked like. Gary's dark hair was disheveled and he gazed questioningly at them.

"Gary, this is my friend, Helen," Josephine said by way of introduction. "Helen, this is Gary. He's the other category six I told you about. He was attacked last night so I let him stay here where he'd be safe."

"Wow! I'm surprised the police didn't offer protection," Helen said.

"They had someone standing outside the condo all night but he must have left before you came over," Josephine said. She turned to her guest. "Would you like some coffee? Alice will be over in a little bit."

"Sure. Let me take a shower first."

Alice arrived a short while later. Soon, the four of them were seated at the dining room table sipping coffee.

"You had an exciting night, young man," Alice commented.

"Yes," Gary said.

The sound of a dog barking caught their attention. Josephine frowned with displeasure. Robert's poodle had a habit of going into barking fits over random time intervals. She never knew when it would happen. Sometimes, it would wake her out of a sound sleep. Robert must not go to bed until well after midnight.

"That damned dog. I'd like to throw it off the side of the building," Josephine grumbled.

"It doesn't bark that often," Helen said.

"You don't live here so you can't hear it as often as I do," Josephine said.

"Paula sent him a letter, didn't she?"

"He's gotten it by now. Obviously, it hasn't helped."

"Too bad they allow pets in this complex," Helen said.

"Isn't he breaking some sort of rules with his dog barking like that?" Gary asked.

"Yes but I doubt they'll kick him out because of it," Josephine said.

"If you keep complaining, they'll send someone to check on him and if he's caught with the dog barking, he'll probably get a heavy fine," Gary said.

"Do you really think so?" Josephine asked.

"Yes, my grandmother lives in a complex in New York. She had a similar situation."

"Hmm," Josephine said thoughtfully.

Gary finished the rest of his coffee and excused himself. He left for work a short while later.

"How long is he staying with you?" Alice asked.

"I don't know. He's welcome to stay until the serial killer is caught."

"That could take forever with someone who's skilled with ignotus enchantments," Helen pointed out.

"I'm sure if it drags on for too long, Gary will move back into his own apartment," Josephine said.

"It's about time to go to the gym," Helen said.

"I'm almost finished." Alice swallowed another gulp of her coffee. "Just give me another minute."

"No need to rush," Josephine said.

"It gets crowded after nine," Helen fretted. "People hog the machines."

"Okay, I'm done." Alice got up from the table and rinsed her mug out in the sink.

The three of them stepped out into the hallway and were struck by a blast of arctic air and snow. Josephine shivered as large bits of snow clung to her hair and clothing. She brushed her arms off and saw Dale dashing down the hall in retreat. She shot off a telekinetic wave but he'd already raised a shield.

"That obnoxious toad," Josephine said.

She made sure to activate her security enchantments before heading for the gym. She knew Dale would probably try to break into her condo while she was away.

"We need to do something about Skanky Toad," Josephine said as she drove down the streets toward the gym.

"Who's that?" Helen asked.

"Dale," Josephine said grimly.

"That's a good nickname. You've always been talented at giving appropriate nicknames to jerks," Alice said approvingly.

"Thanks." Josephine smiled briefly at her then returned her attention back to the road.

She parked in the gym parking lot and the three of them went inside. Robert was on an exercise bicycle off in the corner. Josephine wrinkled her nose with disgust as she noticed the rivulets of sweat running down his body and soaking his shirt. The flabby skin in his legs was wobbling wildly as he pedaled.

"This is just wrong," Josephine said.

"What's wrong?" Helen asked.

"Spots on one of those bicycles." Alice pointed at him.

"Oh!" Helen exclaimed.

"Let's get this over with." Josephine strolled over to the first weight machine and set the adjustments.

When it was time for Robert to leave, he discreetly walked past them and pretended not to notice their presence in the gym. Josephine was relieved and irritated by his reaction. When she and her friends finished their routine, they went to Siesta Key beach. They sat down on lawn chairs and sunbathed in relative silence. Josephine enjoyed the quiet atmosphere and rolling waves. Before the Disaster, this beach had been miserable to visit because of the crowds. Josephine had lived here but had luckily moved away before the Disaster had occurred.

"Alice, I need to talk to you," Josephine said.

Alice turned and gazed inquisitively at her. "Yes?"

"Promise you'll keep this just between us. I'm sure Helen wouldn't approve."

"I promise! Tell me!" Alice said eagerly.

"I've tapped into the vortex here at the beach before," Josephine blurted out nervously.

"You did?" Alice stilled and a horrified look dominated her face. "How could you do something like that? It warps your mind."

"And why exactly would it do that?" Josephine said defensively.

"You know why! You're a category six! If you tap into the vortex, it has a different effect on you than other people."

"The laws existed for so long that I don't believe anyone really knows what happens," Josephine said.

"You always complain that you can't tap into the vortex here. You're kind of predisposed of having an addiction before you even do anything. I'll bet you're connected to the vortex right now," Alice said.

"No, I'm not," Josephine said firmly.

Unfortunately, she felt an uncomfortable urge and desire to connect with it but she was resisting. It didn't feel overpowering like one would associate with an addiction.

"I can choose not to tap into its power at any time. I've only connected with the vortex several times," Josephine said.

"You have to be very careful. Everyone knows that tapping into the vortex is what made Brenda crazy and that she eventually caused the Disaster."

"I know but I don't think the story is accurate. I think she may have already been crazy."

"You don't know that for sure, do you?" Alice asked.

"No, but I can't just blindly accept everything I've been told anymore."

"You're allowing your addiction to cloud your judgment."

"I'm not addicted," Josephine said evenly. "After I've tapped into the vortex, I have much greater control of my abilities."

"It's like being on a high," Alice pointed out.

"I don't think so."

"I can't tell you what to do but I really think you should be careful," Alice said after a lengthy pause.

"Don't worry. I'll be careful."

"When's the last time you tapped into the vortex?"

"About four days ago."

"You should avoid tapping into it for two weeks and see how you feel," Alice advised.

"Maybe I will."

Alice sighed and turned back to her original position facing forward out to the ocean. She didn't bring up the subject again for which Josephine was grateful. She'd been hoping for more support than what had been provided. Alice didn't cling to the rules so Josephine had been surprised by her reaction. Josephine was forced to admit that the way she felt was similar to an addiction. However, she'd never heard of anyone born with an addiction and she'd always felt drawn to power vortexes. All category six wizards shared this discomfort which was why most of them lived far away from these natural phenomena.

"It's strange how life is sometimes," Josephine said.

They returned to their condos and Josephine worked on making enchantments in her empty wands and pendants which is what she did when she was bored. She mainly worked with protection and telekinetic enchantments since they were one of the most basic ones. She also had a teleportation wand she was working on. It had always been too advanced but now that she was free to practice whatever form of magic she could, she had experimented with it. It was very complex and required vast quantities of power. Fortunately, she had more than enough power. The ability to align the energy matrix just right was the tricky part. Josephine lost track of time as she worked on the spell. She finally called it quits when her stomach rumbled loudly.

She popped a frozen dinner in the microwave and waited for it to finish. Gary arrived while it was still heating. He was wearing a pale blue uniform and name tag which identified him as a pharmacist.

"I didn't realize you were a pharmacist," Josephine said with surprise.

"Most of my family works in the medical field. My brother, Dan, and my Dad are both doctors," Gary said. "Dad has a doctorate in magical medicine but Dan's only a category three so he has the standard degree in medicine."

"Why didn't you become a physician, too?"

"I can't stomach the thought of cutting people open," Gary said with chagrin. "It's something I could never overcome."

"I can understand that," Josephine said. "Would you like something to eat?"

"No, I stopped by McDonald's on the way here and had a burger."

"Okay."

Gary paced the room as Josephine sat down with her dinner.

"I wasn't able to stop by the beach and tap into the vortex because a police car was following me. They're keeping a close eye on me. I need to get my trace energy shield back up. The psychic impressions are terrible. I can't concentrate and it's making me very anxious."

"Maybe your brother could help you," Josephine suggested.

"I tried calling him before but he won't return my calls. He told me if I moved here, he wouldn't help me anymore."

"That's terrible!" Josephine exclaimed. "But why did you move if you knew he wouldn't make trace energy protection enchantments for you anymore?"

"I was tired of depending on him. I've been roommates with him ever since I moved away from my parents and I've been very dependent on his magic for practically my entire life and I needed to be on my own for a change," Gary said.

"Good for you," Josephine said encouragingly.

"Except that I'm starting to depend on you now. I didn't feel safe by myself so I spent the night here. After tonight, I'm returning back home."

"If you're sure that's what you want. Of course, you're welcome to stay here."

"I appreciate that but I need to do this," Gary said. He took a deep breath, sat down on the couch, and squeezed his eyes shut. "Maybe the meditation CD that I listen to everyday will help. My brother gave it to me to help relax. It's supposed to give me more resistance to trace energy impressions so I can control what I receive better."

"That's probably a good idea," Josephine said.

"I think I'm going to go to bed now," Gary said.

"Really? It's only a little after eight."

"I'm hoping the extra sleep will help me recover from the stress of the trace energies," Gary said.

"Good night," Josephine said.

"Good night."

Chapter 11

"Josephine!" a panicked, male voice cried out.

She opened her eyes in the pitch black and struggled with the sheets as she sat up in her bed. Her eyes honed in on the alarm clock which indicated it was shortly after one in the morning. Josephine wondered if she'd been awakened by a bad dream.

"Josephine! Help!" Gary's terrified voice drifted from three different directions.

She realized now that it was a magical projection. Her heat hammered in her chest as she wondered if the serial killer had somehow broke into her house. She brought up a shield as she grabbed two telekinetic wands she kept under her mattress for emergencies.

"Josephine, help!" Gary's panic-stricken voice echoed all around her.

She fumbled with the handle of her door and tried to open it quietly. She stepped over to the guest room door and threw it open. A hot wind slammed into her and an almost complete darkness greeted her. She flicked on the light to find that Gary was alone in the room hovering half a foot above the bed in the grip of a nightmare. His sweat dampened tee shirt and boxers clung to his skin as hot air blasted around him.

"Josephine!" his voice cried out from several directions around them. "Help me, please!"

Josephine sighed with relief and brought her personal shield back down.

"He's going to kill me," Gary's terrified voice drifted to her.

140

"Gary! Wake up!" Josephine said.

She wasn't surprised that the sound of her voice failed to elicit any sort of reaction from him since the lights hadn't woken him up. Sweat broke out on her forehead and arms as the hot air continued to blast over her. She approached Gary and gently pushed him down to the bed so he wouldn't drop and hurt himself when waking up. He started to lift again but she pressed firmly and began to nudge him with her other hand.

"Josephine!" his voice cried out from directly behind her.

"Gary, wake up!" Josephine said.

"He's going to kill me!"

Josephine gently shook him and his eyes popped open. She backed up a step and smiled reassuringly at him.

"You were sleeping," she said by way of explanation.

"Josephine!" his terrified voice drifted at her from different angles and his lips didn't move.

His eyes stared up vacantly up at the ceiling.

"Gary! You're having a bad dream. Wake up!" Josephine said loudly.

Gary gasped and his eyes centered on her. The hot air in the room abruptly died away and he sat up.

"What's going on?" he asked.

"You were having a bad dream," Josephine explained. "You woke me up."

"I was talking in my sleep?" Gary asked.

Josephine hesitated for a moment. "Yes. You were calling for help."

Gary's face flushed with embarrassment and his gaze shifted away from her for a moment.

"I'm sorry," he murmured.

"It's okay." Josephine reached out and squeezed his shoulder. "I was just worried about you."

"Thanks," Gary said.

Josephine straightened to her full height and took a step back. "Time to get back to sleep."

"Yep."

Josephine didn't sleep well and she doubted that her guest did. She knew he was seriously frightened in order to have an episode like that. She woke up earlier than usual feeling disturbed and anxious. She couldn't help but feel that Gary shouldn't move back into his apartment so soon. She had taken her shower and was cradling her first cup of coffee in the living room when Gary stepped into the room in his work uniform. He clutched his suitcase in his right hand. It looked like he was packed and ready to go. His eyes were guarded and anxious as he smiled at her.

"Sorry about last night," he said.

"That's okay. It wasn't your fault," Josephine said reassuringly. "Would you like some coffee?"

"No, thanks. I want to get my stuff back to my apartment," he said.

"You're welcome to stay here a few more nights or as long as you need," Josephine said. "I can understand it if you don't feel safe returning just yet."

"I'll be all right. There's a police officer that's been tailing me. It's why I haven't been able to go to the beach and get my trace energy shield back up."

"It's a shame your brother won't help."

"I'll try calling him again." Gary shrugged and headed for the front door. "Thank you for letting me stay here. I appreciate it."

"You're welcome. Stay in touch." Josephine followed him to the door and opened it for him.

She couldn't help but feel he was making a big mistake. A short while later, Alice and Helen arrived for their morning coffee. Once they were seated in the dining room, she informed her friends of what had happened last night.

"Wow!" Alice exclaimed.

"That's terrible!" Helen said passionately. "Gary needs to stay with you. The killer is obviously targeting him."

"There's more to it than that, I'm afraid," Alice said dourly.

"What?" Josephine was surprised by this reaction.

"This shows that his subconscious mind has suffered a major trauma. Nothing else would cause an episode like that."

"I assumed that since he was a category six that sometimes nightmares could cause that kind of thing to happen," Josephine said.

"Obviously, he's been traumatized earlier in his life and his subconscious has adapted to try and protect him from further dangers," Alice said. "He needs to see a psychiatrist."

Josephine mulled this over as she took a drink from her mug. She hadn't considered that Gary had more problems besides the killer targeting him.

"Are you sure it wasn't just a nightmare?" Josephine asked.

"No, I think his subconscious picked up clues from the crime scenes he's read and realized he would be in danger," Alice said.

"He was attacked at his apartment with psychokinesis," Josephine said.

"Psychokinesis is an erratic talent. You can't control it very well," Alice said. "It's unlikely the killer would use that type of enchantment to murder someone. Now that you've told me about this episode Gary had last night, I believe it's much more likely that Gary's subconscious mind manufactured the attack to give him an excuse to stay with you."

"That's ridiculous!" Helen argued. "Psychokinesis is very complicated magic."

"Yes, it is but the subconscious mind is capable of doing a lot more than our conscious minds," Alice said. "Trust me. After a lifetime of being a psychiatrist, I've seen enough cases to know what I'm talking about."

Josephine choked on her coffee as a brilliant idea struck her. She coughed and set her mug down on the table.

"Are you all right?" Helen asked.

"I'm fine," Josephine said weakly and coughed a bit more. "Alice, you can help Gary. You're good at sensing injuries to the subconscious and helping to facilitate healing."

"Oh, no! I'm retired! I'm not good at that kind of stuff anymore!"

"Sure you are! You've done it a lot," Josephine said.

"I can't just sit down with someone and heal their mind with a snap of my fingers! It requires numerous sessions and the patient's complete cooperation."

"Will you at least try to help if I can talk Gary into coming over here?" Josephine asked. "Please?"

Alice sighed wearily. "All right. But don't expect any miracles."

"Thank you!" Josephine smiled gratefully at her.

144

Alice grunted and took a large swallow of her coffee.

"Why do you want to help Gary so badly?" Alice asked.

"I feel sorry for him. Besides, the killer will go after me once he's finished with Gary. We're both a threat to exposing his identity with our psychometry," Josephine said.

"It's a shame you have to work for the police," Helen said.

"Yes, it is," Josephine said. She gazed thoughtfully at Alice. "What sorts of mental trauma can cause the kind of episode Gary had last night?"

"Childhood trauma is a major cause. Any number of things can happen to us when we're young to cause an adaptive response in our subconscious."

"But something unusual must have happened for Gary to be susceptible."

"Probably," Alice said.

"I guess there's no way to guess, is there?" Josephine asked.

"No. That would be a waste of time." Alice finished her coffee and stood up. "I think I'll be going. I'll see you later."

"Okay. Bye."

Helen sipped some more of her coffee. "It's really nice that you want to help Gary."

"I just feel a kinship with him," Josephine said.

"Maybe it's the fact that he's a category six."

"That's a big part of it," Josephine admitted.

"There's nothing wrong with that," Helen said.

A short while after Helen left, the phone rang.

"Hello?" Josephine said.

"Hey, it's me," Jake said cheerfully. "How're you doing?"

"I'm fine, thanks. What are you up to?"

"Vickie just woke up from her coma. She wanted me to tell you thanks. She knows she wouldn't have survived if you hadn't discovered she was still alive," Jake said.

Josephine smiled and a surge of gratification coursed through her.

"I'm so glad that she's going to be okay," she said.

"The enforcers have placed a topaz ring with an aequitas enchantment on her hand," Jake said. "She's going to have a rough ride learning to discipline her powers."

"Probably. I can imagine it will be difficult not to summon explosive energy when her entire life she's had to really work to use magic. Now, it will be a piece of cake. In fact, it will be too easy," Josephine said. "Do you think the police will be able to protect Gary from the killer?"

"I don't know. He's pretty powerful to use psychokinesis. Maybe that was his only psychokinetic enchantment though. There's a police officer assigned to you as well, by the way."

"I'm glad I have some protection," Josephine said even though this would curtail her visits to the beach.

"I'd better get back to work."

"Okay, honey. It was nice talking to you."

"It was nice talking to you, too, Grandma. Bye."

"Bye."

Josephine hung up the phone and stared off into space. She wondered if she was overlooking any course of action. She was tired of allowing this serial killer to run loose. She wasn't accustomed to having an open-ended case last this long. Josephine dialed Gary's home number even though she knew he was working. She left a message for him asking if he would be willing to allow Alice to try and

146

help him. If his subconscious was traumatized, it might explain his lack of control in reading trace energies. It was rare for category six wizards to suffer this affliction for their entire lives. Normally they outgrew it as teenagers. The door knocked and Josephine went to answer it. She brought up a deflection shield just as she opened the door because she'd had too many pranks performed on her lately. She flinched as the shield lit up and reflected whatever spell had been shot at her.

Josephine turned to see Dale flinch as his magic was turned against him. His eyes widened in astonishment and he opened his mouth in surprise which allowed a loud belch to escape. Josephine giggled at this childish prank. Dale's face flushed and he glared at her in reprisal.

"Well, if it isn't Mr. Skanky Toad," Josephine said smugly. "You thought you'd cast another jinx on me."

Dale opened his mouth to hurl a sharp retort but whatever he'd been about to say was lost in a series of belches. A loud rip escaped from his derriere and Josephine burst into boisterous laughter. Dale started to yell something but couldn't get past the loud belch that took over.

"Why don't you get lost, Mr. Skanky Toad?" Josephine taunted.

She couldn't resist hurling a spell of her own. Dale's trousers fell to his ankles and he tripped as he tried to back away. He lost his footing and fell flat on his back which released another fart as well as a belch. Dale quickly drew his pants back up and stumbled down the hall as fast as his arthritic legs could carry him. Josephine closed her door and reactivated the security enchantments. That had been too much fun. She laughed again and shook her head with mirth. It was a good thing that she'd created that deflection shield. Maybe Dale would think twice before pulling any more pranks on her. Speaking of which, she still owed him a payback for the last spell he'd cast on her apartment.

Josephine was bored so in the late afternoon, she paid a visit to the Sarasota Memorial Hospital. She was allowed to see Vickie who had a police officer posted just outside her room. Josephine walked inside and introduced herself.

"I'm glad to meet you. I'm grateful I survived the attack. I want that monster locked up," Vickie said passionately.

The lights above her bed flickered erratically and a frigid gust of air whipped over Josephine for several seconds.

"Your emotions will trigger your magical abilities for awhile," Josephine said. "You'll find that you can draw upon power extremely easy now."

"I can't believe I'm a category six," Vickie whispered fearfully. "At least I'm alive though."

"There are a lot of advantages to your new abilities."

"I guess it doesn't matter too much since I was a category two before this attack. I won't have to be restricted from anything that I was used to doing."

Josephine smiled faintly at her. "Yes, that's a good way of looking at it. Category two wizards can't really do much. Even though you won't be able to do spells that are more complicated than what you could do before, you'll find that you can create a lot more of them in a much shorter time period."

"That's good," Vickie said.

"I'm going to see if I can read the trace energies. I've never been able to find anything new by going to the same scene but this is a public place and there were so many energy particles that I may have missed something," Josephine said.

She opened her second sight and began reading the room. She took her time but didn't find any knew information. After a lengthy period of time, she gave up.

"Nope. I'm sorry," Josephine said.

"That's okay. It was nice for you to come over and try again," Vickie said.

"I'd better be going. You need to rest," Josephine said.

"I'm feeling fine. The only reason they're keeping me here is for observation. I'm glad to be out of ICU."

"I'm glad you're doing better but I'm going to take off. I'll talk to you later."

"Okay. Bye."

Josephine anxiously waited for Gary to call. She worked on a crossword puzzle that had come with the daily newspaper and watched the Science Fiction Network. It was still early in the evening by the time she began pacing and glancing impatiently at the clock. She knew that Gary had probably returned to his apartment by now but he'd failed to call her. She picked up the phone and dialed his number. Unfortunately, his answering machine picked up.

"Gary, it's me, Josephine. I'd like to talk to you about something important. I didn't tell you something that happened last night. You were kind of sleep walking and using magic. You were asking me for help and worried that the serial killer is after you. I'm sorry I didn't tell you before but I thought you might be embarrassed. Anyway, I have a friend who I think could help you. I think your subconscious might know something about the serial killer. I think you picked it up while reading one or more crime scenes. Please call me."

149

She hung up the phone and sighed. She wondered if he would be too embarrassed to return her call. She sat back down in front of the television and tried to focus on the show but her mind was too preoccupied on Gary. She dialed his number again but he still wouldn't pick up. She sighed dismally and hung up the receiver without leaving a message this time. She should have told him about his sleep walking episode when she'd awakened him in his room. She hadn't realized at the time that it was an indicator of something more serious. Josephine mentally chastised herself for being so short-sighted. She would never forgive herself if Gary ended up dead because of any shortcomings on her part.

Josephine dialed his number again but wasn't surprised when he once again failed to pick up. She went to bed late that night because she found it difficult to unwind and relax. She abruptly awakened to an almost complete darkness.

"Josephine! I need your help!" Gary called out.

She groaned dismally when she realized his subconscious was projecting again.

"Josephine! He's going to kill me!" Gary's terrified voice echoed from all around her.

"Gary, can you hear me?" Josephine asked.

"Josephine! He's going to kill me!"

Josephine wondered if she could communicate with his subconscious mind. Would he be responsive to her voice? She decided it was worth a try.

"Gary, tell me who the serial killer is," she said.

"I don't know who he is."

"You have to know something. Tell me about him," Josephine said.

"He's going to kill me."

"Why don't you stay with me? We would be safer together."

"You have to help me," Gary's voice sounded more panicked now. "He's going to kill me unless you stop him."

"How do I stop him? Is there a way I can find him?" Josephine asked.

"You have to find him."

"How do I find him?" Josephine's heart pounded wildly in her chest and adrenaline coursed through her veins as Gary's terrified voice continued to echo through the room at her.

"He's going to kill me."

"Tell me how I can help you!" Josephine shouted with frustration.

The room was plunged into an eerie silence. She expected a response but it never came. Josephine sighed heavily and got up from bed. She'd never sleep after a disturbance like that. She fixed herself a large mug of chamomile tea and sat down in the living room with the lights out. She closed her eyes as she nursed the hot ceramic mug. She wished that Gary had returned her calls. He was such a guarded and stubborn person. His subconscious mind seemed to realize he was in serious danger. She couldn't help him though unless he cooperated with her efforts.

Chapter 12

Josephine sometimes wondered if on days like these if one could die of boredom. She was lying on her couch staring up at the ceiling as she literally waited for time to pass. It had been two days since she'd called Gary and she had failed to hear from him except at night when his subconscious projected his voice into her bedroom. It was an obnoxious and frustrating phenomenon. She wished she could get a decent night's sleep for a change and also was tired of feeling guilty over a situation that she had no control over. How could she help Gary unless he cooperated? The television was tuned in on a soap opera and was blaring because she'd turned the sound up in order to annoy her ex-husband next door. If he was allowed to have an obnoxious dog that broke into fits of barking at random intervals throughout the day and night then she logically assumed that she was permitted to occasionally turn the volume up on her television.

Josephine got up from the couch when the phone rang. She rushed over to answer it and was surprised to hear Gary's voice.

"How are you doing?" Josephine said cheerfully.

She crossed the room and turned the television off so she could hear him more clearly.

"I would like to take you up on your offer to meet with your friend if you're still willing to help me. I'm not going to stay at your apartment though," Gary said.

"Sure, I'll talk to Alice and see if she can work with you tonight," Josephine said. "What caused this change of heart?"

"I woke up to a message on the wall in my bedroom," Gary said. "I think I'm sleep walking."

"What did the message say?" Josephine asked curiously.

"It just said that you could help me."

"Well, I think you should listen to yourself," she said flippantly.

"What time should I come over?"

"How about nine o'clock. Is that okay?" Josephine said.

"That's fine. I'll be there."

"Okay. I'll see you tonight. Goodbye."

"Bye."

Josephine immediately called Alice to let her know. Unfortunately, Alice wasn't thrilled by the news. Apparently, she hadn't really expected Gary to accept the offer. Alice came over in the late afternoon to prepare a claro mentis enchantment which would allow her to delve into the subconscious of Gary's mind. Alice carried a copper bracelet in her right hand which she slapped down on the coffee table of the living room.

"This is what I'll use to encase the claro mentis enchantment until I'm ready to work with Gary," Alice said.

"I see," Josephine said.

"Usually, it takes three days to prepare an enchantment like this. Since I'm retired, I can't afford to go out and buy one. Besides, you have to have a license to purchase something like this. My license has expired a long time ago."

"We don't have three days. I want you to work with Gary tonight," Josephine said sharply.

"If you provide me with a steady stream of power, I can finish the enchantment in about three hours," Alice said.

"I can do that."

"I thought you could." Alice sat down on the couch and frowned irritably at her friend. "You owe me big time for this."

"I know."

Alice held her hand out and Josephine clutched it with her own and began flowing a stream of power to her friend. Alice held her other hand out toward the bracelet and furrowed her brows in concentration. It was a long and cumbersome process. When Alice finished, she lowered her hand and smiled widely.

"It's finished," she said. "I knew I could do it but it's the only time I was able to do this so quickly."

"It's amazing what you can accomplish with an endless supply of power."

Alice nodded in silent agreement and carefully picked up the copper bracelet as if afraid it would break. She put it on her right wrist and nodded with satisfaction. Now that they had the enchantment performed successfully, it was time to wait. Gary arrived as soon as he'd promised. He'd changed out of his uniform and wore jeans with a blue tee shirt. His expression was guarded as he sat down on the living room couch.

"I'm going to need you to relax," Alice said in a soothing voice. "It won't hurt at all. I promise."

"Okay," Gary said cautiously.

"Take slow, deep breaths," Alice said as she sat down beside him. She waited silently as he followed her instructions. After several moments she said, "Good. Now, close your eyes and continue breathing."

Josephine could tell that Gary wasn't relaxed but Alice didn't seem to be in a hurry.

"I want you to concentrate on relaxing your body. We're going to start with your feet. Concentrate on your feet and will them to relax. Allow the tension to ease out of them," Alice said.

She continued instructing him to relax various parts of his body until Josephine wanted to leap to her feet and shout in frustration. This was so boring that she wasn't sure if she could stand much more of it. Josephine forced herself not to fidget and tried to followed Alice's instructions that she gave Gary. By doing so, she may be able to stave off the excruciating boredom that plagued her. Finally, Alice raised her right hand and activated the claro mentis enchantment. A gentle, golden luminescence spilled from the bracelet and directed itself over Gary's head.

"I'm beginning to link with your subconscious mind. All is well. You're continuing to relax. You're completely safe," Alice said in a soothing tone. "Are you ready for me to proceed?"

"Yes," Gary said softly.

"I'm beginning the procedure," Alice said calmly.

Her eyes lost their focus and the bracelet's glow intensified.

"I can see the surface. It's very turbulent. You've been under a lot of stress but you're safe now. Everything is going well. You must lower your block for me to help you. Can you do that?"

"There is no block," Gary said.

Alice didn't respond immediately and Josephine shot her a questioning look.

"The block is completely unconscious in nature. I'll have to slip past it as gently as I can. There will be no pain but you may feel a little confusion. It's important that you stay relaxed and remember you are safe," Alice said. "Do you understand?"

"Yes."

"All is well. You're safe," Alice said. "I'm looking for a way in."

A long quiet ensued and Josephine fought the urge to shuffle her feet or squirm. She wondered how much longer this would take. She had no idea there would be so much involved in this process. A powerful wave of magic built up in the room with remarkable speed. Josephine turned her attention back to Alice with surprise. She hadn't realized the enchantment was that strong. Alice suddenly floated into the air and hurtled backward until she was pinned against the wall by an invisible force. Gary's eyes popped open but he was staring off into space.

"The serial killer must be stopped," Gary's voice drifted from several different directions. His lips didn't move and the words were strained and hardened.

"Gary! You need to wake up now!" Alice shrieked.

Gary slowly stood up and turned to face her. His eyes didn't focus on anything in particular but seemed to be looking in her general direction.

"You're the serial killer," he said in a hardened voice that materialized from various parts of the room. His lips were relaxed and unmoving as he spoke. "You must be stopped."

"Gary! She's not the killer!" Josephine exclaimed and rushed toward him.

Before she could take more than a couple of steps, her body lifted from the floor by several feet and she hung in the air suspended. A powerful dampening field had gathered around Gary which was difficult to create and would take a great deal of time to neutralize. She couldn't cast any spells on him for quite some time. She focused instead on the telekinetic spell that encompassed Alice. It was possible she could free Alice but it would take awhile. Josephine began flowing the magic she would need to accomplish this goal.

"Gary, you must let her go. She's trying to help you," Josephine said. "She's not the killer. She was with me when one of those murders happened. She can't be the killer."

"She's attacking me," Gary said.

"She's trying to help you heal your mind and discover who the serial killer is. Don't you remember?" Josephine said.

Gary's attention was centered on Alice but he hadn't yet made any further moves against her.

"Let her go!" Josephine said forcefully.

"She'll kill me."

"Release her!"

Josephine noticed that the bracelet on her friend's hand was still glowing.

"Alice, deactivate the claro mentis enchantment," Josephine ordered.

"Okay," Alice said quietly.

The golden light radiating from the bracelet began to fade for several seconds then abruptly died away.

"Gary, let her go now!" Josephine said forcefully.

Alice and Josephine slowly lowered to the floor. Josephine breathed a sigh of relief. Gary's eyes cleared and he weaved as though dizzy. He focused on Alice and blinked with surprise.

"What are you doing over there?" he asked.

"Sit down, Gary," Alice said.

"Okay." He shot her a puzzled and frightened look as he reluctantly complied.

"Your subconscious mind has taken a lot of trauma over the years. I'm afraid it's developed some rather robust defenses. It sensed a threat as I was connecting with you and took over. It's not exactly a split personality. You were sleep walking and believed me to be the serial killer," Alice said.

"Oh my God! Did I attack you?" Gary asked.

"Yes, but I'm all right."

"I'm so sorry!" Gary abruptly stood up from the couch and guilt twisted his features. "I should be leaving now."

"We should talk about this. You need some professional help," Alice said.

"No, I can't," Gary said as he headed for the door.

"Gary! You need to listen! After what she's gone through to help you, you owe her that much," Josephine said forcefully.

"Okay."

A sullen expression dominated his face as he sank into one of the couches and crossed his arms across his chest. Josephine threw her friend an expectant look as she took a seat beside Gary. Alice remained standing and eyed Gary warily.

"I wasn't able to sense much because I only established a very shallow link to your subconscious," Alice said slowly. "It has been invaded by magic for years. Someone has been casting spells on your mind and I'm not sure as to the purpose or what enchantment or enchantments were used."

"That's not possible! I'd remember if I was attacked!" Gary protested.

"Let me explain the many ways that a wizard can invade the mind of another," Alice said. "One way is that he or she can attack the victim directly with a wide variety of enchantments and then remove their memory of the incident. If this is done repeatedly, the subconscious usually develops defenses to ward off the invader even though no memory exists of the attacks. The wizard will find it more and more difficult to keep attacking the victim."

"Why would someone invade my mind?" Gary asked.

"For power," Alice said. "You're a category six. You can supply a limitless flow of energy to a wizard that can help to accomplish many enchantments that couldn't otherwise be accomplished."

"If what you're saying is true. I would have large pieces of time missing but I don't."

"That's not necessarily true. What if the wizard uses you at night when you would be sleeping?" Alice suggested. "You wouldn't notice any missing time in that case."

"There are some days that I'm extremely tired. Maybe those are the nights that I don't get enough sleep. So you're saying I'm being controlled?"

"Yes although I can't be certain of the type of enchantment being used. It has been lodged in your subconscious mind and is strengthened periodically. Your mind would heal on its own and the enchantment would dissipate if the mind invasions would stop and you would no longer be susceptible to further attacks because of how you've adapted. It will take anywhere from a month to three months for the enchantment to leave your mind depending on how long a duration of time you've been attacked."

"I don't want to wait that long," Gary said looking sick at the thought of the invasive spell residing in his head.

"I don't blame you," Josephine said. "I think we need to dispel it."

"That can be done but you'd have to undergo another claro mentis. It would need to be a deep link so the wizard could get close enough to dispel it," Alice said.

"Do you think you could do it tomorrow?" Gary asked.

"I'm not willing to try again," Alice said adamantly. "Your subconscious has adapted in ways I don't understand. It attacks and I'm not going to put myself in harm's way again. I don't know what you would have done if Josephine hadn't managed to awaken you. Your subconscious mind had convinced itself that I was the serial killer."

"You think I'd attack again?" Gary asked. "I'm sure I wouldn't now that I know all this."

"No one can know their unconscious minds; especially ones that have been invaded with mind control spells. You need to contact the police and they'll arrange to have a wizard psychiatrist help you," Alice said.

"I won't trust a stranger to link with my mind even if there are police present. Besides, I don't trust the police," Gary said anxiously.

"I'm a stranger and you let me cast the claro mentis on you."

"That was different. I trust Josephine and she's a friend of yours," Gary argued.

"I'm not willing to do it again. It's too risky."

Josephine rose to her feet and determination shone in her brown eyes. "I'll help you, Gary. I'm willing to perform the claro mentis."

"You can't do that," Alice squawked. "You have to be a professional."

"It's just a spell. If you make the enchantment for me, I can just activate it," Josephine said. "It should be a piece of cake."

"It's not that easy. You don't understand the workings of the mind."

"I can learn. I may not be able to dispel the mind control enchantment on the first try but I'm sure it won't take more than a few attempts," Josephine said.

"You have no idea how to create a claro mentis. It takes years of practice," Alice said.

"You can make them," Josephine said. "We'll do what we did this afternoon."

"I'd be putting your life in danger if I did that."

"I'm willing to take the risk. I don't think Gary will attack me. His subconscious knows I'm not the serial killer. He'll know that on a purely instinctual level. Everything will be fine."

"You don't know what you're talking about. The human mind is completely unpredictable. You have no idea what's going to happen when you start tinkering with his subconscious," Alice said heatedly.

"I know what will happen if I don't try. The wizard will attack him again during the night and strengthen the mind control enchantment. Gary will be an unwilling tool for some user indefinitely unless I can stop it."

"The police are keeping a watch on him at night. No one will get near him," Alice argued.

"I think he's been attacked recently. That's why his subconscious keeps communicating to me at night. It's trying to get help!" Josephine exclaimed.

Gary's pleading eyes fixed on Alice. "Please, help me."

Alice grunted with displeasure and squeezed her eyes shut for several seconds. She sighed loudly and opened them again.

"All right. I'll create the claro mentis enchantments but I'm not performing them," Alice said.

"Thank you," Gary said.

When Gary left, Alice whirled to confront her friend.

"I can't believe how reckless you've become," Alice said.

"It's not that great a risk."

"I'm a retired psychiatrist. I know the risks involved but you just won't listen."

"Sometimes, we need to help our friends in spite of the dangers," Josephine said evenly. "I'm surprised you don't understand that. It's not like you to be such a stick in the mud."

"You know that I'm not a cautious person," Alice said carefully. "But I've seen firsthand what horrific things can happen to people when things like this go wrong. You could end up in a coma or go crazy or you could even die. Especially when Gary's subconscious has a tendency to lash out."

"He lashed out once. I'm a familiar face and his subconscious has been calling to me for help. I don't think that will be a problem," Josephine said.

"There's no point in arguing with you about this," Alice said.

"You've known me for years. I'm surprised you've tried talking me out of it for this long," Josephine teased.

"I surrender." Alice held her hands up in a placating gesture. "I'll help you make the damned claro mentis enchantments. We can work on it tomorrow afternoon."

"Good. Thank you."

"You're not welcome." Alice strode for the front door and threw her an irritated look before leaving the condo.

Josephine locked the door and reactivated the security enchantments. She was certain that everything would turn out for the best.

Chapter 13

Josephine's gaze dragged down to the copper bracelet on her left wrist once again as she tried to pay attention to the news on television. Alice had finished making the claro mentis enchantment early this morning right after their habitual coffee drinking. Josephine's stomach tightened and restless energy made her unable to concentrate. Alice had warned her yet again that this was a dangerous procedure because she wasn't trained in psychiatry. Alice was seldom cautious so her warning was unsettling. Josephine wanted to help Gary catch the serial killer who would strike soon. Gary's unconscious was warning him that his life was in danger. It stood to reason that Josephine would be the next target. She turned off the television and paced the room for a moment. She flinched when the telephone rang.

"Hello?" Josephine said.

"Hi, it's Vickie. I was wondering if you would be willing to help me."

"Help you?" Josephine said dully.

"Yes, I'm having a terrible time with my powers. I can't do anything anymore." Frustration tinged her words as she spoke in a rush.

"I'm not sure I'm qualified to train you on the use of magic," Josephine said warily.

"No one's willing to train me because I'm a category six now!" Vickie said. "I'll pay you."

"I'm not looking for money," Josephine said.

"Can't you help me? I've always been a category two but I've always been proficient with restoration spells. My career is in general repair work and I just can't do it anymore. They've made me take two weeks off to rest. If I don't find a way to get back to the way I was, I'll lose my job. My life will be ruined," Vickie said desperately.

"If you're a category six, you may never regain your proficiency at restoration enchantments. I can certainly try to help but I can't make any promises. You're the first person that's become a category six that wasn't born that way except of course, those who were hit by the shock wave during the Disaster," Josephine said.

"Are you willing to help me regain control of my ability again?" Vickie asked.

"Okay. I'll drive down to your house some time."

"Could you come over tomorrow afternoon?" Vickie said.

"Okay," Josephine said reluctantly. "How did you find out my phone number? I'm surprised the police would tell you."

"I went down to the station and begged them for help. One of them finally gave it to me if I promised I wouldn't tell who it was," Vickie said sheepishly.

"I'll bet it was Howie. He's such a softie," Josephine said. "Okay. I'll stop by your house around one tomorrow."

Vickie gave her directions to her house and thanked her profusely.

"Don't thank me yet. I'm not sure I'll be any help," Josephine said.

"At least you're trying. I'll see you tomorrow. Bye."

"Bye."

Josephine hung up the phone and sighed wearily.

"Why is everybody wanting my help all of a sudden?" Josephine said moodily.

Her ex-husband's poodle began barking rapidly. Josephine wished she could make her walls soundproof. She pounded angrily on the wall to get Robert's attention.

"Shut up your damned dog!" Josephine shouted.

"Why don't you shut up?" he retorted.

"You don't want to mess with me, Spot."

"There's nothing you can do to me in here. You might as well get used to it," he taunted.

Josephine smiled grimly as she began generating energy. She raised her hands and pressed them flat against the wall. A cold wind whipped over her as she prepared a hail storm. She opened her second sight and directed the energy into Robert's condo. The room in his place slowly dropping and a layer of fog was accumulating around the ceiling.

"What in the hell are you doing?" Robert shouted.

"I'm showing you what I can do, Spot," Josephine said flippantly.

"Cut it out, you stupid bitch!" Robert shouted.

The temperature continued to fall and Josephine had gathered enough moisture so that a nice thick cloud cover currently resided overhead. She shivered as the cold air brushed against her skin. Unfortunately, she couldn't completely prevent the effects from spilling into her own environment. She lacked that kind of control but with practice, maybe she'd eventually learn how to achieve it. Josephine smiled with satisfaction as hail began to drop from Robert's ceiling. Robert's dog had fallen silent now which was a nice perk.

"Stop it!" Robert shouted.

"If you ask me nicely, I'll think about it," Josephine said.

The hail pattered against his furniture, the walls, and the tiled floor in the kitchen. Josephine flinched when some of the hail began pinging against the walls in her own place. She continued to feed the hail storm with power that flowed easily from her.

"I can keep this up all night, Spot."

"All right! Will you please stop?" Robert said.

"If you get a muzzle for your dog, I'll do it."

"I'm not going to get a damned muzzle for David," Robert said.

"That's pathetic! I can't believe you gave your dog a human name."

"It's just a name," he said defensively. "What would you name it?"

"I'm not the idiot who was stupid enough to get a dog in the first place," Josephine said moodily. "Now, are you going to buy that damned muzzle or would you like to have a lot of hail storms inside your condo forever?"

"All right! I'll get a muzzle," Robert said.

"Okay. I'll get rid of the hail then," Josephine said.

She smiled with satisfaction as she concentrated on dispelling the energy matrix that was feeding the hail. Soon, the cloud cover had dissipated and the temperature was quickly rising back to normal. Josephine's stomach tightened as power continued to course through her. She backed away from the wall and concentrated on stopping the flow of magic. Pain lanced through her stomach and chest. Josephine stumbled into the kitchen. She clutched her stomach and leaned against the counter. Unfocused power shot from her in uncontrollable waves. Two of her cupboard doors burst open and several cereal boxes flew out. Frost gathered on the mug laying on the counter top. The cupboards crashed as a huge telekinetic wave pounded against it.

Abruptly, Josephine succeeded in stopping the power. The pain in her body swiftly evaporated and she straightened to her full height. She breathed deeply and took stock of her surroundings. She stepped into the living room to see if anything had happened in there but found no signs of damage. Luckily, she'd regained control in time to prevent any costly repairs. Josephine returned to the kitchen, picked up the cereal boxes and shoved them back into her cupboards. Her power had always been completely manageable when she'd been connected to the vortex. Josephine wished she could venture to the beach right now. Unfortunately, as long as the police were watching her she couldn't risk any such trips. Then again, it occurred to her that she should be wondering why she was experiencing problems with control. She hadn't tapped into the vortex in awhile so it could be withdrawal symptoms. Maybe there was truth to the teachings that category six's were natural addicts to power vortexes. Josephine hated to think that but it sometimes seemed that way.

She waited anxiously for the evening when Gary would come. Alice's dire warnings had made her edgy and she wanted to get the session with Gary finished. Josephine tensed when it finally came time for him to arrive. The doorbell rang and she went over to invite him inside. Gary walked stiffly into her living room and smiled nervously at her.

"We need to relax if this is going to have any chance of working," Josephine said.

"I know," Gary said.

"We'll try to duplicate the relaxation process that Alice did yesterday," Josephine said.

"That sounds like a plan."

"Have a seat." Josephine motioned to the couch.

Gary obediently sat down with his back straight and looking vigilant. Josephine instructed him to lean back and close his eyes then guided him through the relaxation exercise that Alice had given him last night. She knew she wasn't doing as good a job but she didn't have the experience that her friend had. Josephine was seated in the armchair facing Gary. She nervously eyed the copper bracelet secured to her wrist and hesitated before activating the claro mentis enchantment. Josephine took a deep breath and cast the spell. The bracelet immediately began radiating a soft golden luminescence and she felt herself connecting with Gary's subconscious. It was a strange experience. She felt a smooth, glassy barricade and realized it was some sort of protection that his subconscious had erected to protect itself. Alice had warned her about this.

"Gary, you're keeping me out," Josephine said softly. "You have to relax and lower your guard."

"I don't feel anything," he said.

"But you're still keeping me out," she said. "You need to lower your guard."

"I'll try."

Josephine waited patiently but nothing happened. She could feel a weak connection but it was only on the surface. As long as the barricade remained, a stable link couldn't be established. Josephine didn't have the skill to ease her way past the unconscious barriers that the mind created. It was a shame that Alice had refused to help with this process. The lights flickered for a second and a hot breeze rushed over them. Magic flared into existence all around them.

"You may enter, Josephine," Gary's voice materialized from three different points in the room but his lips remained closed.

Josephine shivered in spite of the heat and felt the barrier protecting his subconscious fall away. She was immediately assaulted by a myriad of jumbled memories. There were so many fragmented images, sounds, and thoughts that nothing made sense. Anger burned through his subconscious. It was suppressed from his conscious mind but barely contained. Josephine's body tightened and she tried to sort out the impressions that raced through her mind. The hot wind continued to sweep over the two of them.

"Gary, I can't make sense of this," Josephine said anxiously.

"I have been betrayed," Gary's voice rang out from all around her.

"What do you mean?" Josephine asked.

He didn't respond and she couldn't make sense of the barrage of psychic impressions that continued to pound at her mind. A throbbing began to pound at her temples as the connection between her and Gary's subconscious held. Josephine tried to focus on single impressions to gain some useful information but they slipped from her grasp every time. It was chaos. Josephine's surroundings faded into blackness and she realized she'd passed out. Rage, desperation, and a sense of betrayal tore at her as she swirled blindly through the disordered memories. Josephine realized she should end the spell and leave his subconscious but couldn't summon enough strength to do so. Her identity felt as though it was being consumed by another. She could barely think straight.

"Gary! Stop what you're doing!" Josephine shouted.

"We need to stop him. We're the only ones who can," Gary said desperately.

"I intend on finding the serial killer but you need to let me go!" Josephine shouted anxiously. "Please! Stop this!"

"I'm not trapping you here."

"Why can't I leave then?" Josephine demanded.

"We're the only ones who can stop him. He wants to kill us both."

"Let me go!" Josephine screamed.

"I'll help you to leave," Gary said.

A powerful bright, gold light flared around her and Josephine opened her eyes. She could no longer feel any connection with him. She was staring up at her living room ceiling. Josephine sat up and realized she was lying on the floor. Gary was lying on his side on the couch. The hot wind was no longer whipping through the room. Josephine slowly rose to her feet and gazed down at Gary. She held her wrist up and inspected the copper bracelet. The enchantment had been depleted completely. She would need Alice to create another one before she could perform another claro mentis spell. Of course, after this experience, Josephine wasn't sure she ever wanted to perform this type of magic ever again.

"Gary," Josephine said tentatively.

His eyes snapped open and he abruptly sat up with a start. He quickly took stock of his surroundings before his gaze locked onto hers.

"Did it work?" he asked.

"The spell worked but I didn't accomplish anything, I'm afraid," Josephine said sadly. "Everything was so chaotic that I couldn't make sense of anything. There was just too much psychic input for me to process."

"You did your best. That's all I can ask," Gary said with a faint smile. His eyes reflected his disappointed though.

"We'll do this again in a couple of days. Don't worry. We'll get rid of that enchantment that's lodged in your unconscious," Josephine said.

"I really appreciate your help," Gary said.

"You're welcome."

He left her condo and Josephine locked the door behind him. She wished she could have solved his problem but she'd failed. Alice had warned her that the claro mentis spell was tricky and would need many sessions before any progress could be made. Josephine should have listened to her. She went to bed feeling discouraged and awakened early the next morning feeling unbalanced and off-center. Josephine started the pot of coffee and showered. She decided to wear jeans and a pink tee shirt today. She gazed in the full-length mirror secured to the closet door and frowned speculatively. She couldn't shake the suspicion that something was seriously wrong with her body. She opened her second sight and immediately all of the subtle energies in the room became visible.

She gasped in horror at the bright red string of energy that emerged somewhere from above which was lodged securely in her head. She was connected to something powerful. The bright red strand pulsed with a strong magic that rivaled her own. It had to be Gary. Somehow, she'd formed a connection with him last night when she'd cast the claro mentis. The doorbell rang and she went over to answer it. Alice stood with a guarded look.

"What happened?" she said anxiously. "Did everything go all right?"

"I just discovered something very disturbing," Josephine said.

"Okay," Alice said slowly.

"Come inside and have a cup of coffee," Josephine said.

Helen appeared down the hallway and hurried when she saw
that the door was already open.

"Hey! How did things go last night?"

"Not good," Josephine said.

"I was afraid of that," Alice said dourly.

"Yes, you were," Josephine said irritably. "You warned me
like crazy not to try it."

Alice cocked a brow but didn't take the bait. Helen breezed in
through the open door and Josephine closed it behind her. They
gathered in the dining room with mugs of coffee and Josephine
informed them of the night's events and her discovery that morning.

"This isn't good," Alice said dourly.

"I know," Josephine said despairingly.

"I suspect that your subconscious mind is connected to his
which means he can draw on your power," Alice said.

"Can't you help me to sever the connection?"

"It's not that simple. I can do a claro mentis enchantment but
your mind needs to settle for at least a couple of days before I try. It
will probably take numerous sessions for me to remove the link," Alice
said.

"How many times would you say? Just give me an estimate."

"There's no way to tell until I can examine the connection
with the claro mentis. Anywhere from three sessions to a dozen."

Josephine choked on her coffee because she hadn't been
expecting this kind of news.

"A dozen? If you have to wait two days in between each
session, that could take over two weeks," Josephine said.

"Yes."

"Isn't there some way you can rush this process?" Josephine said hopefully.

"I wish." Alice grimaced and shook her head sadly. "The mind is a complex thing and I tried to warn you that there could be problems that would develop if you tried this procedure with Gary."

"I needed to help him," Josephine said.

"You need to learn to set limits for yourself."

"Whatever," Josephine said dismissively.

She frowned at her friend with annoyance before gulping some more coffee. Alice was usually carefree and supportive. It really irked Josephine to be put on the defensive like this. One would think she made a habit of making irresponsible decisions the way Alice was treating her.

"Everything will be okay," Helen said reassuringly. "I'm sure the connection between you and Gary can't be too strong when you two haven't even interacted very much."

"That's not true. The connection may be very strong," Alice contradicted her.

"You're just full of good news today," Josephine said sardonically.

Alice shrugged helplessly. "Sometimes the truth hurts."

Chapter 14

Josephine stepped up to Vickie Richardson's massive, two-story white house. She had a spacious, well-maintained yard with a rose garden positioned near the front door and miniature palm trees dotting the landscape. Pineapple bushes lined the driveway with several growing fruit. Vickie lived on Siesta Key about a mile from the beach. Josephine knocked on the door and Vickie answered almost immediately. She wore a pink blouse and jeans. Her eyes reflected fear and despair but a touch of hope. She wanted to believe that Josephine could teach her to use her ability again.

"Thank you for helping me with my problem," Vickie said. "Of course, I'll be happy to pay you."

"I can't accept payment. I'm not a certified trainer and I don't know if I can help you or not," Josephine said bluntly.

"I appreciate whatever you can do," Vickie said. "Please, come in."

The two of them gathered in the living room and Vickie offered her a seat on one of the large, red sofas. The living room was large with a huge entertainment center, massive television, surround sound speakers, plush gray carpeting, a crystal chandelier, and gold painted walls.

"Would you like a drink or anything?" Vickie asked. "I have tea, coffee, soda, and red wine."

"I'll have some red wine and I think you should too," Josephine said.

"Why is that?" Vickie asked with a perplexed frown.

"You'll need to relax if you want to control your new power."

Vickie nodded and wordlessly left the room. She returned with two glasses of wine.

"I have a video which shows how I do my work. The company uses it to show potential clients," Vickie said.

"Okay. That may be helpful."

Vickie played the video tape which showed her standing in a shop in front of a red, antique mustang with a smashed hood and broken windshield. Vickie had on a blue business suit and her curly brown hair was pinned in a bun that gave her a more powerful look. She clutched a wand in her right hand and held it out toward the severely damaged car. Josephine glanced at Vickie whose curly hair was draped loosely down her neck to her shoulders. She looked a lot different in the video.

"What kind of wand are you using?" Josephine asked.

"It's programmed with a restoration enchantment. I was never able to generate much power so I had to have that work done for me," Vickie explained.

Josephine nodded and returned her attention to the television screen. A green shimmering light radiated from the car. The damaged hood rippled as though it had become very flexible and soft. As the ripples continued to flow over the hood and windshield, it slowly reshaped itself until it was restored completely. The ripples dissipated and the green shimmering faded away into nothingness. The mustang was now in pristine condition and the camera zoomed in for a closer look. Josephine was impressed. This was category five work. Vickie was definitely talented and lucky to possess such a gift when she was merely a category two. Of course, that was not the case now. The next clip showed Vickie restoring a large, antique vase which had been shattered.

"Okay. I've seen enough," Josephine said.

Vickie turned off the television and nervously gulped the rest of her wine.

"I need to see you cast a restoration spell," Josephine said.

"Okay."

Vickie left the room and returned with a wand and a tray containing a blue mug that had broken into three pieces.

"I broke some cups I bought at garage sales to practice on," Vickie explained.

Josephine opened her second sight so she could see the energy flow as Vickie set down the tray on her coffee table and stepped back.

"Do you want me to go ahead and cast the spell?" Vickie said.

"Yes," Josephine said.

Vickie aimed the wand and took a moment before casting the spell. Power exploded from both her hands and distorted the enchantment in the wand as it was activated. The tray and mug were tossed up like leaves and hurtled across the room. Josephine flinched at the unexpected burst of power. Unfortunately, magic continued to explode from Vickie's hand chakras and twist around the room.

"You need to concentrate on stopping the flow of power," Josephine said.

Josephine created a dampening field around her body to protect herself from the unpredictable tendrils of power flapping wildly around the room. One of the couches abruptly lifted a foot from the floor and slammed back down violently. The topaz ring on Vickie's finger had turned green in warning. She didn't have much time before the aequitas enchantment knocked her out. Untamed magic continue to

177

spill from her hand chakras as Vickie closed her eyes and concentrated on turning off the power. The chandelier jangled as it was struck by an unseen force. Vickie flinched at the noise but kept her eyes closed. One of the couches toppled forward and over. Something pounded against one of the walls. Josephine knew that more than a moment had passed since the topaz had turned green yet Vickie was still conscious.

She felt a couple of tendrils of power brush against her dampening field but she was still safe. Josephine waited for several moments for Vickie to regain control. She was relieved when this finally happened. Vickie's topaz ring turned blue again and she opened her eyes. She nervously regarded Josephine as she waited for a response.

"This is very strange," Josephine said slowly. "You seem to somehow be immune to your aequitas enchantment. Has it knocked you out at all when you've been practicing on your restoration spells?"

"No, it hasn't knocked me out since I was in the hospital," Vickie said.

"Interesting," Josephine said. She mulled this over for a bit then shrugged it away. She needed to focus on the issue of what was holding Vickie back from casting the restoration enchantments. "I think I may know part of the problem."

"Really?" Vickie looked hopeful.

"Yes, I'm almost one hundred percent certain that you're trying too hard," Josephine said. "You need to have a completely different mind set now that you're a category six. The power comes without effort. You're used to exerting a lot of effort but you're no longer a category two."

"I wasn't trying hard at all," Vickie protested.

"You weren't trying nearly as hard as you used to try," Josephine said. "But I think I can help you."

She picked up the tray and pieces of the mug that had fallen to the carpet to set them back on the coffee table.

"You're not going to use a wand for this. You're going to use telekinesis," Josephine said.

"Why?" Vickie asked.

"It's the easiest spell you can do and I want you to realize what it feels like when you control the amount of power you use," Josephine said.

"Okay." Vickie frowned at her uncertainly.

"Concentrate on one of the pieces of the mug and cast a telekinesis spell but don't try to tap into any power at all," Josephine said.

"Nothing will happen," Vickie said.

"Trust me."

Vickie shrugged and gazed at the broken mug. After a moment, one of the pieces jiggled and lifted an inch into the air. Vickie exclaimed joyously and the piece clattered back against the tray.

"You see?" Josephine said. "Power comes without effort. Cast the spell and the power will follow. You were concentrating on the spell hard enough that you gave your chakras a gentle nudge for power."

"That's incredible!" Vickie said.

"Let's see if you can do it again."

Vickie gazed at the broken mug and furrowed her brows in concentration. One of the pieces slowly lifted into the air and hovered above the tray.

"Do you feel how much power you're drawing now? That's how much you'll need to generate to work your magic," Josephine said.

"It's going to take a lot of practice to get this under control," Vickie said.

Josephine crossed the room and shot her a congratulatory smile.

"After a bit of practice, you'll be used to your new ability, I'm sure," she said.

"Thank you so much!" Vickie said.

"My pleasure."

A sense of accomplishment suffused Josephine's body as she left Vickie's house. Too bad that all of life's problems couldn't be solved so easily. The fact that Vickie seemed to be immune to the aequitas enchantment had her puzzled and piqued her curiosity. She wondered if there were other instances of this happening. Josephine noticed that a police car was on her tail as usual. She drove down to the beach and strolled along the shoreline. She connected with the vortex as she walked and power surged through her body. She continued to walk normally as a pleasant smile transformed her face. She became aware of all the subtle energies and thoughts surrounding her. She turned to gaze directly at the vortex and was startled to see that it was churning with an angry red energy.

Josephine swallowed nervously and wondered if she was doing anything to influence the vortex. After a moment, she could tell that she wasn't causing this behavior. She focused on the vortex and realized the red swirling energy was slowly calming down. Only a category six could do something like this to a vortex which meant that someone had recently tapped into it. Josephine glanced nervously around her but couldn't sense any category six wizards nearby. She realized she may look conspicuous standing here staring at the vortex so she tore her gaze away from it and continued her walk. It was a risk for her to connect with the power here but it was a calculated one. The police officer currently assigned to her may or may not be a wizard and probably couldn't even tell she was connected if he or she used their psychometry. After all, only a category six could use psychometry very well.

Josephine picked up the pace so that she was almost jogging. She figured it would look less suspicious because anyone watching her would assume she was exercising. Josephine lost track of time as the pleasant sensations from the vortex washed over her. She abruptly realized she was standing perfectly still and decided to sit down. She was still breathing heavily so she couldn't have been inactive for very long. She closed her eyes and wondered if she could cast a psychokinetic spell. She had never tested her abilities while being tuned into the vortex. This was a good opportunity to practice a little. She directed the power into the proper matrix with ease and directed it at her condo, concentrating on moving the armchair across the room. She pictured it lifting in the air and slowly drifting to the far end of the room. Josephine knew psychokinetic spells were extremely difficult and she probably hadn't done a thing but it had been fun to try.

She got up and headed back the way she had come. By the time she reached her car, her connection with the vortex began to waver. She took another look at it and could see that the angry red tendrils had receded to be replaced by the typical blue and green. She wondered why anyone would tamper with the vortex. She and Gary were the only category six wizards in the county so it was probably Gary. She wondered if his subconscious had taken over and cast a spell at the vortex for some unknown reason. She couldn't fathom what would compel him to tamper with something so powerful. Of course, there was the possibility that there was an unregistered category six in the city. Sometimes, people managed to hide their abilities until they lost control of their ability in public.

When Josephine returned to her condo, she was amazed to find that the armchair she'd imagined had moved about twelve feet across the room towards the corner and that it now rested on its side. She righted the armchair and moved it back to its original position. She chuckled as she finished working and straightened to her full height. She couldn't believe it had worked! She had successfully cast a psychokinetic spell from miles away! She was absolutely thrilled and astounded by her accomplishment. Josephine wished there was someone she could share this victory with but no one would understand. Alice had expressed disapproval when she'd discovered Josephine had tapped into the vortex and would certainly not be pleased to find out she hadn't followed her advice.

The doorbell rang and Josephine headed for the door. She checked the peephole to discover Robert waiting outside. Josephine frowned with irritation and created a deflection shield as she opened the door. Robert held his hands up defensively.

"I'm just here to talk!" Robert exclaimed with wide-eyed panic.

"What do you want, Spot?" Josephine snarled.

"I wanted to apologize for letting David bark his head off so much and wanted to reassure you that it won't happen again."

"It better not or you'll find yourself freezing your ass of in a snow storm," Josephine said moodily.

"I'm tired of fighting with you. We've been fighting for years. Can't we just stop?"

"I don't see why I should stop. You're a creep and a bastard."

"I'd really like for us to have a truce. I don't think it's all that healthy to be enemies like this."

"I'm not about to kiss and make up with you. After you betrayed me and dumped me for another woman, I don't think we'll ever become best friends," Josephine said coolly.

"I don't expect us to. Can't we just be neutral with each other? Why do we have to be enemies?" Robert said. "I was younger and more stupid back then. I'm sorry for hurting you. Can't you forgive me?"

Josephine wanted to shout no and to slam the door in his face. Or better yet, to hurl a jinx at him. Unfortunately, his words stirred a modicum of sympathy and she realized how old he'd gotten. She was lucky enough to still have her youth but he had lost it. Maybe she should give him a chance.

"I'll think about it," Josephine finally said. "I suppose it may not make sense to hold onto a grudge for so long."

"Thank you," Robert said cautiously.

"We can talk more later," Josephine said slowly.

"Okay."

Josephine gently closed the door and locked it. She wasn't sure what she should do. Robert had a point but he'd also been an asshole. She wasn't sure she was ready to forgive him just yet. On the other hand, it had been practically another life when they'd divorced. He was an elderly man now and not really capable of posing much of a threat anymore. It seemed kind of cruel to continue her attacks on him. Josephine reminded herself that she had more pressing issues such as the link between her subconscious mind and Gary's. She also didn't like the idea of the serial killer running loose in Sarasota. She suspected that she was a target along with Gary but didn't know why. Maybe the police had figured something out. She dialed Alex's cell number.

"Detective Riley," he said tersely.

"Hi, it's me," Josephine said casually. "I was calling to see if you'd made any headway regarding the serial killer."

"No, I haven't and it's not your job to solve the crimes."

"What in the hell are you talking about? I solve every crime I come in contact with," Josephine said haughtily.

"It's your job to use psychometry to read the crime scenes and if it ends up helping me to solve the case then that's a good thing but you're not a detective."

"You're splitting hairs. I usually know the name and address of the killer," Josephine said.

"You have a very unique gift but you're not a detective."

"So you haven't discovered anything new about the serial killer. That's strange. I would have thought after all this time you could have come up with some sort of clue," Josephine said with disappointment.

The dial tone sounded in her ear so she hung up the receiver with a frown of displeasure. Detective Whiney was a very trying individual at times. Josephine made several protective enchantments anchored to different pendants since she had nothing better to do. The rest of the day passed by slowly as she worried about how many sessions it would take to sever the link between her subconscious mind and Gary's and how long it would take to track down the serial killer. Late in the evening, Josephine lay on her bed struggling to sleep. It was so difficult to relax when she had so many problems plaguing her mind. When she awakened, she found herself lying in the middle of the bathroom floor. Josephine abruptly sat up and took stock of her surroundings. Various odds and ends lay scattered around her such as lipstick, makeup, a hand mirror, wash cloths, and towels. She slowly picked herself up off the floor and saw more hand towels in the bathtub.

The mirror over her sink had a message scrawled with her bright red lipstick: "Find the killer before it's too late. You are not safe."

Josephine grabbed some paper towels and some glass cleaner and wiped the mirror clean. She was disturbed to find this mess here. Obviously, she had walked in her sleep. She warily stepped out into the hallway where she could see into her bedroom. All of the sheets had been ripped off the mattress and tossed carelessly on the floor. Josephine gasped in dismay as she entered the room to find clothes strewn everywhere. All of the dresser drawers were open and emptied of their contents which was why the floor was such a mess.

"I don't think I like my subconscious very much," Josephine said irritably.

She stalked into the kitchen which was spotless and orderly. It was such a relief to have at least one room untouched. Josephine started the pot of coffee then ventured into the living room which was also fine. She cleaned up the bathroom, took a quick shower, and heard the doorbell ring just as she was drying off. Josephine hastily threw on a pair of shorts and a blouse so she was presentable. She opened the door and let Alice inside.

"Did you sleep in this morning? It took you awhile to answer the door," Alice said.

"I did sleep in a bit because of my stupid subconscious," Josephine said irritably. "I must have walked in my sleep because my bathroom and bedroom are a mess. And of course my subconscious left a message for me."

"What was the message?"

Josephine told her and Alice nodded with understanding as if this made perfect sense.

"I was expecting something like this. You'll suffer from a similar affliction that Gary does because your linked now," Alice said. "Don't worry about it. You'll be safe."

"But my bedroom is a mess! What if my subconscious decides to trash my place the next time I go to bed and it actually does some damage this time?" Josephine said. "I don't know if I dare go to sleep."

"Don't be ridiculous. Your subconscious isn't going to harm you. It's a part of you. It's just reflecting Gary's symptoms as a way of communicating the stress it's feeling."

"It's too early to listen to this psycho babble," Josephine said moodily.

Helen chose that moment to arrive which saved Josephine the torment of listening to any further weirdness from her friend. The three of them gathered in the living room where Josephine filled Helen in on what she'd missed.

"I can start our first session tomorrow morning," Alice said. "I'll be able to determine how quickly the link between your subconscious and Gary's can be severed once I've worked with you."

"Good," Josephine said.

"You'll need to help me create a claro mentis enchantment sometime today."

"We can do it right after we're finished with our coffee," Josephine said.

"Okay."

"I had the strangest conversation with Robert yesterday," Josephine said.

"Tell me about it." Alice's eyes shone eagerly and she leaned forward a bit.

Josephine filled her in on what had happened and her indecision to forgive Robert.

"That scumbag doesn't deserve a reprieve," Alice said. "You shouldn't give him a truce. If anything, I'd be even more relentless until that bastard is driven out of this complex."

"I think you should let bygones be bygones," Helen said. "It takes a lot of energy to have enemies. Why not just be at peace with him? Dale is obnoxious enough without having your next door neighbor as an enemy too."

"You've got a point there," Josephine said thoughtfully. "Maybe I should just make this a temporary truce until things are settled between me and Dale. I never know when he's going to break into my condo and jinx something in here or when he's going to jinx me."

"So you're going to forgive Robert?" Helen asked hopefully.

"Don't do it!" Alice said. "You can't trust Spot! He'll stab you in the back when you're least expecting it!"

Helen threw her a reproving look. "Don't be ridiculous. Robert is tired of this rivalry. It's time to put it to rest."

"Yes, I think you're right," Josephine said slowly. "I'll call a truce with Robert but it will probably be temporary."

"If you're going to forgive him, you'd better not let him get away with anything," Alice warned her.

"Don't worry. I won't."

Chapter 15

Josephine was reclined in her armchair with Alice seated on the large sofa facing her. Alice wore sky blue pants and a blouse and the gold bracelet on her right wrist which contained the claro mentis enchantment. She was patiently guiding Josephine through the relaxation process that she'd performed with Gary but Josephine was a more difficult patient.

"I'm just not buying this," Josephine said.

"There's nothing to buy. You need to relax," Alice said calmly and patiently.

Josephine frowned at her friend and crossed her arms over her chest.

"Can't you just go ahead and do the spell? It's taking too long. I'm getting nervous," Josephine said.

"This is why psychiatrists need to maintain a professional distance from their patients," Alice said in reprisal. "I really need your cooperation for this procedure to work. I'm doing you a favor."

"I'm sorry," Josephine apologized. "It's just that this relaxation process that you do seems phony to me."

"It's what all psychiatrists use," Alice said. "But since it's not working, I'll just have you relax on your own and tell me when you're ready. How's that?"

"Sounds good."

Josephine closed her eyes again and relaxed. After several moments, she indicated she was ready to proceed. Alice activated the claro mentis enchantment and the bracelet began to shimmer with a beautiful golden glow.

"You're subconscious is blocking me. I can't make the connection," Alice said.

"I don't feel like I'm blocking you," Josephine said.

"Have open thoughts. Open your mind."

"I am."

"No, you're not. You're not even trying," Alice said with annoyance.

"Okay. Just a second."

Josephine concentrated on feeling more open and instructed herself to allow Alice access to her mind. It sounded corny but maybe it would work. Josephine felt a strange sense of disorientation and fast movement as though she were falling. Her eyes opened and she found herself lying on the floor on the other side of the room. Alice stood over her with a concerned expression dominating her face.

"Are you okay?" Alice demanded.

"Yes, I'm fine," Josephine said weakly. "What happened?"

"You entered a fugue state like Gary and were telling me that I needed to leave the connection between the two of you alone," Alice said.

Josephine sat up and frowned at her friend. "I hope you aren't going to listen to my subconscious."

"I'm afraid I am. I've retired and I'm not going to make any progress if your subconscious wants to stay connected with Gary's. You need professional help."

"I can't believe this," Josephine said dismally. "It's not what I want."

"A part of you does want this or it wouldn't be happening, my dear," Alice said.

Josephine stood up and brushed herself off even though she wasn't dirty. She couldn't believe she was losing control of her life like this.

"What if I talk to Gary," Josephine said.

"What would be the point?" Alice asked.

"I guess that would be a waste of time."

"Yes, it would. You need to call and hire a psychiatrist," Alice said.

"I'll wait awhile. Once the serial killer is found and locked behind bars, my link with Gary should go away on its own, right?"

"Theoretically. I wouldn't count on it though."

"Sometimes, you can be a real pessimist," Josephine said.

"I'm a realist. I've worked with all kinds of patients in my career. I know what I'm talking about," Alice said.

Josephine abruptly felt dizzy and reached for the back of the couch to prevent herself from falling. She flinched and gasped with surprise when her surroundings were replaced by the Siesta Key beach. The sun was shining down on her and the waves were gently lapping the shore a couple of feet in front of her. Josephine's knees buckled but she managed to remain on her feet. She noticed Alice standing next to her on the right and shot her a frantic look.

"How did we get here?" Josephine said as icy chills prickled down her spine.

"You slipped into the fugue state and said I needed to drive you to the beach now," Alice said.

"This is so creepy," Josephine said fearfully.

"Do you have any idea what's so urgent that you need to be here? I don't see anything wrong," Alice said as she regarded her friend in concern.

"Let me check something."

Josephine opened her senses to the psychic energies in the atmosphere and immediately noticed the power vortex was plagued with angry, swirling tendrils of red energy just like the other day. She stiffened reflexively and wondered how her subconscious had sensed this from her condo. She knew that the subconscious could sometimes perform incredible feats that wizards normally failed to achieve no matter how much they practiced but this really astounded her.

"What's wrong?" Alice asked.

"It's the power vortex. The other day, its energy was turbulent and disruptive. It's the same way right now. I think someone's been connecting with it and doing something to cause a temporary imbalance."

"Why would anyone do that?"

"I don't know. I've never tried to manipulate the energy of a vortex before. Only a category six is capable of doing that. I would be afraid of trying," Josephine said.

"This is very serious. We need to tell the police," Alice said.

"I can't expose myself."

"You wouldn't be exposing yourself. Just tell them we were visiting the beach and you sensed something wrong so you used your psychometry to feel it out and discovered that someone's been tampering with the power vortex," Alice said.

"You really think the police will believe it? They'll think that I'm the one who did it. There are no category six wizards in this area except for me and Gary. Gary's at work and has an alibi. They'll think

I was fooling around for some reason and messed up with what I was doing and trying to get them to fix it."

"Vickie's a category six," Alice pointed out.

"She's not the one doing this. She was at home the last time this happened," Josephine said.

"You can't know that for sure."

"There's no need to tell the police what's going on. The vortex will heal up on its own. Already, it's looking better," Josephine said.

"Oh my God!" Alice exclaimed. "It's the serial killer! He's an unregistered category six!"

"I think you're right."

"You do?" Alice blinked at her friend with surprise.

"It makes perfect sense. I picked up that he was very disciplined. If he was never registered, he was free to experiment without limitations because he wasn't restrained by an aequitas enchantment. He could be very skilled."

"And powerful," Alice said. "We need to tell the police what happened. We'll let them know about the link between you and Gary and how it clued you in on the vortex here."

"It's too dangerous. I can't let anyone find out that my aequitas enchantment has been neutralized," Josephine said. "If we let the police know what's going on, they won't be able to use this information to find the killer."

"If they watch the beach, the killer will probably come here again soon and link with the vortex."

"They would have to have either me or Gary here because we're the only ones who could sense the connection and the vortex being manipulated," Josephine said.

"You see? This is an opportunity to catch the killer," Alice said triumphantly.

"I guess so." Josephine couldn't shake the uneasy feeling that clung to her. She really didn't want to take the chance that the police would figure out her aequitas enchantment was neutralized. On the other hand, if she didn't do everything possible to catch the serial killer, she could end up being the next victim.

"Wait a minute." Alice's eyes reflected a sudden panic. "We can't go to the police. It's illegal for me to cast claro mentis spells without a license and my license expired years ago."

"Can't we just tell them the connection happened by itself?" Josephine asked.

"No, they'd never believe that. It would be too suspicious."

"Then what do we do?"

"We could tell them that we had decided to go to the beach and that you sensed something wrong with the vortex while you were here," Alice said.

"That works for me."

The two of them went down to the police station and were immediately allowed to walk back to the offices to speak with Alex Riley. Unfortunately, he was located at his desk typing carefully at the computer. Josephine had hoped she would be permitted to file a report with someone else. She hated working with this obnoxious detective. Her grandson was also working on a report at the desk beside Alex and several other officers were in the room as well.

"Detective Riley," Josephine said as she stepped into the room.

Alex's head whipped up and his gaze fixed on her with surprise which was quickly replaced with irritation.

"What do you want?" he said.

"I came to inform you of something disturbing," Josephine said.

Alex noticed Alice standing off to the side and slightly behind her friend.

"Why is your friend here?" Alex said sharply.

Josephine ignored his hostility and launched into her story. When she'd finished, Alex looked shaken.

"Okay." Alex was clearly at a loss for words and his gaze flitted between Josephine and Alice as though expecting her to jump in with further information. "We need to have this vortex watched."

"Good idea," Josephine said.

"Yes, we'll need to have it under surveillance. Will need a category six posted there at all times," Alex said. "I'll have to assign you and Gary."

"That's fine. I'll be happy once we catch this guy," Josephine said.

Alex nodded thoughtfully. "I'll assign Howie to go with you for the first shift. Gary can have the overnight shift."

"He'll love that," Alice murmured.

It took great restraint for Josephine to keep from shushing her friend. The last thing she wanted was for Alex to give her the night shift. That would suck.

"Howie will meet you at the beach. You can go now, I hope?" Alex said.

"Of course."

"Meet him in the main parking lot," Alex said.

"Okay."

Alice drove Josephine back to her condo so she could pick up her car.

"I'm worried about you. Be careful," Alice said,

"I know what I'm doing," Josephine said confidently. "And I'm always careful."

"Good bye," Alice said.

"Bye." Josephine hopped into her car.

Josephine stopped by a Checkers fast food restaurant to pick up a chili burger then headed for the beach. She parked her car there and started on her dinner. She'd only just finished eating the burger when Howie arrived in his civilian car wearing a red, tropical print shirt, shorts, and sandals. Josephine had never seen his muscular legs before and they were something to behold. Howie saw her and grinned as he strode over.

"Why are you out of uniform?" Josephine asked.

"I'm undercover. We don't want the serial killer to know there's any police in the area," Howie said. "I'll get a couple of chairs we can sit on at the beach."

"Okay."

The two of them made their way to the beach with the chairs, picked a spot, and waited. Unfortunately, Josephine doubted the killer would connect with the vortex so soon. A couple hours later, she stiffened reflexively when she saw the familiar angry swirls of red energy appear. Josephine connected with the vortex as well since the killer was likely to use powerful magic against them.

"The killer is tapping into the vortex," Josephine said.

"Already?" Howie asked with surprise.

"Yes."

Josephine led the way down the beach as she traced the path of the link. Howie pulled out his cell phone and requested backup. Her heart hammered wildly in her chest as she continued walking. Soon, she began to sense the minds around her and realized that the killer would be able to feel hers. He'd know she was coming. Josephine swallowed nervously and chills danced along the nape of her neck as she realized the killer wasn't on the beach but farther up the road.

"He may be in the parking lot or a couple of blocks down the street," Josephine said.

"Really?" Howie said. "I didn't realize it was possible to link that far."

"It is," Josephine said.

Howie eyed her appraisingly. "There's something different about you."

"It's nothing. I'm just worried."

"I don't think that's it," he said.

"The killer may be able to sense us when we get closer. We'll need to act quickly," Josephine advised.

She stumbled as she sensed a surge of power behind her. Josephine turned to look at the vortex which was not only churning with turbulent force but manifesting an energy matrix within its center. The matrix rotated and collected the energy around it as its shape became more intricate.

"The killer is doing something with the vortex," Josephine said in horror.

"What is it?" Howie asked.

"Some sort of enchantment."

Josephine tried to disrupt the matrix but couldn't seem to produce any results. It stopped weaving itself which meant the spell was complete and ready for casting. Chills of apprehension danced along her spine as she wished there was some way to escape. An explosion of red energy burst from the vortex and rushed over the people. Josephine was still connected to the vortex and used the power to create a shield around herself and Howie. Screams of pain sprouted from all around her as the red wave of energy whooshed through the beach and continued down the roads.

"What's going on?" Howie asked.

Many people were either shouting or covering their heads with both hands. Some were running madly as if trying to escape something only they could see. Josephine's shield had offered complete protection from whatever spell the killer had unleashed. Soon, people began passing out until Josephine and Howie were the only ones remaining conscious.

"We need to get moving," Howie said.

"Right."

"Can you still follow the killer's link to the vortex?" Howie asked.

"Yes."

Josephine walked briskly along the path of energy and could sense the only conscious mind besides Howie's. It was very dark, disciplined, and focused. The killer sensed her and was already strategizing new ways to incapacitate her. She began jogging even though it was difficult to track the link when she was exerting herself like this. Being connected to the vortex helped her though. She felt another energy buildup as the killer prepared a spell. Josephine knew he was too far away for her to reach in time. Suddenly, she felt a release of power as a spell was unleashed. Howie lifted into the air unexpectedly and floated high above her head. Josephine sensed the killer's intention to drown him in the ocean. She concentrated on creating a dampening field but the killer was blocking her attempts so it would take some time.

Howie's body slowly floated towards the ocean and he linked with the vortex. Josephine didn't think he was strong enough to create a dampening field but with his efforts added to her own, they may be able to stop the killer. Josephine yelped when she lifted into the air. She flailed her arms reflexively until she quickly realized it wouldn't do her any good. Howie was continuing to head for the ocean and she was following behind. Josephine concentrated on creating a dampening field around her own body and immediately began to lose altitude. Soon, she was standing on the shore. Howie was now over the water. Josephine kept her own dampening field up as she focused on creating one around him. He abruptly fell into the ocean but she knew she hadn't succeeded in releasing him. The killer had intentionally dropped him into the water and was going to hold him under until he drowned.

Josephine dashed into the ocean and continued her efforts on protecting him. A dampening field was beginning to form around him. His body was pressed firmly against the sandy floor as he struggled to push himself up. Josephine stumbled but managed to stay on her feet. Adrenaline coursed through her body when she could tell that he was too weak to push against the sand anymore. He was losing consciousness. Desperation made Josephine forget about keeping the dampening field around her own body so she could spend as much energy on saving Howie as possible. She sensed the psychokinetic enchantment being deflected from him but Howie's body still rested against the bottom. Josephine raised him to the surface of the water with telekinesis then held his head above the water. She pulled him to the shore and his eyes snapped open. He gasped then rose to his feet.

A strange red mist formed a couple of feet in front of Josephine's face. She backed away from it and watched as it coalesced into a face.

"Hello, Josephine," it said in a raspy voice.

"What do you think you're doing?" Josephine asked.

"I'm practicing," it said. "You don't have much time left before I kill you."

"I'm too strong for you to do that," she said with false bravado.

"I'm definitely stronger than you but it will be a struggle," it said with amusement. "You and Gary are running out of time."

"Why are you even bothering to talk to me?" Josephine asked.

"Because you have been annoying to me and made things complicated. I wanted you to know how little precious time you have left to live," it said.

The red mist abruptly lost its form and dissipated. Howie and Josephine exchanged horrified looks. She could no longer sense the killer's connection to the vortex which meant he was probably on his way off the island.

"I need to talk to Detective Riley about this," Howie said.

Josephine shrugged and followed him to his car. Howie spoke to Riley for several moments then disconnected and turned to face her.

"It's too risky for you to come here when the killer is connected to the vortex. He's too powerful for any of us to stop when he's tuned into so much power," Howie said. "You're going to have two officers assigned to you at all times and will need to stay away from the beach until we catch this guy."

"All right. I'll definitely stay away from the beach," Josephine said. "You realize that Gary is probably in danger as well, right?"

"Yes, Detective Riley has assigned two officers to watch Gary just like you," Howie said.

Chapter 16

When Josephine opened the front door, there was a tall lanky man in his early thirties who she'd never seen before. He had black hair, piercing blue eyes, a long nose, and a hawk-like face which gave him a severe, dangerous look. His body thrummed like an electric line with intense but controlled power which gave him away as a category five wizard. He wore jeans and a black, long-sleeved collared shirt. Howie stood beside the man with a guarded expression on his face.

"Hi, Josephine. This is Morgan McKinley. He's an enforcer whose been assigned to protect you. You'll need to give him your full cooperation as he investigates the clues which means you'll need to tag along with him when he looks over evidence that's been collected from the various crime scenes left by the serial killer," Howie said.

"Okay," Josephine said evenly as anxiety coursed through her body at the thought of an enforcer spending so much time with her.

"I'll be spending the nights in your condo as protection against the killer who seems to be one of the most powerful wizards on record according to the police reports I've reviewed on this case," Morgan said.

"He's certainly powerful," Josephine said. She realized she was standing in front of the door and stepped aside. "Please, come in."

"Thanks," Howie said nervously.

No one liked dealing with enforcers who worked for a higher branch than the police department. Enforcers were category five wizards with remarkable power and control of their magical abilities. To become an enforcer, one had to follow a strict training program which last a couple of years. Category five wizards weren't as rare as sixes but not too many existed in comparison to fours and lesser wizards so they made a great deal of money. Many wizards growing up aspired to become one but only a handful of them were gifted and talented enough to attain this goal. Morgan had a different ring on each finger which probably contained an assortment of enchantments. He also wore a pedant around his neck and there were probably six wands stashed in an inner pocket of his pants.

"Would you like some coffee?" Josephine asked.

"That would be nice," Morgan said.

"No, thanks. I've got to run. I just came with Morgan to make sure you were properly introduced. We've already verified his identity so you don't have to worry about him being the killer," Howie said.

"Okay," Josephine said.

She poured herself a cup of coffee in addition to her uninvited guest.

"Would you like cream or sugar with your coffee?" Josephine asked.

"Both, please," Morgan said.

Josephine prepared both coffees then returned to the living room and handed him his mug.

"I suppose you have a lot planned on the agenda," Josephine said.

"Yes, I do," Morgan said. "We'll be going to the beach to patrol."

"But that's too dangerous. The serial killer is too powerful."

"I'm a lot stronger than he is. I've had years of training and experience working with vortexes," Morgan said confidently. "Gary has an enforcer assigned who will also be doing patrols. Our times are coordinated to provide the maximum coverage for keeping Siesta Key under surveillance."

"All right."

The two of them went to the beach a short while later in Morgan's black sedan. Josephine knew that enforcers carried power wands and various enchantments in hidden compartments in their vehicles so she supposed she was as safe as she could be from any attacks the serial killer may attempt on her. Morgan and Josephine stayed in the car to wait for anything to happen. Morgan sat and watched while Josephine read her novel. Even though Morgan didn't complain, she had the distinct impression that he didn't approve of her not keeping her undivided attention on the beach. It wasn't until late in the afternoon that she sensed a disturbance. Josephine opened her second sight and gazed at the vortex which was beginning to show signs of distress.

"It's happening," Josephine said.

"I suspected he wouldn't stay away," Morgan said. "Track the connection to the killer."

"Okay."

Josephine began creating a dampening field around herself as she followed the path toward the killer. She sensed Morgan connecting to the vortex and creating his own protection. He got out a cell phone and dialed one of his colleagues.

"It's Morgan. The target is tapping into the vortex." Morgan listened to whatever his colleague was saying. "Okay. Bye."

"Who were you talking to?" Josephine asked.

"That's none of your concern," he said tersely.

Josephine rolled her eyes with exasperation but continued following the energy path. She wished she wasn't assigned to an enforcer because then she could connect to the vortex and protect herself better. Unfortunately, Morgan had better psychometry than the average wizard and the risk was greater that he would sense her connection. Josephine could sense an enchantment forming in the vortex.

"He's doing something to the vortex. He might be getting ready to hit everyone with a knockout enchantment like yesterday," Josephine said.

"Don't worry. I can protect us," Morgan said. "You must hurry. We can't let the killer get away this time."

Josephine walked briskly but couldn't concentrate on tracking the link if she went any faster. A moment later, a wave of energy exploded from the vortex behind them. As promised, Morgan protected them from the enchantment. Josephine watched the enchantment rush past her and down the street. It was much stronger this time and may actually reach the city before it dissipated. There were shouts and screams from many who didn't pass out right away but after a moment, only she and Morgan were conscious at the beach.

"A lot of people are going to get hurt if the spell reaches Sarasota," she said.

"There's nothing we can do about that," Morgan said.

This statement confirmed the rumors that Josephine heard about enforcers being cold-hearted bastards. She felt magical power gathering around her and Morgan and knew an enchantment was being cast. She abruptly slammed into something solid and was knocked backward. Morgan caught her before she could fall and frowned at the space ahead of them.

"We're surrounded by a psychokinetic field," Morgan said. "It'll take me a minute to break it."

He stared off into space and Josephine waited patiently. Soon, a strange silver ripple danced in the air around them and she could feel the psychokinetic field torn away with violent force. Morgan had tapped into some serious energy to make that happen. It made Josephine a little nervous. She continued following the path. The killer tried creating a psychokinetic field around them a short while later but Morgan was ready this time and prevented it from forming.

"I'm starting to sense the killer," Morgan said.

"You are?" Josephine asked.

"Yes," Morgan said. "When I tap into a vortex, my mind expands and I become aware of the thoughts and emotions of those around me. People are like sheep; spewing energy mindlessly that can be picked up and read like a book. There are no secrets."

"I see," Josephine said. "So you're picking things up from me?"

"No, category six wizards don't give off junk energy. It's a shame that there aren't more of them. They make useful tools," Morgan said.

"Thanks," Josephine said sarcastically.

"I was just stating a fact. It's a matter of genetics, I suppose. Something you were born with," Morgan said.

"Vickie wasn't a category six until she was attacked by the serial killer. The Disaster turned a lot of people into category sixes," Josephine pointed out.

"We don't have time to talk about this. The energy from the disaster merely awakened a dormant potential that already existed.

People can't become what they're not. You need to hurry," Morgan said.

Josephine sensed a buildup within the vortex once again. An energy matrix was forming within the disturbing red mass of energy. Josephine warned Morgan of the new threat.

"I can sense it. You don't have to worry. I'll protect us."

Josephine sensed they were drawing closer to the killer. It wouldn't take much longer. Suddenly, the enchantment in the vortex was released. A wave of sickly green energy tore through the air. It passed harmlessly over Morgan and Josephine. Josephine sensed a different type of enchantment had been used. Many unconscious beachgoers stirred and awakened. Josephine didn't pay attention to them until they turned to face her and Morgan and walk purposefully toward them.

"What's going on?" Josephine warily eyed a group of people who were steadily drawing closer.

One of the closest, a man in his early forties, suddenly leapt for Morgan. He bounced off Morgan's protection and was thrown backward several feet. The rest of the group shouted and dashed toward Morgan and Josephine. Morgan pulled out a wand and cast a wide-range knockout spell which took care of the attackers. Unfortunately, more of the unconscious beachgoers were awakening and sharing similar violent tendencies aimed at Morgan and Josephine. It took quite awhile for Morgan to take care of all the humans and wizards that mindlessly attacked in a rage. By that time, the killer was no longer linked to the vortex and Josephine had lost the trail.

"This is going to be a lot more difficult than I anticipated," Morgan said stonily. "I wonder how a category six can cast so many spells like that. His control is remarkable and stronger than anything I've encountered before."

"Stronger than an enforcer?" Josephine asked.

"Of course not. I would say he was just as good as I was but his psychometry allows him to attack from a distance."

"I see," Josephine said.

"I know about the connection between your subconscious and Gary's. I'm going to remove that connection tonight," Morgan said.

"I don't think that's possible," Josephine said.

"Yes, it is. I've mastered the claro mentis enchantment."

"Alice used to be a psychiatrist and she says it would take numerous sessions to remove the link."

"She doesn't have the resources that I do," Morgan said.

"It doesn't seem like a good idea to me," Josephine said.

Morgan cocked a haughty brow at her. "Are you refusing to cooperate?"

"Of course not." Josephine forced a tight smile on her face. She couldn't believe the misfortune she'd received in being assigned an enforcer. Of course, she should have expected it after what had happened at the beach with the serial killer. The police just weren't equipped to deal with the kind of power that was being wielded. Morgan drove them back to her condo then instructed her to have a seat and relax.

"I will begin the claro mentis soon," Morgan said. "But I must prepare first."

"You're going to prepare?" Josephine asked.

"I'm going to perform a meditation that will temporarily enhance my abilities," Morgan explained.

"How long will this take?"

Morgan merely closed his eyes as he sat down in her armchair without responding. Josephine frowned at him then leaned back in the sofa. She didn't know what to expect but she wasn't looking forward to it. She shifted impatiently as time dragged on and Morgan remained motionless and silent.

"What on earth is taking you so long?" Josephine asked irritably. "Did you fall asleep or what?"

Morgan's breathing was slow and deep but not heavy as one would expect from an individual who'd fallen asleep. Josephine frowned at him with annoyance and stood up.

"Sit down," Morgan said in a chilling tone.

Josephine abruptly sat down and regarded him nervously. She flinched when his eyes opened and radiated with a powerful, golden glow. Dizziness abruptly assaulted her senses and she clutched the side of the couch for support as the room seemed to rock violently beneath her and threatened to toss her body.

"You need to lay down and close your eyes as I instructed you to do earlier," Morgan said tersely.

Josephine leaned back and closed her eyes. A feeling of nausea gripped her as the dizziness continued to pour relentless into her.

"I'm not feeling so well," she said.

"You're subconscious mind is resisting me," Morgan said with disapproval. "You can't stop me."

"Whatever," Josephine said weakly.

A cold wind abruptly tore through the room. Uncontrolled power gathered around her and swirled throughout the room. Josephine's head pounded and she felt something cold and wet brushing against her body. She opened her body to discover snow blowing through the room; however, there were no clouds anywhere. The snow was materializing from the middle of nowhere and whipping through the room.

"Stop resisting me," Morgan said in a demanding tone.

"I'm not doing anything," Josephine said.

She shivered as the small snow flakes continued to brush against her and gather in her hair and clothes. Morgan was having the same problem. She was surprised he could concentrate. He cast a knockout spell which somehow deflected away from her by a mysterious force. She couldn't detect the source of magic within the room. Abruptly, everything went black as she passed out. When Josephine awakened, she felt exhausted but no longer cold. She sat up and took stock of her surroundings. The snow had long since evaporated and Morgan lay unconscious on the floor on the far side of the room. Josephine swallowed a lump of fear as she wondered if the serial killer had attacked.

She stood up on legs that threatened to collapse with fatigue. She felt so weak that she didn't know how long she'd be able to stand. Josephine made her way over to Morgan and knelt down beside him. She checked the pulse at his neck to make sure he was alive. Josephine wondered if her subconscious had attacked Morgan while he'd performed the claro mentis enchantment on her. A cold lump of fear settled in the pit of her stomach as she gazed down at the living room phone with indecision. Morgan still lay unresponsive on the floor. She picked up the phone and dialed Riley's cell number.

"Detective Riley," Alex's typical terse voice came over the line.

"It's me," Josephine said shakily. "Something happened to Morgan while he was performing the claro mentis enchantment on me. We may need a medic."

"I can't believe you took out an enforcer," Alex said with a mixture of accusation and surprise.

"I did no such thing, Detective Whiney," Josephine snapped. "You might want to quit wasting time and send some help."

She slammed down the phone and turned to examine Morgan's unconscious body once again. As far as she could determine, he hadn't stirred since she'd awakened. Josephine gazed down at her topaz ring and realized it was extremely risky to allow her aequitas enchantment to remain dormant like this. She concentrated on summoning power and carefully charged the ring. Josephine paced the room as she waited for the police to arrive. She checked Morgan's condition periodically to make sure he was still okay. She didn't look forward to his reaction over this debacle. It didn't take long for Alex to arrive with a medic. The medic wore the typical uniform consisting of a purple uniform with the wizard proficiency insignia emblazoned with gold on the right shoulder and upper-left hand corner of the chest. He was a young man in his late twenties with blue eyes and short-cropped brown hair. His name badge identified him as Dustin.

"The subject passed out while performing a claro mentis enchantment on you?" Dustin asked in an efficient, business-like tone.

"That's right," Josephine confirmed.

"Can you remember any details of this session leading up to his losing consciousness?" Dustin asked.

Josephine supplied the few details she could remember before passing out herself.

"Okay. Let me take a look at him," Dustin said.

He knelt down and took out a short, thin fluorite wand which he held over Morgan. The fluorite wand shimmered with a soft, green glow for several seconds then went dark again. Dustin pocketed the wand and took out a clear quartz one that was the same size as the fluorite. A spark of white light materialized at the tip of the wand as Dustin pressed it against Morgan's forehead. After a moment, the light winked out and Dustin pocketed his medical device. Morgan's eyes opened and he abruptly sat up then jumped to his feet. Josephine felt a sudden surge of power from the enforcer before it went out. She assumed he was checking to make sure all of his magical tools were accounted for. His cold, disapproving eyes honed accusingly on Josephine.

"You knocked me out," he said.

"You performed a claro mentis enchantment under very unwise and inadvisable circumstances," Dustin stepped in. "From the pattern of energy that encompassed your mind earlier, you had received a backlash of unfocused energy which was unintentional. You weren't attacked."

"Are you certain of that?" Morgan said sharply.

"I'm sure."

"All right," Morgan said coolly. "I suppose this lets Josephine off the hook."

Alex regarded Josephine guardedly as if he wasn't sure what to think of the situation. He probably suspected that Dustin had assessed the condition incorrectly and that Josephine had indeed attacked Morgan. Josephine supposed she should probably be more agreeable to Alex. It wasn't wise to antagonize him like she did. Suddenly, Josephine sensed a massive amount of power building within the room.

"Something's happening," Josephine said.

"It's the killer. He's getting ready to cast a psychokinetic spell," Morgan said. "Everyone needs to build up a dampening field for protection."

Josephine instantly set to work on this but couldn't create as much protection as she would have liked because of the aequitas enchantment. She silently chastised herself for activating the topaz ring. She could feel the power hovering over them, gathering like a storm and preparing to unleash itself. Alex wasn't a wizard so he couldn't protect himself. Dustin must be a category three or less because his dampening field was weaker than Josephine's. Morgan extended the dampening field to encompass the others in the room. They waited in tense silence for the serial killer to either strike or abandon his efforts. Josephine saw the power slowly leave the room and gather into the kitchen. She warned Morgan of what was going on.

"I can see what's going on," Morgan said coolly. "He's probably going to try to use something as a weapon and toss it with enough force so that the object's momentum will carry itself to its intended target."

"And that intended target is probably me," Josephine said shakily.

A dull pounding began at her temples and dizziness rocked her backward a couple of steps. She sensed the connection between her subconscious and Gary's had become active again. It probably sensed the danger in the room and was preparing to do something. Unfortunately, Josephine couldn't be sure if whatever course of action either hers or Gary's subconscious chose to take would be productive. The buildup of magic continued at an alarming rate.

"There's so much power in there," Morgan said warily. "He must be tapped into the Siesta Key vortex."

"Maybe you should call for backup," Alex said nervously.

"I can't afford to be distracted right now. Something could happen at any moment and I have to be ready." Morgan's eyes remained watchful and he held a wand in each hand.

There was a clattering sound in the kitchen and one of the drawers violently flew open and crashed onto the floor. Half a dozen knives floated into the air and two of them darted out with shocking speed and force. As soon as the knives passed through the dampening field, the psychokinetic spell was no longer active and the knives were being carried by mere momentum. One of the knives stabbed Dustin's right foot and the other sliced Josephine's right arm. Hot spears of pain shot up her body but luckily it was only a flesh wound. Josephine cried out and clamped her left hand over the wound. The dampening field that Dustin had manifested weakened considerably as he extracted the dagger from his foot. Two more knives hurtled into the living room. Dustin had raised a telekinetic shield that protected him from both attacks but the dampening field was severely hampered by his lack of concentration. Josephine activated the shield in her pendant and felt its protection snap into place around her body. The last two knives darted into the room like missiles. Their speed was so fast that they managed to penetrate Dustin's shield. One of them stabbed Morgan in the chest and the other dug into his right thigh. The dampening field which was protecting them from psychokinetic attacks dissipated completely as Morgan passed out. The pounding in Josephine's head sharpened intensely as magic poured from her and into the aequitas enchantment in the topaz ring. She sensed the enchantment neutralize which gave her the freedom to work the full extent of her abilities. Blackness crept along the edge of her vision as the pain in her temples continued relentlessly. The knives in the living room began to raise as psychokinetic force from the killer set to work unimpeded. Everything went black and abruptly Josephine awakened standing up and leaning against the couch. The pain in her head had decreased to a dull ache and the dizziness was gone. Dustin was kneeling beside Morgan with the two knives still embedded in his chest and thigh. Josephine opened her second sight and was relieved to find that the killer's magic had fled the scene. She caught sight of Alex a short distance beside her as he warily eyed the room for any suspicious activity.

"How long was I out?" Josephine asked.

"If you mean how long were you all weird and creepy, I'd say about five minutes," Alex said.

"What happened? Was I able to keep the dampening field up?" Josephine asked.

"The knives fell to the floor and nothing seemed to happen. You were just staring off into space," Alex said.

"You brought up a powerful dampening field that seemed to protect the entire condo rather than just this one room," Dustin said. "I've never seen such a big dampening field before. Of course, in my line of work I haven't had to use them much."

He was still pointing his clear, quartz wand at Morgan with the tip radiating a bright, glowing spark of luminescence. Two more medics arrived and carefully removed the knives from Morgan's body before carrying him to the ambulance. This left Josephine alone with Alex.

"My God. There's no stopping the killer," Josephine said fearfully. "He's too powerful. Not even an enforcer was able to protect himself."

"You'll be okay. We should go to the police station and wait for another enforcer to be assigned to you," Alex said.

The door knocked just as they were getting ready to leave. Josephine checked the peephole to discover Jake. She opened the door and gave him a fierce hug.

"Grandma, what happened?" Jake asked.

Alex filled him in on what had transpired. Jake had heard about the attack from the dispatcher at the station but hadn't known the details. Alex cleaned Josephine's arm and bandaged it. Fortunately, the bleeding had stopped all on its own and it was a very minor cut. Josephine knew she had been extremely lucky and that her time was running out.

Chapter 17

Morgan stood over the three elderly women like a dark, sulking cloud waiting to pour rain over unsuspecting victims. His knife wounds had completely healed last night thanks to the proficiency of magic performed by the wizards at the hospital. Not even a trace of a scar had been left in spite of the seriousness of the injuries. Josephine took a sip of her chocolate-mint flavored coffee as she struggled unsuccessfully to block all thoughts of the surly enforcer from her mind. Alice and Helen were trying to ignore Morgan as well but kept glancing nervously at him. It was easier for Josephine because she had her back to him.

"Half of the people in Sarasota blacked out because of the knockout spell that the serial killer cast from Siesta Key beach yesterday. It's horrifying to think any individual has that much power," Helen said.

"I know," Josephine said. "No one should have that kind of power – not even someone in law enforcement."

"What's that supposed to mean?" Morgan asked in a surly tone.

"I'm just stating a fact," Josephine said coolly. "If you take any offense to my remark, it's only because you internalized it."

"It sounded like you were talking about me."

"I was being completely hypothetical. I didn't name anyone specifically. Are you saying that you could do what the serial killer did with the knockout spell?" Josephine said challengingly.

"As a matter of fact, I could do more than what he did," Morgan said crisply. "I could probably take out the entire city if I wanted and maybe even extend the spell farther. I could possibly take out parts of Venice and Bradenton."

"Whatever," Josephine said before taking another drink of her coffee.

Helen blanched at the enforcer's bragging and exchanged a concerned look with Alice. Josephine hoped Morgan was just blustering because no individual should have that kind of power. She hated having him in her personal life like this. She couldn't even enjoy a simple chat with her friends in the morning without him intruding on her privacy.

"That knockout spell caused a lot of injuries," Helen said. "People who were driving on the freeway had major accidents. There were some fatalities too."

"Were we going to the gym this morning?" Alice asked.

"Yes," Josephine said. "I don't see any reason to change our plans."

"We need to go to the police station to look at evidence from the crime scenes," Morgan said.

"We can do that after we go to the gym," Josephine said firmly.

"That's fine but you can't spend all day goofing around," Morgan said.

"In case you didn't notice, I'm retired. I've worked my entire life and I'm old now. Retired people are supposed to be able to enjoy themselves," Josephine said.

"You're a category six. You could be working another sixty or eighty years before you need to retire," Morgan said coolly.

Josephine frowned over her coffee and wished she could hurl a jinx at him without needing to worry about consequences. He was such a slime ball. A pressure began to build in her temples and the room seemed to slowly shift from side to side. Josephine shivered as chills danced along her skin.

"Josephine," Helen said in a choked, anxious tone.

"What is it?" Josephine asked.

She screamed as pain suddenly tore through her head. She passed out and awakened abruptly sitting up. A thin layer of snow covered the living room floor and she was shivering uncontrollably. Morgan, Alice and Helen were standing a safe distance away from her. Josephine's mug of coffee was hovering in the air to her right. She grasped it and cringed at the cold. The remaining coffee had frozen inside the mug.

"It's about time you woke up," Morgan said.

"What happened?" Josephine asked.

"You were in a fugue state. You were completely unresponsive."

"So I made it snow in here?" Josephine asked.

"Yes," Morgan said. "You also made some things float and some things you dropped and broke on the floor."

Josephine gazed down and saw that there were several broken mugs which had previously been safely stowed away in the cupboard.

"What's happening to me?" she asked.

"Your subconscious is being strained by the link to Gary. It needs to be severed," Morgan said.

"You tried before but you couldn't do it," Josephine pointed out.

"I intend to do it with help this time," Morgan said. "Jennifer will be coming over shortly to assist me."

"When are you going to do it?" Josephine asked.

"As soon as she gets here. It should be in another few minutes or so. I called her while you were doing your whammy on the room."

"That wouldn't be a good idea," Alice said authoritatively. "You should wait at least several hours for her mind to recuperate."

"If we do that, she'll be able to resist us better. We have to link with her while her energy is low," Morgan said.

"A category six wizard never has low energy. I would think that someone of your abilities and experience would realize that," Alice said.

"I realize that," Morgan said with a trace of annoyance. "But we are severing her link to Gary. It's too unstable and makes her vulnerable to the serial killer's attacks."

"So far, the link has helped to save her from the serial killer's attacks," Alice said in a reasonable tone. "Maybe it would be best to leave it for now."

"The unconscious mind is completely unpredictable. Just because she was lucky enough to be protected in one or two instances, doesn't mean that her subconscious will continue to behave in the same manner."

Alice cocked a bemused brow at him but let the matter rest.

"I'm afraid I need to ask you all to leave," Morgan said to her and Helen.

"We're going to the gym as soon as you perform the claro mentis enchantment," Josephine said. "I'd like for them to stay."

"I must insist that they leave now. You can call them when we're finished and you want to go to your little gym," Morgan said frostily.

Josephine rolled her eyes with annoyance but a sense of foreboding took root in her mind.

"We'll see you soon," Helen said.

"Talk to you later. Nice cup of coffee," Alice said in a strained voice.

When Josephine's friends left, Morgan activated the security enchantments on the door and turned to face her.

"We need to talk," he said.

"About what?" Josephine asked nervously.

"Your aequitas enchantment is no longer active," Morgan said with a grave frown. "This means either your subconscious deactivated it while you were in the fugue state or your body has adapted to the enchantment. We need to find out for sure before a decision can be made. Of course, you must reveal none of this or you'll be sent to jail for treason."

"Of course," Josephine said quietly.

"If you're body has adapted to the aequitas enchantment which does occasionally occur among category six wizards, you'll need to go to training camp to become an OC enforcer," Morgan said.

"What's that?" Josephine asked.

"Basically, it means you learn to control your abilities and agree to take assignments across the United States when needed. You'll be completely undercover so no one will be able to know what you're doing – including the local police. When you do your assignments, you'll need a disguise and false identification so you're not discovered."

221

"Why do you have such a program?" Josephine asked.

"It's an option to keep you useful and to keep your powers under control. If you fail your training, you'll need to wear a constrixi enchantment which will bind your powers. The constrixi is tied to a topaz ring and will keep your power under wraps. If you ever take it off then you'll be knocked out and the enforcers will be immediately notified."

"I think you're jumping the gun a little bit," Josephine said shakily. "Probably what deactivated the aequitas enchantment was my subconscious mind when I was trapped in the fugue state."

"I believe that is the case but I wanted to let you know what would happen if I found out otherwise," Morgan said crisply.

"That's why you want to sever my connection with Gary as soon as possible," Josephine said.

"Yes. That and the reason that I mentioned in front of your friends regarding the unpredictability of your subconscious mind."

Josephine's mind swirled with possibilities. She wondered if she would end up being forced to become an OC enforcer or if she could hide her ability to neutralize aequitas enchantments from Morgan. The doorbell rang and Morgan went to answer it. A thin woman in her early thirties stepped into the living room. She had frizzy red hair, intense blue eyes, and barely restrained power hummed from her body as if ready to explode at any moment.

"This is Jennifer," Morgan said. "Jennifer, this is Josephine."

"Nice to meet you," Jennifer said.

"You're a category six," Josephine said.

Jennifer turned to fix Morgan with a questioning look. "She knows?"

"Yes."

"You are correct. I'm an OC enforcer," Rachel's disquieting, blue gaze focused on Josephine.

Something about Rachel was deeply disturbing and it wasn't just the intense power. Josephine wished she knew for sure what the source of this intuitive warning came from but she had learned through her life to trust her instincts. She dreaded the claro mentis enchantment she would be forced to endure and wished there was a way to halt the process.

"Sit down so we can get started," Morgan said.

"Shouldn't we discuss things first?" Josephine said.

"There's nothing to discuss," Morgan said.

"What if you aren't able to sever my connection with Gary?"

"With Jennifer's help, the claro mentis enchantment will definitely be successful," Morgan said.

He pulled out a wooden wand with a gold handle engraved with rune-like symbols. Jennifer wordlessly took out a similar wand.

"Close your eyes and relax. If you don't, this process will be more difficult for you," Morgan said.

Josephine reluctantly closed her eyes but knew this would not be a pleasant experience. Her head began to pound with pressure and an overwhelming dizziness tore through her. The pressure in her temples quickly escalated and she clutched the cushions of the couch as hot shards of pain rushed through her body. The temperature in the room plummeted and she could feel cold moisture pressing against her skin. She opened her eyes to find that it was gently snowing in the room. Morgan's and Jennifer's eyes were glowing with a bright, golden luminescence. Their brows were furrowed with concentration and the same gold light spilled from the tips of their wands which they had pointed at Josephine. She squeezed her eyes shut and instructed herself to relax but it was hopeless. The dizziness and pain were so overwhelming that she longed to pass out. Soon, she got her wish. Josephine found herself floating several feet above her body a short while later. Her consciousness felt restricted and she couldn't control her movements. She was floating helplessly in the air watching Morgan and Jennifer continue to perform the claro mentis and snow gently falling from the ceiling. Oddly enough, Josephine's body was sitting straight up and her eyes were open and vacant.

"The link with Gary must remain in place," Josephine's authoritative voice boomed from several locations in the room.

Josephine realized at this point that her subconscious had taken over and that she was somehow able to retain her awareness of the surroundings.

"Stop resisting us," Morgan said intently. "You're only making it harder on yourself."

"I won't let you into Josephine's mind," Josephine's voice boomed throughout the room. "The link must remain in place until the serial killer is found and locked away."

"I will find the killer. You must sever your link with Gary," Morgan said forcefully.

"The killer must be stopped."

"I will stop him but you're hindering my investigation. You must allow me to sever your connection with Gary."

"No, you are not powerful enough. If I let you work on your own, Josephine will end up dead. Only her connection with Gary can save her." Josephine slowly rose from her chair and her vacant gaze remained fixed on nothing although she faced Morgan.

He scowled at her and moved his wand so that it remained pointed at her chest.

"Sit down," he ordered.

A powerful dampening field quickly formed around Josephine. The claro mentis enchantment was only partially established and would break if they didn't strengthen the spell enough to compensate.

"Stop resisting us or we will have to bind Josephine's power," Morgan ordered.

"You can bind her power but you can't bind mine," Josephine's voice boomed in a threatening tone. "I will make you very sorry if you take such a course of action."

Morgan's body began to shake with exertion and the golden glow at the tip of his wand dimmed. He breathed heavily and seemed to gather more strength because the golden luminescence flared back to its former bright glow once again. Jennifer's hand trembled as she continued her work. A tremendous flow of power streamed from her body with such potent force that Josephine was surprised it didn't completely dissolve the dampening field that protected her body. Josephine realized that she was a lot stronger than she had ever imagined if her subconscious could ward off two enforcers like this; especially when one of them was a category six like herself.

"I don't think we can do this," Jennifer murmured.

"Don't stop," Morgan said intently. "We must sever their link."

"This is hopeless."

"Be quiet," Morgan said sternly.

Jennifer sighed loudly and her arm continued to tremble. Morgan pulled out another wand and activated a powerful telekinetic spell at Josephine which ripped a sizeable tear in the dampening field. Before he could make any progress, the dampening field quickly strengthened and prevented him from deepening the connection to her mind. Morgan's body slowly lifted into the air until he was hovering about a foot above the floor.

"Put me down," Morgan snarled.

"If you don't stop helping the serial killer, you will be sorry," Josephine's voice boomed at him.

"I'm trying to catch the killer – not help him, you idiot!"

"If you don't stop helping the serial killer, I will make you suffer. Stop performing the claro mentis now."

Morgan glared at her with fury but the glow at the tip of his wand and his eyes quickly died away. Jennifer also stopped her efforts and an expression of relief dominated her face. Morgan's body slowly lowered to the floor.

"You'll pay for this," Morgan said.

"If you let the killer get to Josephine, I will make you suffer," Josephine's authoritative voice echoed eerily throughout the room.

Morgan blanched but quickly hid his startled reaction. Josephine's consciousness abruptly returned to her body and her knees crashed to the floor. She desperately grabbed the edge of the armchair to her right to keep from falling flat on her face.

"Oh my God," she said.

She leaned against the sofa because her body felt so weak at the moment. She remained in her kneeling position clutching the armchair until her strength began to return. She slowly lifted herself into a standing position and saw Morgan scowling at her. It would probably be best if she feigned complete ignorance.

"Did you sever the connection with Gary?" Josephine asked.

"No, I didn't," Morgan said frostily.

"What happened?" Josephine asked.

"I changed my mind," Morgan said abruptly. "I decided after some careful thought that it may be in our best interest to keep your connection with Gary in place."

"Really?" Josephine asked.

She glanced at Jennifer and could see that she looked surprised by this revelation as well. Jennifer quickly hid her surprise and looked stoically at Josephine with her intense, blue eyes.

"Yes," Morgan said. "Your subconscious can lend extra help during our investigation. Yours seems to be more stable than most people's and it can perform magic a lot better than anyone I've met. We may need the help if the serial killer catches us off guard."

"Okay," Josephine said.

"You may go to the gym with your friends now, if you wish," Morgan said.

Josephine bit back a scathing remark that would probably make him even more obnoxious than he was currently behaving. It was almost like being in house arrest. She had no privacy and couldn't run her life the way she wanted to. He reminded her of a pesky mosquito that flew too quickly to swat unless you let it sting you. She would be so glad once she was rid of Morgan. Josephine called her friends and she drove them down to the gym with Morgan positioned in the front passenger seat. She had wanted him to sit in the back but he'd insisted that he couldn't protect her as well and had refused to comply with her wishes. Jennifer had left without saying a word. Josephine walked over to the ab cruncher machine and began her workout routine. Alice and Helen chose the two machines on either side of her. Alice half-heartedly pushed on the weights but Helen wasn't even pretending. Helen was lounging in the leg extension chair watching the other gym members exercise.

227

"Oh my God!" Alice exclaimed.

Josephine hadn't realized how stressed she was until she jumped at her friend's unexpected show of surprise and she almost lost her grip on the handles of the weight machine. Josephine brought herself back to the beginning position and slid her gaze over to her friend.

"What is it?" Josephine asked.

"Spot's working out across the room," Alice said.

"Dale and I have an understanding. We've decided not to antagonize each other anymore," Josephine said.

"Really?" Alice said. "I'm surprised to hear that. You sounded like you weren't going to take him up on his offer of a truce the last time you talked about him."

"My life is too complicated without making new enemies. I have a serial killer to catch and an enforcer breathing down my neck," Josephine said. "I'd like to kick Morgan's ass and shove him down a flight of stairs."

"You're awful violent today," Alice teased. "I think you need to drink less coffee."

"Coffee is what keeps me sane in this crazy world."

"Yes, coffee is known for its calming effect," Alice said flippantly.

Dale caught sight of them and waved. Josephine smiled and waved back. She resumed her work on the ab cruncher even as she mulled over how strange it felt to make such a civil gesture to Dale. It felt counteractive to her instincts to be friendly to him although she only had a small desire to toss a jinx at him. She was definitely making good progress in regards to her feelings for him. Josephine finished the set and began her resting period. She liked to do three sets on each machine because that required less moving around. She glanced behind her and saw Morgan talking on his cell phone across the room. His gaze was fixed in her general direction but he looked to be engrossed in a conversation. Josephine wondered what was being discussed.

"How long do you think it will take for the enforcers to find the serial killer?" Josephine asked.

"I don't think it will take long at all. Enforcers have a vast array of magical tools at their disposal," Helen said.

"That doesn't mean they'll be able to track down a serial killer," Alice said derisively. "Look at how Morgan's doing. We've already seen him screw up a claro mentis."

"You said it takes years of psychiatric practice to perfect that enchantment," Helen said.

"Enforcers have to go through a two year training course and continue their practice for five additional years. If Morgan is the best that the MEA has to offer then I don't have too much confidence in their competency," Alice said.

"Me neither," Josephine said. "The Magical Enforcement Agency is supposed to train their field agents for the highest caliber of work and provide the best equipment. I'm certainly starting to have doubts about them."

Morgan ended his conversation and pocketed his phone. His gaze honed in on Josephine and she stiffened reflexively. She never felt comfortable being the object of his attention even if he was here to protect her. He'd already noticed that her aequitas enchantment had failed. She fervently hoped she could hide the fact that she knew how to disarm the aequitas enchantment intentionally because if she couldn't, he would force her to enroll in the OC enforcement program. It sounded like a nightmare. If she became an OC enforcer, she'd never be able to retire. Sometimes, it really sucked to be a category six wizard.

Chapter 18

Josephine quickly took in her surroundings as she abruptly found herself standing at Siesta Key beach facing the gently lapping waves. It was early in the evening and the sun had set. The night was rapidly approaching and she'd somehow ended up here. She knew that she must have slipped into a fugue state and her subconscious had taken over. It had brought her here for some inexplicable reason. Hardly anyone occupied the beach at this point. Josephine weaved as dizziness crashed into her body like a physical force that threatened to knock her off her feet. She stumbled and abruptly left her body so that she was floating about a dozen feet behind herself. She tried to get back but had no control of her etheric body at this point except to turn her gaze.

She watched helplessly as her body slowly stepped towards the edge of the water. Her body stopped walking as soon as her feet reached the ocean waves. Josephine's arms raised and her subconscious connected with the vortex. She watched in astonishment as unimaginable power flooded through her body. It was disheartening to experience this lack of control. The vortex turned an angry shade of red and a violent wind whipped through the beach.

"What are you doing?" Morgan stepped into view wearing black pants and a black silk collared shirt.

"Leave me alone," Josephine's voice drifted from many directions and echoed eerily.

"You need to tell me what you're doing," Morgan said forcefully. "This is what the serial killer does. Are you the serial killer?"

Josephine's head turned and she was shocked to see that her face was transformed to look like Brenda Kirkland. Spittle dribbled from the corner of her mouth and her eyes conveyed madness.

"You will be healed once I have accomplished my mission. You will learn to repent," Brenda said.

"Why have you changed your face? You look and sound like Brenda," Morgan said.

"You may be left behind when the rapture comes but you will learn from Jesus and you will be healed," Brenda said.

"Do you think you're Brenda?"

"I am Josephine," Brenda said.

She turned back to face the vortex and began creating an enchantment within its massive depths.

"You're performing similar magic to the serial killer. Why?" Morgan said forcefully. He regarded her intently and waited for an answer. When none was forthcoming, he took a couple of steps back and snapped, "You will answer my questions or I will stop you from doing whatever it is you're doing."

A powerful dampening field popped into existence around Josephine's body. She had never seen one created so quickly. Morgan immediately began to work on dissipating it.

"You must be the serial killer. You must be stopped," Morgan said.

"I am not a killer!" Brenda screamed and whirled to confront him. Her crazed eyes glowed with an eerie red light. "You will be cleansed!"

She brought her arm up and shot out a powerful telekinetic wave at Morgan which he managed to deflect. He immediately connected with the power vortex and began to create his own dampening field.

"You will be cleansed!" Brenda screamed.

Josephine's mind whirled with confusion and terror as she watched Brenda fire another telekinetic wave of energy at Morgan. He brought up a shield but it collapsed under the attack. He was no match for Brenda. Josephine wondered why her subconscious had cast an illusion of Brenda onto her body. It was strange. She could see now why Morgan had wanted to disconnect her link with Gary. The subconscious was something that couldn't be predicted. It was a wild card and it was powerful. Morgan brought up another shield but it didn't completely protect him from the next blast. He was thrown backward and fell to the sandy ground. Brenda took several steps toward him and fired another bolt of telekinetic energy. He deflected the attack but he really looked exhausted. He wouldn't be able to fend her off for much longer.

"Stop what you're doing!" Josephine shouted.

Brenda flinched and threw her a troubled look.

"You can't tell me what to do," Brenda said with confusion.

"I am you!"

"No, we are separate from each other. I take control when you are weak and in danger," Brenda said.

"Why do you look like Brenda?" Morgan asked.

Brenda's attention snapped back to him and her crazed eyes narrowed into angry slits.

"You will be cleansed!" she screeched.

233

She launched another volley of telekinetic power which Morgan partially fended off.

"I've had enough!" he said icily.

A blinding white light erupted all around them and Josephine opened her eyes to discover it was early in the morning and she was laying in her bed. She abruptly sat up and checked the time. It was only shortly after six in the morning. What had just happened to her? She sighed with relief when she realized she'd only had a nightmare. Unfortunately, she had the disturbing sense of Morgan's presence as though he occupied the room with her. Josephine shoved the sheets aside and slipped out of bed. Her door opened unexpectedly and Morgan stood there in his black outfit.

"You had an interesting dream," Morgan said.

"What?" Josephine froze and fear took hold of her.

He'd somehow been snooping in her dreams. It must have been a somnium inviso enchantment. That was a spell used in psychiatric therapy and sometimes criminal investigations if a warrant was issued.

"I hope you got a warrant before you decided to invade my dreams," Josephine said tightly.

"Of course I've got a warrant," Morgan said and reached into his pocket to pull out a neatly folded document. "This is just a copy so you can have it."

"Thank you for your generosity," Josephine said snidely.

She snatched it from his hand and glanced over the legal document. Unfortunately, she could tell it was probably legitimate.

"Why was it necessary to intrude on my privacy like that?" Josephine asked after a lengthy silence.

"A somnium inviso enchantment allows peripheral access to the subconscious. If I perform the spell several more times, it will be a lot easier to do the claro mentis enchantment which will allow me to sever your link with Gary."

"Why did you lie about changing your mind and deciding to keep the link when you had no intention of doing so?"

"Your subconscious may have noticed the somnium inviso enchantment if it was aware that I still intended on severing its link to Gary. It's imperative that you regain full control. You're a liability with your subconscious running loose like it's doing," Morgan said.

"Its goal is to protect me from the serial killer. I think that's a benefit."

"It's not natural for the subconscious to be fractured enough to control your conscious mind and put you in those fugue states. It's creating a pressure on your mind and body that isn't healthy."

"I seriously doubt you're concerned over my wellbeing," Josephine said haughtily.

"I'm more concerned about catching the serial killer and making sure you don't screw up this investigation with uncontrollable behavior," Morgan said impatiently. "Is that what you want to hear?"

"I want you to leave me alone and get the hell out of my home!" Josephine shouted.

"That's not going to happen," Morgan said coolly.

Josephine sighed with frustration and turned her back on him. She wished her subconscious would take over and slap him around a little. Unfortunately, that wouldn't help her situation. She didn't need any more complications in her life. Josephine turned around and discovered Morgan was quietly watching her. She walked briskly past him and out of the room. She made her way into the kitchen and quickly set up the coffee maker. After finishing this task, she took a quick shower and waited for her friends to arrive. When they all settled at the living room table with their cups of coffee, Josephine launched into the unsettling experience she'd had regarding Morgan invading her dream. Helen kept shifting her gaze nervously to take in Morgan's reaction but he stood impassively with a mug of coffee in his hand as if nothing out of the ordinary had occurred.

Alice leveled him a dirty look. "You should be ashamed of yourself. That's an invasive spell."

"It's the only way I'll be able to successfully cast the claro mentis spell on Josephine and free her of the link to Gary's subconscious," Morgan said.

Alice rolled her eyes with exasperation but let the subject drop. Josephine wished the police or the enforcers would catch the serial killer so her life could return to normal. She hated feeling trapped and watched like this. It felt like everything she did was under scrutiny.

"I must warn you that he'll be able to pick up some of your stray thoughts. It's one of the side effects of the somnium inviso enchantment," Alice said regretfully.

"He can read my mind?" Josephine asked.

"He'll pick up some stray thoughts but not really read you," Alice explained.

"Do you have something to hide?" Morgan said with what appeared to be a forced casual air.

"Of course not!" Josephine said indignantly.

She tried to squash the rise of panic that threatened to consume her mind as she drank some more coffee. She couldn't let him know about her ability to deactivate the aequitas enchantment. If he found out, her life would be ruined. She'd be forced to go through an intense training camp for enforcers which would be extremely arduous and stressful. If she didn't pass, she'd probably be sent to prison. Once she did pass the training, she would be like a secret agent. She would never be able to relax without worrying about when her next mission would be foisted upon her. She couldn't stand the thought of living like that. Josephine took another swallow of coffee and tried burying her thoughts. The more upset she was, the stronger she broadcasted telepathically. She needed to control her thoughts and keep herself as calm as possible.

Morgan's gaze locked onto hers and a hint of a cold smile curved his lips. She wondered if he'd already found out what she could do and was just biding his time before he reported her to the MEA. She dragged her attention back to her friends and forced an awkward monologue from her lips. Helen was only too happy to pretend everything was fine and talk about mundane topics. Alice played along but occasionally threw disapproving glares at Morgan. The enforcer's cell rang and he answered it. His eyes widened in surprise at whatever was being said and he swiftly stepped out of the room.

"I wonder what's going on," Alice said with obvious amusement. "I've never seen him react like that before."

"Must be something serious," Helen said dourly. "Whatever the news is, it can't be good."

"Not for him anyway," Alice said snidely.

When Morgan returned to the kitchen, tension dominated his face.

"You two will have to leave now. Josephine and I are needed at the police station," Morgan said brusquely.

"I haven't finished my coffee!" Alice said indignantly.

"The serial killer just murdered someone in Seattle, Washington," Morgan said.

"How can that be?" Alice asked.

"Obviously, he must have taken a plane. That's the only way he could have gotten there fast enough after the last time he connected with the power vortex at Siesta Key," Morgan said.

"Why do you and I need to go to the police station?" Josephine asked.

"You and Gary will look over the evidence together," Morgan said. "Gary's subconscious mind should be able to pick up things that his conscious mind hasn't."

"Why do you need me there?" Josephine asked.

"Since you're linked, it's more likely that his subconscious will act if you're there working with him," Morgan said impatiently. "Do I have to explain everything to you?"

"It was just question."

"You two need to get moving." Morgan shot Alice and Helen severe looks and they quickly excused themselves.

"I hope you're happy," Josephine snapped. "You're alienating my friends."

"We're on important police business."

"I'm an old, retired woman. I don't work for the police. I'm merely a part-time consultant."

"You have the body of a woman in her early thirties. Don't whine to me about being old and retired," Morgan said bluntly. "Get your lazy ass out of that chair and into the car."

Josephine crossed her arms across her chest and glared defiantly at him. "I will go when I'm ready. I haven't even finished my coffee."

Before she could react, the mug flew from her grasp and smashed into the wall, shattering into a myriad of pieces.

"You're finished now," Morgan said.

Josephine's head pounded as she stood up from her chair. The temperature seemed to plummet as chills danced along her skin. She headed for the front door and Morgan quickly followed. The pressure in her skull abated somewhat but threatened to explode at any moment. Her body was tense and she couldn't calm herself. She wanted to jinx Morgan so badly she could almost taste it. When they arrived at the police station, Gary was already waiting for them in one of the waiting rooms with Jennifer, the enforcer currently assigned to him. Plastic baggies spread across the table as Jennifer observed Gary from one corner of the room. She was leaning slightly against the wall with her arms crossed over her chest. Her disturbing, blue eyes were unreadable but her overall body language suggested impatience. She nodded silently in acknowledgment at Morgan as he entered the room.

"What have you learned so far?" Morgan asked.

"Not much," Jennifer said. She pulled out a notepad and read some notes. "This is the same information that he picked up before which is next to nothing."

"Josephine, sit down beside him," Morgan instructed.

Josephine wordlessly complied with his instructions and Morgan grabbed one of the bags of evidence. He tossed it in front of the two of them.

"You will both work on this piece of evidence at the same time," Morgan said.

"Why did you choose that one?" Gary asked.

"It was a random selection," Morgan said impatiently. "Are you going to give me a hard time about this?"

"No," Gary said warily.

Jennifer sat down in a chair behind them with her notepad ready. Josephine opened her second sight and sought out any trace energies in the unicorn figurine which was sealed in a plastic, evidence bag. She wondered why the police had deemed this appropriate for collection. It didn't contain anything she could read. She glanced at Gary and he shook his head.

"You're not trying hard enough," Morgan chastised them.

"We're doing the best we can," Josephine said moodily.

"Obviously, it's not hard enough because you're failing to come up with any clues."

Josephine whirled around and glared at him. "You're such a jerk. I can't come up with something if there's nothing to read."

"There's always something." Morgan's eyes suddenly flared with a bright, golden light.

The pressure in Josephine's head exploded and agony ripped through her body. She realized now why Morgan had wanted her here with Gary. He wanted to prod her subconscious into taking over. A frigid wind whipped through the room and Josephine abruptly found herself outside her body and watching the scene unfold as a helpless observer. Josephine's body slowly stood and regarded Morgan impassively.

"You need to read the evidence," Morgan said forcefully. "Find the killer before he finds you!"

Gary's eyes had also glazed over but he remained seated and staring straight ahead.

"Read the evidence!" Morgan shouted.

Jennifer gazed warily at Josephine but her pen still rested on top of the notepad, ready to take down any useful information that came up. Obviously, Morgan and Jennifer had planned this incident to occur.

"I will assist you," Josephine's voice echoed from various parts of the room.

The bags of evidence shifted then lifted several feet into the air. Josephine extended her hands toward them with her vacant eyes staring in that general direction. A heavy silence encompassed the room as everyone waited for her to speak. Josephine wondered how long she'd be trapped in this fugue state.

"The killer is someone who knows Gary," Josephine's authoritative voice materialized from many different directions. "He has known Gary for many years. He has been planning on killing him for several months now. He cast a pertorqueo sententia enchantment on Gary many years ago and activates the spell in his mind on a regular basis."

"The killer has been thinking of murdering Gary for several months?" Morgan asked sharply. "Why has he waited?"

"I don't know. I'm not picking up much. There isn't much to read. That's all I can tell you other than the fact that the killer is a life-long friend."

Josephine's hands were still poised over the table as if preparing to play the piano. The evidence bags abruptly dropped and Morgan's clothes disintegrated into a fine black powder. His cell phone, wallet, and magical tools abruptly clattered to the floor. He gaped at Josephine who still had her back turned to him. Jennifer's notepad slipped from her grasp as she ogled her naked colleague.

"A small price to pay for your insolence," Josephine's smug voice drifted from all around them.

241

She abruptly returned to her body and braced herself against the table to keep from falling. Jennifer glanced at her appraisingly then returned her attention to Morgan who was glaring irritably at Josephine. Without warning, the door burst open and a police uniform hurtled into the room. Morgan clothed himself with the pants, shirt and jacket as the door slammed shut on its own. He picked up the magical tools and shoved them in his pants and jacket pockets. Gary shifted uneasily in his chair as he silently took in the situation.

"Gary, do you have friends who you've known for years living nearby?" Morgan asked in a surprisingly stoic tone.

"No," Gary said.

"You used to live in Washington before you and your brother moved to Florida," Morgan said. "Do you keep in contact with any of them?"

"Yes, why?"

"What are their names?" Morgan asked.

"Why do you want to know?" Gary asked warily.

"One of them is probably the killer," Morgan said in a chilling tone. "We need to know who they are."

"One of them is Tim and the other is Frank."

"I'll need their addresses." Morgan began to pace the room as he jotted notes in his notepad.

"I don't have them memorized," Gary said hesitantly.

"We're all going to take a trip down to your apartment then," Morgan said. "Jennifer, why don't you take care of replacing the evidence bags while I take everyone to Gary's apartment for more information."

"Okay." Jennifer slipped the notepad into her pants pocket and stood up.

"Let's go," Morgan said.

Josephine and Gary followed him out to his car.

"It may not be a friend of mine. It may just be someone who's been stalking me," Gary said.

"Unlikely," Morgan said. "It's go to be a friend."

"Why?"

"Because your subconscious mind wouldn't be so damaged otherwise. It's a personal betrayal to have a friend doing this to you. It's the only reason your mind would be reacting this way."

"Don't you think it's possible his subconscious is trying to adapt to the spell that's controlling him? It must be horribly invasive," Josephine said.

"I don't think it would be enough to fracture his mind like this."

"My mind isn't fractured," Gary protested.

"Sure it is," Morgan said in a matter-of-fact tone.

When they reached Gary's apartment, they stepped inside and Gary got Tim's and Frank's addresses and phone numbers.

"Thank you," Morgan said crisply as he jotted the information down in his notepad.

"I think you're wrong about this," Gary said.

"You don't want to admit that your friend is a killer but that's what's probably happening here. You heard what Josephine said. The killer has known you for many years," Morgan said. "How strong a wizard is Tim?"

"He's a category two."

"What about Frank?" Morgan said.

"He's a category five."

"It's probably Frank then."

"Why do you say that?"

"Because the killer is a category six. He's extremely powerful and it would be easier for him to pretend to be a category five rather than a two. Unfortunately, we can't rule out Tim completely until we've got Frank."

"What are you going to do?" Gary asked nervously.

"I'm not going to do anything. I'm just going to send my findings to the MEA," Morgan said.

"Can't you wait until we know more?" Gary said.

"No, I can't wait," Morgan said stonily. "If you'll excuse me, I'm going to make a phone call."

He whipped out his cell phone and walked away from them to afford himself some privacy. Josephine patted Gary on the shoulder sympathetically.

"It'll be okay. I'm sure your friends aren't killers," she said.

"The MEA will send enforcers to harass them," Gary said. "They don't deserve to be treated like that."

"Everything will be fine," Josephine said and wished she could believe that.

Morgan finished his conversation and pocketed his cell. Josephine strode over to him as her mind suddenly glommed onto an idea.

"Don't you think it's odd the serial killer has been killing in Florida for so long when he really lives in Seattle?" Josephine asked.

"The murders occur about a month apart on average so it's very conceivable that the killer flew down here on short trips when he committed the murders," Morgan said.

"That's a lot of trouble to go through. It sounds pretty far fetched to me."

"The killer is very calculating. What better way to throw off the police then to choose victims clear across the country?" Morgan said pointedly.

"Why are you so determined to believe Tim or Frank is the killer?"

"Why are you so convinced it isn't them?" Morgan said coolly. "Do you fancy yourself a detective now? Do you think you can solve this case by yourself?"

Josephine turned away from him and stared at the wall. If she argued with him, it would only frustrate her so she decided to just ignore him for the moment. She wondered how she could possibly track down the real killer. Too bad Morgan was in charge of the investigation. Of course, Alex and Jake were also working on the case but didn't have any further clues to ponder over.

Chapter 19

A pile of leather-bound books lay at Josephine's feet as she stood in the library of her two-story house frantically searching for information. Once again, Josephine became aware of the fact that she was dreaming. She'd performed an enchantment on herself just before going to bed to aid in lucid dreaming. She needed to maintain complete control of her mind if she wanted to keep Morgan from successfully performing the somnium inviso enchantment. Josephine could no longer remember what she was searching for or why she was living in her old house again. She focused on the present and kept a vigilant eye out for Morgan. She had sensed his presence earlier and blocked him. She could feel it happening again now. Josephine brought up a mental block but this time, Morgan was more persistent. She resisted his efforts for as long as possible but wasn't strong enough to prevent the somnium inviso enchantment from taking hold. Morgan materialized behind the massive, oak desk a short distance in front of her. He was reclined way back in the black, fake-leather chair with his feet propped up on the polished surface of her desk.

A duplicate Josephine materialized on the other side of the desk. She was facing Morgan so Josephine couldn't see her face but she wondered if she looked like Brenda. Morgan smirked at the duplicate Josephine. Suddenly, a metal cage came into existence around him and the desk. Morgan's amused smile didn't waver.

"You're a fool if you think you can trap me here," he said.

"I can do anything to you," the duplicate Josephine said.

Morgan's feet dropped away from the desk as he straightened in the black chair and leveled a stern look at her.

"You're sadly mistaken if you think you can intimidate me," he said frostily.

He stood up and made to pass through the bars as if they weren't there but his body met solidly against them. His expression transformed into surprise then anger.

"Nice trick," he said.

"Thank you," the duplicate Josephine said.

Gary stepped into the room with a frantic look on his face.

"We're all going to die," he said.

"Everything is fine," the duplicate Josephine said.

"No, the killer is coming."

"You should listen to him. Let me help you," Morgan said in a reasonable tone.

Josephine cautiously approached them and Morgan turned to glance appraisingly at her.

"There are two of you?" he asked.

The duplicate Josephine turned to look at her and Josephine could see that her eyes were black as though her pupils had completely dilated and swallowed the irises whole. Apprehension made Josephine hesitate as she drew closer. She wondered if her subconscious was negative or if it was a blend of her subconscious and Gary's. The link may have more of an effect on her mind than she realized.

"We must protect ourselves," the duplicate Josephine said authoritatively. "Morgan is helping the killer."

"Why do you say that?" Josephine asked.

"He's trying to make us weak. We must keep our link to Gary or we'll be vulnerable. There is strength in numbers," the duplicate said.

"We can't be fragmented like this. It would be best if the link was broken," Josephine said.

"You should listen to her," Morgan said.

"No!" the duplicate shouted.

"We need to find the killer," Gary said anxiously.

The duplicate held her right palm out toward Morgan and he vanished along with the cage. She turned to Josephine and regarded her with desperation.

"He suspects you can deactivate the aequitas enchantment. He's been using psychometry to try to find proof that you're able to do it. Once he knows for sure, he'll report you to the MEA and you'll have to go to the training camp. Your life will be ruined," she said.

"The killer will get to us first," Gary interjected.

"Why are you telling me this?" Josephine asked. "There's nothing I can do to stop him from finding out about me."

"You must guard your thoughts well. Don't think about aequitas enchantments or worry about it or you will expel energy which can be read through psychometry," the duplicate warned. "I'm afraid it may be too late. He may already know."

The duplicate's eyes widened with fear as Josephine sensed Morgan's presence once again. A moment later, he appeared in front of them.

"Hello, again," he said smarmily. "Did you miss me?"

"Not especially," Josephine said.

"You have interesting dreams," Morgan said.

"You will not sever my link with Gary," the duplicate Josephine said.

"That's not your decision to make," Morgan said forcefully.

The scene abruptly changed. The duplicate was now driving Josephine's car with Josephine seated in the passenger seat while Gary and Morgan were tucked away in the back. Their car was speeding on a freeway with myriads of abandoned cars and trucks pulled over on the sides with emergency lights blinking. Pieces of shredded tire, twisted metal fenders, windshields and other items lay strewn across the road. The duplicate Josephine had to turn sharply every few seconds to avoid the various hazards. Dark, writhing storm clouds completely obliterated the sky and unleashed a series of lightning spears. Josephine clutched the door handle for support as the car continued to shift wildly from one lane to another. Adrenaline surged through her body as a couple of lightning strikes stabbed the road nearby. Thunder crashed violently and the car thumped as the duplicate Josephine accidentally ran over a blown tired. A woman suddenly appeared in the middle of the road running madly towards one side to avoid being hit. Josephine abruptly awakened from her dream. She sat up in her bed with the morning light sifting in through the curtains of her window.

She took several deep breaths and tried to calm herself. Her heart pounded wildly in her chest and adrenaline still pumped through her body. She couldn't believe what a vivid and disturbing dream she'd just endured. The door swung open and Morgan stepped into the room garbed in his typical black clothing. A cold, unyielding expression dominated his face as he gestured at the door to close it telekinetically while keeping his gaze locked onto Josephine's.

"What do you think you're doing?" Josephine said with outrage.

Morgan wordlessly stared her down as a golden luminescence spilled from his eyes. Josephine's head pounded with sudden pressure and the room seemed to rock violently. She was tossed from her body as her subconscious took control in order to defend itself against the claro mentis enchantment. Morgan grasped a wand in his left hand which spat gold sparks and light as the stored power became active. He had raised a dampening field and was quickly strengthening it; however, he was slowly being lifted into the air with psychokinesis as Josephine's body stood up from the bed and a frigid blast of air tore through the room.

"You can't stop me this time," Morgan said with quiet resolve.

His brows furrowed in concentration as he continued to point the wand at her. His body swung backward and smacked against the wall. He gasped in surprise but he must have managed to maintain his concentration because the enchantment remained active. An eerie gold radiance still flowed from his eyes and the tip of his wand.

"I'll kill you," Josephine's hardened voice echoed from many different directions.

Josephine struggled to take control of her body but she was being held a short distance away. She had no idea if her subconscious was capable of carrying out its threat but had no intention of finding out. Morgan completely ignored her and continued with his enchantment.

"If you don't stop what you're doing, I'll kill you," Josephine's powerful voice erupted loudly from various angles of the room.

Morgan was once again tossed back against the wall. He managed to keep his grip on his wand and the enchantment remained active. His feet dangled helplessly above the floor but his dampening field had strengthened a bit more and he was slowly lowering. Josephine could see with her second sight that Morgan had finally succeeded in connecting their minds. Josephine abruptly found herself back in her body and slumped against the bed. Dizziness and chaos danced across her mind as memories flashed randomly. Abruptly, the uncomfortable sensations vanished and Josephine pushed herself back up to her feet. She sensed a distinct absence in her mind and realized that her connection with Gary had been severed. The gold light in Morgan's wand and eyes winked out of existence as a superior smile curved his lips.

"I was successful in removing the link," he said.

"Good for you," Josephine bit out.

"You should be grateful. Your subconscious was blended with Gary's via the link so it may not have been making you behave in your best interests," Morgan said.

"What gives you the right to barge into my bedroom like that? The last time I checked, this was a free country."

"These are extraordinary circumstances. Your mind was being damaged by the link. I had to fix it," Morgan said coolly.

"Now that you've done your work, you can get the hell out of my room, jackass," Josephine snapped.

"All right," Morgan said with a trace of irritation. "But I'm leaving because I choose to do so."

He walked out of the room and Josephine unleashed a burst of telekinetic energy which slammed the door shut behind him. She paced in her room for several moments, wishing she didn't have to come out and face the world. She didn't want Morgan in her life anymore. He didn't feel like he offered any sort of protection against the serial killer. He was a bully and ineffectual even if he had managed to sever the link between herself and Gary. Josephine forced herself to leave her room and start a pot of coffee. Morgan was sitting on her couch talking on his cell phone. He pointedly ignored her as she passed him by. Josephine took a long, hot shower then dressed. Helen arrived a short while later. She seemed taken aback to find Morgan there. Gary joined them for coffee a short while later.

"What are you doing here?" Helen asked.

"Gary and I have to stay together. Jennifer and Morgan will be watching over us and protecting us from the serial killer," Josephine said with scalding sarcasm.

"Where's Jennifer?"

"She's in the other guest room. Morgan spent the night on the couch where he belongs," Josephine said dryly.

She noticed that Morgan was speaking in hushed tones now over his cell and that he vacated the room for more privacy. As if anyone cared about whatever he was saying.

"What an intrusion on your privacy," Helen said. "I don't know how you can stand it."

"I don't either," Josephine said.

"I felt it when he severed our link," Gary said.

"I knew you would," Josephine said.

"What happened?" Helen asked.

Josephine glanced at the living room to be sure Morgan was still out of ear shot then quickly relayed last night's events.

"That's terrible!" Helen exclaimed. "What a terrible violation! He should be punished! I'm sure it can't be legal."

"I'm afraid it is," Gary said sadly.

"The laws need to be changed. Enforcers shouldn't be able to take such actions without worrying about consequences," Helen said passionately.

They lapsed into an uncomfortable silence. Josephine pondered her situation and wondered why she was so unlucky. Abruptly, she realized Alice was extremely late and commented on this observation.

"How strange," Helen said. "It's really unlike her."

"Maybe we should call her condo and see what's wrong," Josephine said.

She dialed Alice's number and she didn't answer. Josephine replaced the receiver with a concerned frown.

"What is it?" Morgan entered the kitchen with an intense, troubled look on his face.

"Alice is late and she's not answering her phone," Josephine said.

"We should make sure she's all right," Morgan said sharply.

"The serial killer is still in Seattle, isn't he?" Josephine asked.

"Yes, he is." Morgan relaxed a little at this reminder but an underlying tension dominated his features.

The doorbell rang and Josephine was relieved to find Alice had arrived.

"Come in. We were worried about you," Josephine said.

"I'm sorry about that. I was watching the news and I wanted to catch all the important details. You and Helen will want to know about this," Alice said.

Morgan stiffened visibly and his jaw clenched.

"You're probably worried about the latest developments," Alice taunted him.

"The MEA is working on the problem," he said tersely.

"What's going on?" Josephine asked.

She shut the door when Alice stepped into the room and followed her to the kitchen.

"The killer has tapped into the vortex in Seattle, Washington three times yesterday," Alice said as she poured herself a mug of coffee.

"Really?" Josephine was surprised to hear this. She would expect the serial killer would start to become more cautious now that he was closer to home.

"Yes, and knocked out practically everyone in the entire county each of the three times. The last time, eighty-nine people were killed because the knock-out spell was much stronger and disrupted the body's autonomic nervous system. Six enforcers guarding the vortex in Seattle were attacked and murdered," Alice said.

"He caught them by surprise. It won't happen again," Morgan said.

Jennifer approached them from the living room. Her intense blue eyes gauged the situation but she refrained from taking part in the conversation. She wordlessly stepped over to the coffee pot and took the last of the coffee.

"I should make some more," Josephine said in spite of the shocking news that her friend had just imparted.

"There is nothing to worry about," Morgan said.

"Why are you so tense then?" Alice asked shrewdly.

"Because the serial killer is still loose. I'm sure his days are numbered though."

"I thought you already figured out who it was," Alice said. "Wasn't it Frank? Why haven't you locked him up yet?"

"He already did," Jennifer cut in.

"What?" Josephine asked with surprise.

"Frank was put in jail yesterday afternoon. The serial killer connected with the vortex two additional times afterward which exonerated him," Jennifer said. "We have no idea who the killer is."

"Sure we do." Morgan pinned Gary with a disapproving look. "We just need to get more cooperation from Gary. Obviously, you didn't tell me all of your friends that you keep in contact with. One of them is the killer. Your subconscious knows it. That's why your mind is so stressed. One of your friends has been controlling your mind periodically throughout your life. You've been used."

Gary's eyes shifted so that he was no longer focused on anything. The temperature in the room plummeted. Morgan shifted nervously and stepped closer to Gary.

"What are you doing?" Morgan demanded.

Gary was no longer aware of anyone in the room. Josephine could tell he'd fallen into a fugue state. Morgan quickly brought up a dampening field to protect himself from magical attacks. Josephine shivered as a frigid breeze wafted over her. It was so cold now. Gary abruptly snapped out of his trance and his eyes roved through the room with disorientation.

"What happened?" he asked.

"You were in a fugue state," Josephine said.

"What did I do?" Gary asked.

"Nothing," Josephine said.

"You made it really cold in here," Alice interjected.

"This is exactly why it was necessary to sever the link between you and Gary," Morgan said to Josephine. "There's no predicting what can happen when you have a splintered subconscious."

"You certainly know how to toss around buzz words and psychobabble," Alice said.

"I do have a general education in the psychology field as do all enforcers," Morgan said stoically.

"Why are you still in charge of this investigation when the killer lives in Seattle?" Alice asked.

"It hasn't been proven that Seattle is his home," Morgan argued. "That was based on deduction from clues that Josephine picked up at the police station and at crime scenes. It's certainly possible that the killer is trying to throw us off track by spending time in Seattle."

"Why would he do that?" Alice said.

"One reason could be to cause the MEA to relocate its enforcers. Maybe he's hoping that Josephine and Gary will no longer be guarded and thus become easy prey."

"That sounds very far fetched," Alice said in a challenging tone.

Josephine had to disagree with her friend. The serial killer possessed a cold and calculating mind. This scenario was certainly a plan that he might come up with if he wanted Josephine and Gary eliminated as threats. She wasn't about to credit Morgan verbally though.

"Maybe we should just relax and talk about something else," Helen said shakily. "I'm tired of thinking about murders."

"All right." Alice smiled tightly at her friend.

After finishing their coffee, Alice and Helen left rather than play cards. They didn't really enjoy it when Morgan was around which was another reason why Josephine wanted to kick his sorry ass out of her condo. Gary and Josephine were still seated at the table with half empty mugs of coffee. Morgan was standing nearby leaning against the kitchen counter. Jennifer was seated by herself and working on her notebook computer. Gary looked stressed and his expression guarded. He obviously wasn't in the mood to be sociable so Josephine just let the time pass.

"Whenever you two are finished, we need to report to the police station and read crime scene evidence again," Morgan said.

"It's such a waste of time. Why do you insist on making us do that?" Josephine asked.

"You've learned something new the last time we went."

"That was when I was in a fugue state because my subconscious was linked with Gary's. I no longer have that advantage. If you'll think back to this morning, you removed that advantage. I don't see why we should continue to waste our efforts," she said.

"We need to keep trying," Morgan said obstinately.

"Isn't there something else we could do instead?" Josephine asked.

"Like what?"

"I don't know."

"Then it's the police station," Morgan said.

"At least let Gary finish his coffee," Josephine said.

"I'm just about done," Gary said.

The doorbell rang and she went to answer it. Morgan was trailing close behind her. She checked the peephole first and was surprised to see Vickie Richardson. She opened the door and opened her mouth to tell her that now wasn't the time but Vickie was faster.

"I'm sorry to come in unannounced like this but I really need your help," Vickie blurted.

"Now isn't a good time," Josephine said.

"I'm sorry to interrupt. It looks like you have company. Would it be all right if we talked privately for a moment?" Vickie said.

"I recognize you from the crime photo," Morgan said abruptly. "You're Vickie Richardson."

Vickie's brown eyes locked with his. "Crime scene photo?"

"Yes, you're one of the victims of the serial killer I'm trying to catch," Morgan said. "I need you to come inside."

"You do?" Vickie asked.

"Yes, please enter."

"Can I see some I.D. first?" Vickie said politely.

Morgan impatiently whipped out his badge and showed it to her. Vickie inspected it closely before nodding.

"Okay, I'll come inside," Vickie said.

"It's actually good to see you," Morgan said. "You may be some help to us. Josephine and Gary have been reading crime scene evidence for the police in order to track down the serial killer. You're one of his victims. You may have trace energy that could be read."

"You really think so? After all this time?" Vickie asked.

"You're a category six now so you won't generate much trace energy of your own. That means you'll have less junk for Josephine and Gary to weed through. Yes, this is a great idea."

"I don't know about this," Josephine said. "The trace energy is probably degraded by now. It dissipates quickly on people."

"Not with category six wizards and sometimes traumatic events like this can create more substantial trace energies," Morgan said.

"What did you need me to do?" Vickie asked.

"Just sit down on the couch and try to relax. Josephine and Gary will try to read your energy," Morgan said.

Gary and Josephine sat down on the couch facing her. Josephine carefully scrutinized the subtle energies that drifted around Vickie. It didn't surprise her to find hardly anything there. She reached out with her mind and brushed the surface of the different strands to determine if any related to the attack that had almost killed her. It didn't take long to find the appropriate one but she wasn't sure there was enough left to read. A series of faint impressions flashed through her mind in a meaningless jumble. She focused harder and could feel the killer's general mood. He was hopeful and anticipating something. No further impressions came to her but Josephine didn't give up. She kept focused on the energy strand and went deeper. Hopefully, more information would surface.

She shivered and realized the room had grown cold. She lost her focus on the energy strand and realized Gary's mind was exploding with energy. She sensed his focus on reading Vickie but something was wrong. There were opposing forces at work in his mind; as if it was splintered and the different parts were working against each other.

"It hurts," Gary said quietly.

His brows furrowed in concentration and he squeezed his eyes shut.

"What are you seeing?" Morgan asked eagerly.

"The killer has been working hard for something," Gary said in a tight voice.

"What do you mean?"

"It's like he has a goal. It's like he's been experimenting or something." Gary groaned softly and clutched his head with both hands. A thin trail of blood trickled from his nose. One of Josephine's lamps toppled over and crashed to the floor. Jennifer and Morgan flinched but their gaze intensified on Gary.

"Keep trying," Jennifer said. "Tell us what you see."

"I see Vickie lying on the floor. The killer presses his fingers against her wrist. He's checking for a pulse and he's disappointed that she's dead. He thought she would be alive."

One of the walls pounded as thought a fist had slammed into it. The front door burst open on its own and the lights overhead intensified then returned to normal.

"Focus on the energy strand! Keep the vision in your mind," Morgan said intently. "Don't let go of it."

"I have to," Gary said.

"You need to keep focused. Don't let the vision leave. You must hang onto it," Morgan said.

"The killer is so disappointed. He'd thought he'd fixed the problem," Gary said.

"What problem? Do you know what the purpose of these murders are?"

"There's some sort of book that he found a long time ago. It gave him the idea," Gary said. "He's been trying to create the perfect enchantment."

"What will the spell do?" Morgan said.

"I don't know," Gary said tightly.

He breathed heavily and the wall pounded loudly once again. The cushion between Gary and Josephine exploded and stuffing burst into the air. Josephine screamed with surprise but Morgan and Jennifer kept their attention fixed squarely on Gary.

"Keep your focus. Hold onto the vision," Morgan said intently.

She realized that he held a metallic object in his right fist which was emitting a red luminescence. Jennifer also had one. An enchantment was enveloping Gary's mind and Josephine suspected it was some sort of mind control. The enforcers were making him keep hold of a vision that was hurting him.

"Stop it!" Vickie exclaimed and abruptly stood up from the couch.

"Sit down," Morgan shouted but he kept his gaze glued to Gary.

"What in the hell are you doing to him?" Vickie demanded.

"We're helping him to read the trace energy left by the killer. Don't impede with this process," Morgan said coldly. "If Gary loses the vision because of your actions, you will suffer the consequences."

Vickie blanched at the threat and reluctantly sat down. The cushion beside her exploded and more white stuffing blew into the air. Vickie screamed shrilly but Gary still seemed focused on the vision.

"I have to stop," Gary said.

"You can't stop. You have to go on," Morgan said forcefully. "Tell us what you see."

"The book is very important. It has lots of information. It's a diary of some sort."

"Can you see a name in the diary?" Morgan asked loudly.

"No, I can't."

"Try harder!"

"I can't see any details. It's just very important. The killer has read about the life of a wizard. I think it has something to do with the Disaster," Gary said pensively.

He shouted loudly and his body jerked as though terrible pain wracked it. He abruptly passed out. His body collapsed in an untidy heap on the floor. Vickie shot to her feet and backed away from him.

"I can't believe you couldn't sit still for a few lousy minutes," Morgan said heatedly.

The unnatural chill that permeated the room was swiftly dissipating. Josephine knelt over Gary and could see that wild energy danced across his body. It was disrupting his autonomic nervous system. She pressed her finger against his neck and could determine the pulse was weak and thready.

"We need to call an ambulance. He's dying," Josephine announced.

"You're wrong," Morgan said.

"There's some sort of spell that's wreaking havoc on his body. He may not survive," Josephine said.

She walked over to the phone and dialed 911. Once she finished with the call, she turned to find Morgan and Jennifer pointing their wands at Gary's unconscious body. An emerald green luminescence spilled from the tips of their wands onto his body. Josephine recognized the energy configuration as a general regenerative enchantment. It wouldn't be powerful enough to cure Gary but perhaps it would buy him some time.

"The spell must be a byproduct of the pertorqueo sententia enchantment. I wonder if it's possible that the wizard who did this to him made a trap that would cause this to happen if he came too close to identifying him," Josephine said musingly.

"That's exactly what this is," Morgan said.

"You knew what was happening when he wanted to stop, didn't you?" Josephine said accusingly. "You forced him to continue anyway."

"Yes, we did," Morgan said. "We needed to find the truth. Unfortunately, he succumbed to the enchantment before he could uncover enough clues for us to identify the killer."

"I didn't realize how inhuman you are," Josephine said with displeasure.

It sickened her to be in the room with Morgan and Jennifer knowing they harbored such disregard for someone's life.

"We needed to stop the killer from taking more innocent lives," Jennifer said passionately. "We were taking a risk by forcing him to hold the vision but in the end, it will help him to shake lose of the pertorqueo sententia enchantment faster. Instead of living with the vile influence of a serial killer in his mind for another two months, he may be free of it within days."

"Or he may be dead in days thanks to you and Morgan," Josephine said coolly.

"We did what had to be done. It's a difficult and thankless job being an enforcer," Jennifer said.

Vickie had remained silent and impassive during the entire exchange but she now shifted uncomfortably and cleared her throat softly.

"I think I'll be going," she said.

"You may go now but we might contact you later," Morgan said.

"Okay," Vickie said apprehensively.

Chapter 20

Morgan stood with his arms crossed over his chest in the hospital lobby radiating displeasure and impatience while Josephine sat nearby in one of the plastic chairs. Jennifer was seated beside Josephine leafing through a magazine with her foot tapping energetically in a most obnoxious and distracting way. Gary had been admitted to the emergency room over an hour ago. Josephine fervently hoped he'd recover from the ordeal he'd suffered at the hands of Morgan and Jennifer. She couldn't believe the two enforcers could be so callous with someone's well being. Josephine was harboring serious doubts about Gary's recovery after so much time had gone by without receiving any news. If anything happened to him, she planned on making sure that Morgan and Jennifer would be held accountable for their actions.

Josephine reached down and grabbed one of the parts of the newspaper which had been broken down into sections. It was difficult to concentrate but as she leafed through the pages, she caught sight of an article focusing on Seattle, Washington. She was shocked to discover that the serial killer had demanded the enforcers vacate the premises surrounding the vortex and to leave it unguarded or many people would perish. Unfortunately, the enforcers had ignored the orders and over four hundred people had died in a spell unleashed at the point of the vortex including all but two of the enforcers who'd been guarding it. The MEA was now under investigation for incompetence and corruption.

"What are you reading?" Morgan demanded.

"The newspaper," Josephine said.

Morgan snatched it from her and scowled at it. "This is utter nonsense. The MEA did everything they could to protect the people in Seattle from him."

"But the MEA couldn't protect them. The killer made a demand that the MEA ignored. As a result, many people died," Josephine said defiantly. "How do you justify that decision?"

"We don't negotiate with killers or terrorists," Morgan said.

"I don't think the government will see it that way," Josephine said. "This is a terrible tragedy that could have easily been avoided."

"We're not going to give in to demands."

"The enforcers could have left the vortex alone until they developed some system of protecting it without being detected or protecting the vortex from a distance. There were many alternatives that the MEA could have taken," Josephine said.

"It's easy for you to say," Morgan said coldly. "You know something? I haven't been completely candid with you. I've been using psychometry to pick up details about your life. I've been investigating you."

Josephine stiffened and shot him a hostile look. "You're supposed to be protecting me."

"There's a possibility of magical abuse going on. You may be breaking the law. You may be intentionally disabling your aequitas enchantment which makes you a liability to this country," Morgan said in a chilling tone. "You need to be controlled and tamed. You need to become disciplined."

"You don't know what you're saying," Josephine argued. "I haven't done anything to jeopardize anyone's lives."

"You're sidestepping the issue like you always do," Morgan snapped. "I have reason to believe you have the ability to disable your aequitas enchantment at will. If this is true, you will need to enlist in the enforcement training camp."

"I don't want to do that. It isn't necessary."

"You may not have a choice. I'm going to perform a full investigation on your daily life and discover the truth," Morgan said.

Josephine swallowed nervously and realized that he would discover her abilities. There was no hiding the truth from him. She would need to devise some way to avoid undergoing such an investigation or her life would be ruined. She became aware of the cold, predatory gaze that Morgan directed at her. She stiffened reflexively and glared at him.

"What is your problem?" Josephine said sharply.

"You're my problem," Morgan said snidely.

Josephine abruptly stood up which caused him to flinch. She took great pleasure in surprising him. Morgan brought up a dampening field in preparation of an attack but Josephine turned her back on him. She forced her thoughts back to the murder investigation and relentlessly reviewed the clues in her mind. She didn't expect to uncover any revelations but it helped to tune Morgan out.

"You're little temper tantrum isn't going to sway my decision," Morgan taunted.

Josephine pointedly ignored him. She ruthlessly dredged up every shred of information she could remember about the serial killer. Abruptly, she made a horrifying realization and shivered as chills danced along her arms and back. Her eyes widened with alarm and she whirled to face Morgan who was still sneering at her.

"The killer got what he wanted," she said softly.

"What?" Morgan said with confusion.

"The killer had a goal and he finally got it when he attacked Vickie," Josephine said.

"He did?" Morgan asked.

"I never paid attention to how his mind felt in that particular way until now. It's not something that would occur to me," Josephine said.

"What in the hell are you talking about?" Morgan said moodily.

"The killer was working on an enchantment to increase magical strength. The murder victims were guinea pigs. He finally made a success with Vickie but thought he'd killed her. He probably didn't realize until he'd read in the newspaper the following day that she'd survived the attack. At that point, he must have discovered that his enchantment was really a success. It just needed a little fine tuning and he did the next experiment on himself," Josephine said swiftly and began pacing as the horror of what had occurred made her sick. "I have never really paid attention before when I read a crime scene but I get short periods of times where I feel the mind of the killer. The serial killer was definitely a lot weaker until after he'd attacked Vickie."

"I think you're right," Morgan said with concern. "No wonder he's been able to do more and more powerful enchantments. He probably experimented in Florida since it was so far from his home. Now that he's so powerful, he feels safe."

"He's becoming more powerful every time he connects with the power vortex," Josephine said with utter certainty. "He's demonstrated an exponential increase in strength every time he's tapped into it."

"If we don't stop him soon, he may become too powerful," Morgan said.

"I think it's already too late," Jennifer said.

Morgan shook his head. "No, I don't think so. He still needs access to the vortex to develop his abilities."

"We need to report this to the MEA," Jennifer said.

"I'll make the call now," Morgan said as he pulled out his cell phone.

He walked a short distance from them as he placed the call.

"That was good thinking," Jennifer said.

"Thanks. I wish I would have thought of it sooner."

"If you would have had more experience as an enforcer, I believe you may have," Jennifer said.

"Wait a minute. You're a category six so you should be able to read crime scenes just as well as I can," Josephine said.

"No, I can't read like that anymore," Jennifer said regretfully.

"Why?" Josephine asked curiously.

Jennifer opened her mouth as a mixture of emotions danced across her face. First, hesitation and fear but then unexpectedly, rage burned in her eyes.

"After I was forced to participate in the enforcer training camp, I lost that ability," she said bitterly. "I can't tell you any more than that."

Josephine shivered with apprehension at the murderous expression on the enforcer's face. Abruptly, the raw emotions were gone and Jennifer's typical unreadable yet intense expression returned.

"It would be best if you told no one about our discussion," Jennifer said crisply.

"Of course," Josephine said.

Morgan ended his call and returned to them.

"The MEA is very concerned. They feel by the killer's behavior over time that Josephine's theory is definitely correct," Morgan said dourly. "We don't have much time to stop him."

"How powerful do you think he can become?" Jennifer asked.

"There's no way to measure it," Morgan said. "And if he reaches his potential, there will be no one around to do so."

"Meaning what?" Jennifer asked.

"If you'll remember, we've had category fives and sixes who've suffered through some sort of trauma or accident become more powerful. With the development of their new abilities, their minds lost touch with reality. In the end, they tried to access the power vortexes. One of them performed an enchantment that looked exactly like the one that Brenda had used to create the Disaster."

"You think that's what the killer will do?" Jennifer asked.

"He's already manipulated the power vortex before. He's experimenting. He's liable to recreate the Disaster unintentionally as he loses his mind," Morgan said.

"His mind never felt like it was deteriorating," Josephine argued.

"You can't really sense someone's sanity through brief glimpses of their mind," Morgan reminded her.

"That's true," Josephine said apprehensively.

"This is the first time anyone has successfully created an enchantment to increase one's magical potential," Morgan said.

"Too bad it's a serial killer who's made this achievement," Jennifer said acidly.

"Once we've got him locked behind bars, we could learn a lot from him."

"Excuse me?" Josephine said heatedly. "You can learn a lot from a serial killer? I hope you aren't going to make any deals with him?"

"We can make a lot of development in the magical field by acquiring the knowledge he's accumulated." A mixture of greed and admiration colored Morgan's words.

Josephine couldn't believe her ears but didn't want to provoke him either. She'd already done enough to irk him for one day. She glanced at Jennifer to gauge her reaction but she wore that same unreadable look that never seemed to change.

"Mr. McKinley?" a doctor had walked up to them without anyone noticing.

All three of them turned to give him their undivided attention.

"What's Gary's condition?" Morgan asked without preamble.

"It's not good," the doctor said. "He's still in ICU but his condition is stable. We managed to remove the enchantment that was causing instability in his autonomous nervous system but the strain on his mind was serious. He's unconscious and may fall into a coma."

"What's the condition of the pertorqueo sententia?" Morgan asked.

"It's unstable and will probably dissipate in several days," the doctor replied. "The patient isn't going to wake up anytime soon. You should probably come back tomorrow afternoon."

"All right, Doctor," Morgan said.

"What are the chances he'll recover from this?" Josephine asked before the doctor could turn and walk away.

"About fifty-fifty," the doctor said.

Josephine cringed inside at the bad news. Of course, it could be much worse.

"If you'll excuse me," the doctor said.

"Of course," Morgan said.

The doctor swiftly walked out of the room. Morgan turned to address Jennifer.

"It's getting late. I'm going to call one of the nearby enforcers and have two of them keep watch at the hospital," Morgan said. "You and I can leave with Josephine."

That evening, Josephine had trouble falling asleep. Anxiety gnawed at the back of her mind even as she struggled to refrain from thinking about her ability to disable the aequitas enchantment and being forced to enlist in the enforcer training camp. Josephine tossed and turned until shortly after one in the morning. At that point, she decided it was ridiculous to just lay there. She got up and went to the kitchen to make some chamomile tea which would hopefully help her to relax. She flinched in surprise when she realized someone was seated in the dark in her dining room. Jennifer perched on one of the chairs with her back straight and her intense blue eyes conveyed a bitter anger and vigilant alertness.

"What are you doing awake?" Josephine asked.

"I've been having trouble sleeping lately," Jennifer said quietly.

"Does Morgan?" Josephine asked.

"No," Jennifer uttered the word as though she found it loathsome.

"What's wrong?"

"I can't talk about it."

"Would you like some tea?" Josephine asked.

"Thank you. That would be nice." Jennifer smiled politely but it didn't change the rage that burned in her eyes.

Josephine prepared both mugs than set them in the microwave. She went to the dining room table and sat down across from Jennifer.

"So you've been having trouble sleeping lately," Josephine said.

"Yes," Jennifer said tightly.

"I've had the same problem."

"I know."

"Morgan seems determined to make my life a living hell," Josephine said glumly.

"He's intimidated by category six wizards. He knows he'll never be able to reach their potential," Jennifer said cautiously. "He wants them under control. He always suspects them of being rogues in some way. He'll try to find proof that you can disable your aequitas enchantment. He'll probably continue to visit your dreams. He'll try to gather evidence with psychometry, too."

"Going to the enforcer training camp won't guarantee that I'm under control," Josephine said defiantly.

"Yes, it will," Jennifer said slowly as if choosing her words carefully. "Once you attend the training camp, you'll never be the same."

Her eyes flitted away from Josephine and stared off into space as though remembering something.

"What do you mean?" Josephine asked.

Jennifer flinched and gasped as though startled then her expression became impassive.

"I really can't say any more," Jennifer said calmly.

"Okay."

The microwave beeped and Josephine went to retrieve their tea. When she returned to the dining room and handed Jennifer her mug, the enforcer offered a stressed smile.

"Thanks," she said.

"You're welcome," Josephine murmured.

"I believe the serial killer is becoming too powerful. I don't think anyone can stop him anymore. We weren't able to prevent him from linking with the power vortex in Siesta Key and it looks like the MEA is incapable of preventing him from accessing the one in Seattle. In spite of their best efforts, the serial killer is repeatedly linking with the vortex," Jennifer said.

"And he's becoming stronger every time," Josephine said.

"Yes," Jennifer said. She cautiously sipped some of her tea. "I'm not sure what the killer intends to do once he's acquired enough power to feel completely safe."

"He's been working for this goal for years," Josephine said.

"Yes, that's true," Jennifer said. "With that type of personality, you would think he'd have other goals in mind."

"Maybe career advancement and personal goals. Maybe he will just blend in with society," Josephine said.

"No, he won't do that. Sociopaths like him who have such utter disregard for human life will continue to find reasons to murder," Jennifer said. "He won't stop until he's locked away or dead."

Josephine didn't like the sound of that. Of course, with the serial killer moving to his home in Seattle, it was no longer her problem. Her immediate problem lay with Morgan and his determination to enlist her in the enforcer training camp.

"I have to do something to stop Morgan," Josephine said. "He's absolutely relentless."

"Yes, he is," Jennifer said tightly.

Josephine sensed a surge of barely controlled power crackling around Jennifer.

"Can you think of a way I can side-track him?" Josephine asked.

"No," Jennifer said slowly as her brows furrowed with concentration. Anger briefly danced over her face and more power swelled around her but she managed to keep it in check. "I'm afraid he's going to do what he does. Once the MEA tracks down the killer and stops him, Morgan will be reassigned. If he hasn't found anything on you at that time, he'll try to assign himself to audit you but that will take some effort."

"It doesn't sound like the MEA has the ability to track the killer much less to stop him," Josephine pointed out.

"It seems that way."

"Is there any way I could somehow get Morgan reassigned and have another enforcer assigned to me instead?" Josephine asked.

"That's not possible," Jennifer said.

Her face turned unreadable again and the power surge around her ebbed.

"I'm going back to bed. Thank you for the tea."

"You're welcome."

Chapter 21

Morgan received a call from the hospital informing him that Gary's condition had improved. He was now stable and had regained consciousness. Morgan had decided to pay him a visit immediately. Currently, he, Jennifer, and Josephine traversed the hallway of the ICU area behind the doctor who guided them toward Gary's room. When they reached Gary's room, they found him lying down with his head propped up so he could watch television. He was pale and had an IV tube attached to his left arm and an electronic monitor beeped steadily beside him.

"I'm so glad you're all right," Josephine said.

"Hey," Gary said weakly.

"You have fifteen minutes and then he needs some rest," the doctor said firmly.

"Thank you, doctor," Morgan said dismissively.

Josephine suspected if Morgan wanted to speak with Gary for longer than fifteen minutes, he would make sure it happened regardless of any orders from a lowly doctor. The doctor jotted down a note on his clipboard and left the room.

"Can you feel the pertorqueo sententia enchantment in your mind?" Morgan asked.

"It's weak enough that I can feel it now," Gary said.

Morgan pulled out a topaz pendant and it began to glow softly with a golden luminescence as he adopted a faraway look. After a moment, the light winked out of existence and his eyes snapped back into focus.

275

"The pertorqueo sententia enchantment will dissipate within several days," Morgan said. "You may start to remember disturbing things about whoever has done this to you. Every time the pertorqueo sententia was activated in your mind by the killer, he suppressed your memory of that time frame. You probably have a lot of suppressed memories which will begin to surface soon. Has this process started yet?"

"No, I haven't remembered anything. I just feel weak and vulnerable as if some sort of boundary is falling away and that it will change everything," Gary said.

"It's normal to feel that way when your mind has been manipulated for so many years. Try to remember. It will help you to speed up the process," Morgan said.

"The doctor said I shouldn't do that. He said the enchantment will dissipate on its own and that if I forced it, my nervous system could destabilize again and I'd be putting myself at risk."

"The serial killer is becoming a lot more powerful every time he connects with the vortex in Seattle. If we don't stop him soon, he may become virtually invincible," Morgan said passionately. "If you choose not to help, you're signing the death warrants of thousands of innocent people who will eventually die at the hands of this killer. Can you live with your conscious knowing you didn't do everything you could to stop him before it was too late?"

Gary flinched at the verbal onslaught and his mouth opened slightly as he seemed at a loss of what to say. Josephine sensed a powerful enchantment rushing towards them. It was coming in so quickly that she didn't have time to warn anyone. She deftly brought up a dampening field just as a powerful wave of magic burst over them. Jennifer stumbled backward and tried to brace herself against the wall.

She slowly slid down until she'd collapsed to the floor unconscious. Gary immediately passed out. Josephine noticed that Morgan had barely managed to raise a dampening field in time to save himself from the knockout spell. The hospital was suddenly eerily quiet as everyone had succumbed to the unconsciousness.

"What just happened?" Josephine said.

"I unleashed a knockout spell from the Siesta Key vortex," a man said from the hallway.

More power than Josephine had ever sensed before emanated from him. He looked to be in his mid thirties with thinning brown hair, brown eyes, and a muscular build. For some reason, Josephine found his appearance oddly familiar.

"Do I know you?" Josephine asked.

"We've never met but I'm sure you recognize the similarities between me and my brother, Gary," the man smirked.

He had reached the doorway now and stood there impassively. A powerful dampening field surrounding him with a protection that would take quite some time to overcome.

"Dan Eslinger," Morgan spat out. "I suspected a family member may be the killer."

"Maybe you should have worked a lot harder," Dan said coolly. "Maybe you would have discovered my identity before it was too late."

"You have two powerful wizards who can take care of you," Morgan said confidently.

Dan chuckled at him and shook his head. "You're absolutely pathetic. It's a shame that I didn't dispose of Gary sooner. He's become a liability. Of course, it almost doesn't matter since I'm so much stronger than any of you."

"The MEA will bring you down," Morgan said threateningly. "If you come quietly, I'll negotiate for leniency for you."

"I don't need leniency." Dan motioned at Gary. "Wake up."

A flash of green lit up behind Gary's closed eyelids. He abruptly opened his eyes and sat up with a vacant look on his face. Morgan unleashed a powerful volley of telekinetic energy that pounded against Dan's dampening field but did little to weaken it. Dan pulled out a revolver and smiled chillingly.

"After I kill all of you, I'll wipe the prints from this gun and have Gary shoot himself. No one will know who the killer is. They'll think that Gary's pertorqueo sententia became active and that he killed everyone and then himself under its influence. I'll return to Washington before I'm missed. After a few weeks, I can return to my home here in Florida with no one suspecting me. The MEA will be determined to believe that I reside near Seattle and keep looking for me there."

"How did you get here so quickly?" Josephine asked with puzzlement in spite of the fear coursing through her veins. Maybe if she stalled for time, some opportunity to save herself would be presented. "You probably flew a plane here early this morning or late last night but how did you unleash a knockout spell on Siesta Key and get here right after it took effect on the city?"

"I've discovered I can teleport quite some distance if I'm tapped into a power vortex. I teleported here from Siesta. It was quite easy after the practice I've done over the last several days," Dan said with undisguised satisfaction. "I did have to take a plane from Washington to Sarasota though."

Morgan abruptly unleashed another volley of telekinetic energy. Dan fired his revolver twice in rapid succession which made

Josephine flinch and scream. He smirked at her as Morgan clutched his chest and stumbled backward.

"You can't imagine the power I have," Dan said.

He pointed the revolver at her and quickly fired twice. Josephine reflexively closed her eyes but oddly enough felt no pain. She opened her eyes and found two bullets hovering several inches away from her chest. Dan regarded her with puzzlement and fired the revolver again and again until no bullets remained in the gun. A group of bullets now floated harmlessly in front of Josephine. Harsh, strained breathing drew their attention to Gary who wore a vacant expression on his face but was looking in their general direction. The bullets abruptly dropped and clattered to the floor which made both Dan and Josephine flinch. A cold wind abruptly whipped through the room. Dan tossed aside his gun with a frown of disgust. He pointed his left hand toward Gary and a flash of eerie green light briefly spilled from it. Gary's eyes briefly sparked with the same green light as he regarded his brother vacantly.

"Stop what you're doing now," Dan ordered.

"You betrayed me," Gary's voice said from multiple directions in the room.

"You must go to sleep now," Dan ordered forcefully.

"You betrayed me," Gary's harsh voice exploded from all around them.

"Go to sleep now!" Dan shouted.

He launched a potent spell at his younger brother but a powerful dampening field had already snapped into place. Gary was unaffected by the attack. Josephine shivered as the frigid wind continued to swirl frantically through the room. She sensed Dan's protection weakening as Gary chipped away at it. Dan narrowed his eyes as he silently worked at his younger brother's dampening field. Josephine concentrated and reached out with her mind to add her own efforts against Dan. Unfortunately, Dan was too powerful. She could see that he was reinforcing his protection at the same time that he whittled away Gary's. It was only a matter of time before Gary became vulnerable. Josephine tensed as she struggled with indecision. Dampening fields only offered protection against magical attacks – not physical ones. She abruptly dashed forward and tackled Dan.

She'd taken him completely off guard. He reflexively grabbed her to ward her off even as they both hurtled to the floor. He bumped his head and shouted with pain and frustration. He threw her off him with a burst of telekinetic power. Josephine's back slammed against the wall on the far side of the room. She slid to the floor but managed to remain conscious. Dan's attention had been distracted long enough from his protection to allow Gary to tear it away almost completely. Dan quickly realized what had happened and worked on reinforcing it. Fortunately, it was weak enough by now that Gary managed to hurl him across the room with psychokinesis. The dampening field dissipated completely as Dan's body smacked against the wall. He stumbled toward Gary but a knockout spell took care of him. Gary abruptly dropped back to sleep and the frigid wind died away. The temperature slowly warmed and Jennifer stirred from her position on the floor. Josephine abruptly remembered Morgan being shot and rushed over to him. She checked his wrist for a pulse but found that he was dead. Josephine left the room to alert a doctor, found one, and returned with him to the room. Everyone in the hospital was awakening now. Two medics scurried into the room to assist the doctor but Morgan was too far gone to be brought back.

Jennifer crossed her arms over her chest in a defensive posture as she surveyed the room. She had handcuffed Dan's wrists behind his back and gave him an aequitas enchantment. Two enforcers arrived to take Dan away. Gary awakened a short while later and Josephine explained to him what had occurred. He gasped and his eyes widened with surprise and pain.

"Yes, I can remember everything now," Gary said quietly. "He used to have me help give him power so he could experiment with the enchantments that he was working on to increase his magical strength. He was having me help him just about every other day."

"No wonder your mind began to develop defenses against that," Josephine said sympathetically. "And that's why you ultimately felt compelled to move out on your own."

"Yes," Gary said. "I was instinctively trying to get away from him. He kept visiting me though and forcing me to help even though he wasn't speaking to me. His visits stopped once I was put under guard."

"I'm afraid my patient needs his rest," the doctor said.

"Okay," Jennifer acknowledged. She smiled encouragingly at Gary. "Everything is all right now. You're going to be fine."

"Yes. I think I will," Gary said with a sense of great relief.

Other books by John O'Riley:

Jigsaw Murders
(Volume 1 of the Kathy Bomar mystery series/ humorous
mystery)

Quik Burger Murder
(Volume 2 of the Kathy Bomar mystery series/ humorous
mystery)

Conspiracy In Bricks
(Humorous psychic investigation/ mystery)

Corruption
(Volume 2 of the Grumpy Old Wizards urban fantasy series)

Made in the USA
Lexington, KY
07 February 2014